To Steal Maggie's Heart

Mail-Order Grooms for Garfield— Book One

Endorsements

Ronda Simpson has written a book filled with twists and turns that will lead to many unexpected surprises. Finding mail-order husbands is a fantastic reversal of an old theme, which Ms. Simpson used effectively to weave this multiple point-of-view saga. *To Steal Maggie's Heart* leaves the reader with a hint of a sequel, so plan on looking forward to another Ronda Simpson book for fulfillment of every expectation.

—Bettie Boswell, author of *On Cue,* and *Free to Love*

For readers who enjoy historical fiction set in the Old West, this story won't disappoint. Ronda Simpson has managed to turn on its head what the cultural norms for a pioneer woman should be. She challenges the traditional female roles with humor. The male and female interactions between Maggie and Garrett were fun to watch. This book will keep you turning pages until the surprising and satisfying ending. The faith element is handled with care and isn't overbearing or preachy. The main characters live their faith and grow through the challenges thrown their way. You'll want to know what happens next in the sequel to *To Steal Maggie's Heart.*

—Jane S Daly, author of *Broken, A Story of Redemption.*

Ronda Simpson's *To Steal Maggie's Heart* grabbed me with its first three sentences: "Mail order husband?" "What?" and

"Ludicrous!" I had to keep reading! Following Maggie Garfield and her creative way of finding husbands for dozens of women in a men-less desert of a town engages, captivates, and challenges readers to read on without stopping. Clear your calendar, grab your favorite beverage, and plop in a comfy chair for marathon reading!

—**Susan Hayhurst**, devotional author and agricultural writer

To Steal Maggie's Heart

Mail-Order Grooms for Garfield– Book One

Ronda Simpson

A Christian Company
ElkLakePublishingInc.com

Copyright Notice

Cover and Interior Design: Derinda Babcock, Deb Haggerty
Editor(s): Peggy Ellis, Cristel Phelps, Deb Haggerty

PUBLISHED BY: Elk Lake Publishing, Inc., 35 Dogwood Drive, Plymouth, MA 02360, 2022

Library Cataloging Data

Names: Simpson, Ronda (Ronda Simpson)

To Steal Maggie's Heart, Mail-Order Grooms for Garfield— Book One/ Ronda Simpson

298 p. 23cm × 15cm (9in × 6 in.)

ISBN-13: 978-1-64949-744-4 (paperback) | 978-1-64949-745-1 (trade hardcover) | 978-1-64949-746-8 (trade paperback) | 978-1-64949-747-5 (e-book)

Key Words: Clean romance books for business women; Inspirational and religious book; Historical fiction about women; Wholesome romance for women; Strong female lead book; Inspirational stories for women; Mail order bride books

Library of Congress Control Number: 2022949272 Fiction

Dedication

In memory of my precious Grandma Juanita, who passed down her love of reading and writing. She always kept a positive outlook and found the fun in life, no matter how dire the circumstances.

Acknowledgments

Without my Savior, Jesus Christ, providing this story, giving me courage to write, and bestowing family and friends to cheer me on, I'd never be able to say I'm a published writer. We serve an awesome God.

Barbara Pyatte was the first one to endure reading my initial draft. I'm sorry, Barbara! A special friend and avid reader, I'm sure she saw how flawed my "masterpiece" was. Yet she encouraged me to get published while providing a reader's insight.

Cristel Phelps and Deb Haggerty saw a manuscript that needed lots of fixes, yet they agreed to take me on as a client. That was a dream come true for me.

Peggy Ellis fearlessly consented to be my editor, knowing this was my first book. Brave lady! She blessed me with her knowledge, patience, kind instruction, and tireless editing. This book is so much better because of her efforts.

My parents and tribe of friends have always believed in me much more than I deserve. Their support gave me the "never give up attitude" I needed to make it to the finish line.

Chapter 1

GARFIELD, MISSOURI, 1898

"A *mail-order* husband?"

"*What*?"

"Ludicrous!"

"No way I'd be a part of this."

"Has she lost her mind?"

"Not a safe choice."

What a disconcerting response to the brilliant idea (at least she thought so) Maggie Garfield, owner of Mando Merchandising, had presented to her employees just a few moments before. The conversation had started well, but ...

"Ladies, I am certain I have a sound solution to our dilemma." Maggie Garfield, the twenty-one-year-old heiress of one of the most profitable mail-order catalog businesses in America, held her chin high and stood on her toes, because she believed tall people exuded more authority. The intensity in the crowd's eyes unsettled her. Maggie cleared her throat to make room for the confidence she needed.

"My inspiration for this idea comes from correspondence I received from my good friend, Hazel. She moved from

Junction City to Montana to marry a wealthy rancher. Hazel found her husband in response to an advertisement for a bride.”

Loud gasps and grumbles filled Maggie's ears, along with thumps from her heart. The ladies' reactions overwhelmed the room. Maggie whistled for attention, bringing instant silence. No one in the state of Missouri could blow out a louder noise from one's mouth than Margaret Eloise Garfield. She shook her head, which made her blonde curls dance as if they were able to help excite the crowd.

“I would not want any of you to answer advertisements from men who seek wives. Without you, neither Mando Merchandising nor the town of Garfield would survive.”

Maggie's eyes crossed as she watched a droplet of sweat roll down her nose until it dripped out of sight. She took in a deep breath and exhaled.

“Hiring women who've aged out of orphanages to work at Mando Merchandising was a dream fulfilled for my father. He wanted a safe place for you to live, as well as to make good wages. However, this has created a town of almost all women. Father and I have been remiss to focus only on our business and the essential needs for you to survive. We both should have realized ladies reared in orphanages would want families of their own.”

Forlorn expressions on their faces were almost more than Maggie could endure. Her shoulders sagged from the weight of responsibility for their needs. She pressed on with her plan because the daughter of William Garfield would not allow herself to disappoint them.

“Hazel's experience has led me to the perfect solution. I'm excited about this because I know every one of you will be delighted. I propose *you* choose your potential husbands. *We can bring them here.* To accomplish this,

I will place advertisements in a few newspapers to find your grooms."

Maggie smiled widely as she waited for their acceptance. Instead, she received intense stares from all eyes. Several spoke at once.

"A *mail-order* husband?"

"*What*?"

"Ludicrous!"

"No way I'd be a part of this."

"Has she lost her mind?"

"Not a safe choice."

Maggie's whistle again brought silence. "I'm sure you're astonished by what I've shared. However, I trust the merits of my proposition will stand out to you. I believe we might have found a worthy path to locate your mates."

Hilary Adams, never one to hold back on her opinions, broke the silence. "Outlandish! Advertisements for husbands? We might as well just list all of us for sale in Mando's catalog. I've never heard of such a thing. Proper ladies do not ask gentlemen to become betrothed. Any man open to this idea is no man we would want. Right, girls?"

"Yes, indeed."

"No man I'd want."

"Not me!"

Maggie raised her voice. "Try to calm down. Let's not rule against this so quickly. Keep your focus on the plan's virtues. You will not be expected to propose. Well ... in reality ... you could, I suppose. What I advocate is letting eligible bachelors outside of Garfield know you're available. I'm certain any fortunate gentlemen we invite will become besotted with our ladies. You'll have to follow your heart to decide if the affection is mutual."

Hilary's voice overwhelmed loud protests. "A man coming here without a source of income is not desirable.

We're not going to work while he sleeps all day, no matter how 'besotted' he might be."

The room echoed with another whistle from Maggie who spoke into the silence.

"I agree with Hilary. No need to worry. Husbands would have many choices of occupations. They could farm or do construction. Some might have abilities to establish their own businesses. Mando Merchandising could use help with our catalog orders and deliveries. The gentlemen could do the same jobs we're all doing now. Eventually, we'll need teachers and a school for our children."

"Take our jobs? Absolutely not! We'll end up on the streets or imprisoned to these strangers. They are *not* welcome here," Hilary said.

Thunderous protests took the proposal down a path Maggie needed to redirect. She paused a few seconds to gather her thoughts before waving her arms to get their attention again.

"Please be assured your jobs are permanent for as long as you want to work. I have no intention of replacing any of you to make room for these gentlemen. Offers of employment to them would be additional positions created due to our growing business and community. I know you don't need husbands to survive. You've proven your ability to live quite well on your own, just as my father and I have always wanted. The homes you live in are all quite lovely. You're excellent at your jobs. However, you have told me self-sufficiency is no longer enough for many of you."

Maggie strained to listen for any murmurs of approval but heard silence.

"We must look outside of our town because there are so few eligible gentlemen in Garfield. Hannibal is close, but we need more options. My business associates at the *St.*

Louis Post, as well as the *Chicago Dispatch*, have agreed to help us in our search. Isn't that wonderful?"

Most of the ladies shook their heads, with chatter exchanged among themselves.

With a sinking heart, Maggie asked, "Do any of you want to leave Garfield?"

"No!" the women said in unison.

"I'm thrilled to hear you want to stay, also relieved. But, if no prospects for marriage become available, I worry you might change your minds."

Maggie perused the room until she spotted Elizabeth Wrigley, a shining optimist in about any situation. "Elizabeth, what about you? Do you want to be married?"

Elizabeth didn't hesitate. "Yes, I do. Families would make Garfield an even better place to live."

Maggie nodded her agreement. "Right now, Garfield is a small town. With Mando Merchandising, along with other businesses being started, I believe our population could grow as large as some of the cities around us like Hannibal, Jefferson City, even St. Louis. We need husbands and children to make this happen."

"We all know your ideas in the past have provided some very nice outcomes," Elizabeth assured her. "I trust you have considered how we will choose only gentlemen of the highest integrity for us to meet. I'm interested to hear how we would get them to uproot their lives to come here."

Sadie Stoddard chimed in. "Elizabeth is right. Garfield is hardly even on the map. Would desirable gentlemen come here just to find wives? If they're desirable, why haven't they found wives where they live now?"

"Maggie has never failed us in her decision-making abilities," Elizabeth said. "She cares for us better than a mother. We can rest assured Maggie has considered these questions."

"Thank you for your kind endorsement, Elizabeth. I also appreciate Sadie's thoughtful questions. I will admit I don't have all the answers. We must pray for discernment. Trust God for wisdom in selecting who is invited. There are undoubtedly many respectable gentlemen in this country who would welcome opportunities to meet a special lady while making an honest living. A gentleman of character would be able to see the merits of this proposal. If he's a man of God, he'll listen to the Lord's prompting and guidance, even if this is a little unorthodox. Ladies, maybe the insecurities you're feeling are because you haven't had time to consider the potential."

"The potential for disaster, I would say," Hilary grumbled.

Maggie's shoulders slumped when several ladies nodded in agreement. She hadn't expected this much resistance. Nevertheless, honesty forced her next words. "I'm reluctant to change the dynamics of this wonderful little community too. However, I believe we must."

Maggie locked eyes with Ruth Calvin, a well-respected supervisor at Mando Merchandising. "Ruth, what do you think about bringing in potential husbands?"

"I guess I could warm up to the idea if it would make our girls happy, as long as we have a proper plan in place."

Ruth's small affirmation encouraged Maggie. Perhaps momentum was shifting in her favor.

"A big part of me likes the way things are now," Ruth admitted. "Yet I've often wondered about having a real family of my own. At the same time, I enjoy my freedom, and find great satisfaction in my job at Mando Merchandising. I don't want to give up those things ... unless I were to have children. Oh my, Maggie, think of the workers we'd lose if they become mothers."

"Yes, but we'd be blessed to have little ones around. God will provide the staff we need. Your children would be priority."

A few murmurs of approval sounded around the room as Ruth continued.

"I'm a bit frightened of your idea, given the types of men who tried to force some of us to marry them to 'save' us from a life of starvation, or worse, when we were beyond the age of the orphanages."

When murmurs of agreement faded, Maggie said, "I'm thankful none of you had to endure such a bad situation. Ruth, perhaps your match would be an understanding husband who is agreeable to you working at Mando. Of course, not all of you want or need husbands. No one will be forced to be married. Fortunately, you can make choices about your future."

"I might not be suited for matrimony, but I will keep an open mind," Ruth assured her.

"Thank you, Ruth."

Maggie gazed around the room, making eye contact with several of the ladies. "I want this to be a sensible situation for everyone. Remember, many of you came to me with your desire for husbands. I have offered a potential solution to find eligible gentlemen to marry. However, I'm receptive to your thoughts. If anyone has a better idea, tell me now, or, after you think about the situation some more. Solutions to problems don't occur overnight."

Silence filled the room as the ladies stared at each other and then at Maggie. Some shrugged while others shook their heads. Maggie straightened her shoulders and forced herself to stand strong. Margaret Eloise Garfield refused to be defeated. She had to be brave in front of them, or they would never agree to this.

"As you know, few gentlemen have permanent residence in Garfield, while there are more than fifty of you ladies. We have the ranch hands, delivery, and construction workers who come and go, if you want to include them as potential husbands," Maggie said.

Sadie's sister, Annabelle Stoddard, laughed aloud. The sisters were twins, but fraternal. Annabelle was of short stature with a pleasant amount of plumpness, and no worries about what she wore. Sadie, on the other hand, was quite fashionable, several inches taller than Annabelle, thin, with intense emerald-green eyes.

"We can forget about the ranch hands and the building crews," Annabelle said. "I know there is no way they've ever spent much time in a tub. I'm not sure they even know soap exists."

To Maggie's relief, chuckles from the rest of the ladies further lightened the atmosphere.

Annabelle added, "Or ... maybe Hank Rothstadt ... if he ever finds a woman more beautiful than a hammer or a fishing pole, a girl might stand a chance."

More laughter filled the room.

"Hank pours much love into creating fine-looking furniture, but doesn't seem to notice the beauty in any of us. Besides, he's more like a brother than a potential husband," Annabelle concluded.

"Annabelle, I think you could charm any gentleman, even Hank, with your outstanding meals," said Maggie.

Annabelle shook her head. "Oh no. Hank *likes* to eat, but catching his food is what he *loves*. I'd never stand a chance of luring him away."

Maggie thought she detected a bit of wistfulness in Annabelle's words about Hank.

The slowly dying laughter lifted Maggie's spirits.

Rose Fairmont rose to her feet. "I'd like to try this, but I'm apprehensive. How do we get to know the gentlemen? Do we choose who would be well suited?"

Before Maggie could reply, Rose's eyes opened wide as she gasped. "Oh my, Maggie! Will we be expected to marry them as soon as they arrive? I wouldn't be ready."

Maggie reassured her. "No one would be ready to get married on the day a gentleman gets here. I'll correspond with those who answer our advertisement to discover if they possess our desired characteristics. Invitations will go only to gentlemen of integrity, who would be an asset not just to a family, but also to the town of Garfield. Interested ladies will be afforded time to discuss any information I have about the gentlemen before they arrive. We'll plan to socialize in groups until anyone feels ready to enter into a courtship."

"What if we don't match well after we spend time with these gentlemen? I don't want to be stuck with one," Rose said amid some murmurs around the room.

"He can go home if you're not well suited. Or maybe he will end up as a better option for someone else. Our boardinghouse has ten rooms available to be occupied, with two beds in each room. We won't bring in too many gentlemen at a time, but if needed, there are a few hotels in Hannibal. Because our announcement will initially go into only two newspapers, the gentlemen should be coming from either St. Louis or Chicago, likely by train. I'll take care of their accommodations for as long as they, and you, need to get to know each other."

"I agree with Elizabeth," Annabelle said. "As we've already said, Maggie's previous ideas have been good, so maybe this one will be too."

"Thank you for your trusting me, Annabelle. There are uncertainties with change, but also potential rewards. Marriage is not for everyone. Those of you who prefer to live independently should continue to do so. For the ladies who desire a family, I know this seems a bit risky.

Let's take a few minutes to think about the risks you took when you came to Garfield. Every one of you responded, 'Yes,' with blind faith, to the invitation my father and I sent to ask you to move here. Do you think you made a sound decision?"

The ladies nodded. Many responded with affirmations.

"Yes."

"The best."

"Such a blessing."

Maggie smiled her relief. She was gaining some ground in the discussion. "Having you ladies here has been a blessing for my father, me, as well as our town. This proposed plan is a similar situation. We advertised for ladies aging out of orphanages they had called home for most of their lives. We needed workers—you needed homes and employment. You are, in a sense, Garfield's mail-order citizens. Why not bring your mail-order grooms here too?"

"We should do this for Mr. Garfield. I think he would want us to have families," Sadie said. "Maggie, I've hesitated to ask about something, but I believe this is the right time. Why did your father do so much for us? I know he was kind, but why take care of us? You've never shared what prompted him to offer such tremendous opportunities."

Maggie's father had died a little over a year before. He was only forty-four years old, far too young to be gone. In the twenty years Maggie had with him, he had prepared her to be at the helm of Mando Merchandising, as well as Garfield. This was the first time any of the ladies had asked why he built the town for them.

"Father adored my mother. They met as children in an orphanage in North Carolina when she was twelve. He was thirteen. My father said it was love at first sight for him. Not so much for my mother." Maggie chuckled at her memory of her father telling the story. "He told me he was relentless in his pursuit until his charm won her over. They were betrothed when she was sixteen. They married on her seventeenth birthday. Sadly, only six years later, she went to be with our Lord. To honor her, he made his lifelong goal to help women like you, specifically orphans."

"Mr. Garfield was an astounding man. I sure do miss him," Sadie said.

Several in the crowd voiced similar sentiments.

Maggie nodded. "Yes, I agree. He was incredible in every way, a wonderful example to all. He told me about many girls in orphanages who were released to the streets as young as fourteen. Those poor girls had nowhere to go, and most were destitute. As many of you know, some ended up in abusive and slave-type marriages. Others were bullied by those who employed them, forced to work long hours with little pay to live in workhouses. In this male-dominated world we live in, women have always had few options. Father believed in women's abilities so much that he built this community for all of you. He made sure you had homes, as well as good incomes. Father carefully created Garfield to be comfortable for all. He didn't want this to be a company town. Father wanted Garfield to be your town. Like me, however, he didn't anticipate—or even think about—your need for families. His goal of bringing mostly women into our town has made this task difficult, but not impossible.

Maggie allowed them a minute to soak in what she had shared. "Shall we take a moment to pray about this situation?"

Several of the ladies nodded their heads.

Maggie closed her eyes. "Lord, we leave this in your capable hands. Give us wisdom and discernment. Open the ladies' minds and hearts if this is best for them. Help us not to be anxious and to feel your peace as we explore this endeavor. Help us to choose kind, trustworthy, Christian gentlemen who will care for our ladies. We ask for your protection and guidance. Amen."

Maggie opened her eyes. "Let's take a look at the details of the plan."

She pulled on a rope at the edge of the platform, releasing a banner. "Here's the wording of the advertisement I plan to use."

> WE ARE SINGLE LADIES LOOKING FOR GROOMS. WE DESIRE COMPANIONSHIP AND FAMILY LIFE. OUR COMMUNITY CAN OFFER EMPLOYMENT AND HOMES TO THE RIGHT HARD-WORKING GENTLEMEN. ONLY RESPOND IF YOU ARE A GOD-FEARING MAN WHO IS KIND, CONSIDERATE, AND SERIOUS ABOUT FORMING A FAMILY. PROVIDE SOME PARTICULARS ABOUT YOURSELF TO HELP US ASSESS YOUR MERITS.

"As I mentioned, we'll begin with placing this notice in two newspapers, the *Chicago Tribune* and the *St. Louis Post-Dispatch*. Mando Merchandising already advertises with them so I believe they are good choices for starters. I've corresponded with our contacts at these newspapers. They have agreed to receive responses and forward them to us to keep our location anonymous. Due to the speed of mail, we can expect the process to take several weeks." Maggie paused. "Those of you who want to be a part of this, tell me now."

"No, no, no! Not me!" Hilary said with a scowl directed toward Maggie. She quickly headed to the outside door. "I'm not going along with this crazy idea. Leave me out." Hilary slammed the door as she left the building.

Ruth stood. "As the leader of these ladies in the warehouse, I feel I should find out what this is all about. I can better guide them if I understand the process. You can count me in. I might end up just being an observer rather than a participant. I'm not sure I want a husband. We'll have to see."

"You're a constant trailblazer who will be important to this endeavor. Thank you, Ruth."

A few others walked toward the exit shaking their heads at Maggie.

"No way."

"This is a terrible idea."

"Anyone who does this will be sorry."

"Just asking for trouble, this is."

The doubters left the building, closing the door behind them.

"What do the rest of you say?" Maggie asked. "Will you try this with Ruth?"

Maggie waited. No one responded. Maggie continued to wait. She counted in her head with plans to speak when she reached one hundred.

At seventy-six, Elizabeth stood. "I believe in you, Maggie. I'm just not keen to meet a stranger in this way. I will pray about the idea. Maybe I can try this in a few months. I hope you understand."

"Yes, I do, Elizabeth. This is a decision that should not be taken lightly. When you feel ready, just let me know."

"Thank you, Maggie. I will support you in any way I can." Elizabeth exited the building with haste.

Maggie's shoulders slumped as she watched her leave.

"I apologize, Maggie," Rose said. "I don't feel ready, either. I'm sure I will in time. I thought I might be able to try, but I don't feel at peace, yet. Don't be upset with me."

Maggie smiled at Rose. "I'm not upset with you, Rose. No need to apologize. This is an important decision. You'll know when the time is right, and you can tell me then."

"I will try your method, Maggie," Sadie said. "At least, new men in town will create some excitement, which is sadly missing in our lives."

"If Sadie will do this, I shall also," Annabelle said. "I can't allow my sister to go on this adventure without me."

"I'm so happy to hear this, ladies. You'll find strength in each other and enjoy this even more." Maggie said.

Several women remained seated.

"Do the rest of you want to participate?" Maggie asked.

She saw shaking heads and heard many noes.

"Ladies, this is a start. A small number of participants should be easier to manage. We'll focus on the three of you for now—Ruth, Annabelle, and Sadie. Thank you for your trust in me. The rest of you can watch and see how the process unfolds. Join us at any time. You're all courageous women who deserve a blessed life with much happiness. This meeting is officially adjourned."

Chapter 2

Garrett Hanley sat in the chair in front of Rex Tillman's desk.

"Hello there, friend. Always a pleasure to have you start a new project for me. I've found you're one of the rare men I can count on. How's your mother?"

Rex's repulsive smile turned Garrett's stomach. "We aren't friends, and my mother is none of your concern. Just stick to business at hand and leave her out of our conversations."

"Garrett, you know I'm quite fond of you and your mother. I care about your welfare, especially after your father swindled us. We're practically family."

"We are nowhere near family. Forgo the niceties. Let's get to why I'm here. You and I both know your bitterness drives the types of jobs you expect from me. What do you want me to build this time?"

"Your daddy made me a bitter man. I had thought he was my best friend until he turned on me. Yet I remain my sweet humble self even when I'm unable to forgive his misdeeds. I don't like to ask you to work so hard. You're like a son to me. I only do what is necessary to keep my businesses profitable. However, today I have a fun assignment I think you'll enjoy. There's no manual labor involved. In fact, we'll step out of the construction business for this one."

Garrett broke the expectant silence. "What do you want?"

"You're going to claim your bride."

"My *bride*? You can't force me to marry anyone. I am *not* your son. I work hard for you, but I won't allow you to control my personal life. No way, Rex. This is where I draw the line."

Garrett started toward the door.

"Hold on there. Sit back down. Trust me. You will want to hear what I have to say. This, my dear boy, could be your final job for me."

Garrett dropped back into his chair. "My final job?"

Rex nodded his head. "Yes, the last one."

"I will not marry someone just so you can get what you want."

"Oh, you don't have to stay married, or even get married. You just need to steal a lady's heart. I found an advertisement in the *Chicago Tribune* about some women who desire husbands. I responded with interest, and obviously, they chose me as a potential candidate. My natural charisma suits me well."

"If you are the chosen one, what does this have to do with me? I do not want a wife. Leave me out of your madness, Rex. I can't imagine there is any financial gain for you to achieve from desperate women seeking men to take care of them."

"You fail to see the entire picture. There is potentially immeasurable profit for me in this situation. However, I need your services to make this plan succeed. I'm not the type of guy they would fancy. You're a somewhat handsome, tall, and muscular fellow. Even though I'm a fine-looking man, they expect someone younger. I hear you can be charming. Seems like the ladies around here go for you. Perfect for this job."

Rex limped to a table where he poured some scotch into a glass. He had been born with a bum leg, which was slightly shorter than his other one. He drank the contents and refilled the glass.

"Drink, Garrett?"

"You know I don't drink. I still don't see how an advertisement for a husband would be beneficial to your pockets."

Rex sat down. "This might be the most lucrative deal I've ever come across. Might even make up for all the money your daddy stole from me when he overcharged me for his company. I received a most unexpected bonus when I answered the advertisement. You see, your daddy was not the only one who did me wrong. I was once William Garfield's most trusted friend. You might have heard of his company, Mando Merchandising."

"Yes, I'm familiar with the company. Leave your comments about my father out of this."

Rex rolled his eyes. "Anyway, I was the mastermind behind the company's success. When the profits rose, Greedy Garfield cut me off and forced me out of town."

"What does Mr. Garfield have to do with ladies who want husbands?"

"I'll get there. Just be patient. I thought this might be an opportunity to gain some land or maybe a nice dowry. Instead, an unexpected gold mine has come my way. This is better than even I could have dreamed up for myself. Before responding to the advertisement for husbands, I had one of my connections at the newspaper find out where the letters originated.

"Fate's lovely head has bowed to me," Rex continued, "as the advertisement came from Garfield, Missouri, the town that's owned by William Garfield, and the location of Mando Merchandising. Apparently, some of the women from Garfield are lonely spinsters."

Rex leaned back in his chair and swallowed a drink. "William talked about his desire to invite orphaned women to his town and offer them employment. He said he wanted to honor his late wife. I never really thought much of her myself, not someone I would want to memorialize. Anyway, he must have followed through and found some desperate creatures. This appears to be my opportunity to get what is rightfully mine from Greedy Garfield. Your job, Garrett, will be to go after his daughter, Miss Maggie Garfield. You must win her heart and take the company for me."

"What?" Garrett's voice rose. "Miss Garfield wants to find a husband from an advertisement in a newspaper? Preposterous! No way would Mr. Garfield allow her to find a gentleman in this way. She must be one of the wealthiest women in America. Your idea does not matter, though, because I am not a man capable of such a horrible endeavor."

"Preposterous, indeed, but this *does* matter. You will do whatever I need you to do, if you care at all about your mother. I doubt Miss Garfield is one of the women involved in this. I agree that William would never allow his daughter to find a husband in this way. I presume the orphaned women are the desperate souls. You must charm your way into Miss Garfield's affections, even though you are presumed to be there for the other eager ladies. By winning her trust and admiration, you'll obtain the company for me. Women are easily led by their foolish hearts."

"You are even more callous than I thought possible. I absolutely do not have the skills or the desire to mislead Miss Garfield, and I certainly would not steal from her.

Count me out, Rex."

"You will do what I say if you want to be free of me. William would give anything to his daughter. I'm sure he'd gladly hand over Mando Merchandising to the man who becomes her husband—or kidnaps her."

"Kidnaps her? I am *not* a kidnapper. No way, Rex."

"Kidnap or marry. Your choice. As her husband, you would have rights to the company, and easy access to transfer ownership of Mando Merchandising to me. If—no—when Miss Garfield falls in love with you, the decision to marry or kidnap her can be made. Either way, William will lose his company and all his wealth to me."

"Rex, this is the most repulsive assignment you have ever asked me to do. I won't play any part in a scheme to harm this young lady or Mando Merchandising."

Garrett headed for the door.

"Who means more to you? Your mother or a stranger?"

His shoulders slumped, Garrett went back to the chair and sat down.

"I used your name in the correspondences, so you're expected," Rex said.

"My name? What did you tell them about me?"

"I have copies of the letters right here—the ones I wrote, as well as the responses." Rex pulled some papers out of a drawer, and handed them to Garrett.

"Read these, so you'll be familiar with your role."

Garrett held up the first page and read the advertisement Rex had saved from the newspaper. "These ladies only want families. If they truly grew up as orphans, as you indicated, they've already had tough lives. Have a heart, Rex. Leave them be."

Rex pounded his fist on the desk. "Have a heart? Did your daddy have a heart when he left me here to take care of his mess? Did William Garfield have a heart when he cut me out of the business we built together? I have a heart all right, ripped apart and crushed by men I have trusted and befriended, so don't tell me about my heart. These men deserve what they get."

Rex refilled his glass and sat down again. He took a long drink and stared at Garrett. "Read the letters."

Garrett read the next page which held Rex's response. Garrett cringed when he saw his own name in the opening line.

Dear Single Ladies Who Desire Husbands,
My Name is Garrett Hanley. I'm intrigued by your advertisement I came across in today's *Chicago Tribune*. I'm a God-fearing, twenty-eight-year-old man, ready to settle somewhere. I would say I'm kind and considerate. I worked so hard in the past, I have neglected any opportunities to find a wife. This has left me lonely. I believe I'm ready to be a husband to the right woman. I've fallen on hard times of late and desire an opportunity to be a good provider and family man. I'd appreciate a new start and a chance to make an honest living. I'm an experienced carpenter and businessman, with many projects to my credit. I get along well with little. I don't expect any free handouts. I ask you to allow me the opportunity to meet my wife.
Sincerely,
Garrett Hanley

"I'm not twenty-eight nor ready to be a husband. I certainly don't have the means to provide for anyone else other than my mother."

"Twenty-four is too young for a responsible husband, so you'll be twenty-eight now. You don't need to worry about provisions for anyone but me. Charming and handsome will be your weapons. Oh, and maybe a dose of your ruthlessness too. I know you have a bit of your daddy in you."

Garrett gritted his teeth. "Ruthlessness? Your plan proves you are the one who is ruthless."

Rex laughed. "Now, don't get all riled up. I shouldn't be the one you're upset with. Your daddy did you and your sweet mama wrong."

Garrett glared at Rex as he held tight to the chair to restrain himself.

Rex emptied his glass. "You might not be a perfect choice, but you're all I have. I'm confident you'll do whatever is necessary to get this done for me. Just read the rest of the letters, then I'll provide you with more details of your assignment."

Garrett reluctantly read on.

Dear Mr. Hanley,
Thank you for your response to our advertisement. From what you have shared, you sound like the kind of man we would consider. What sort of hard times have befallen you? What projects have you created? What qualities do you seek in a wife? Our town is very special and unlike any other. Tell us why we should invite you here. We only want honest and sincere men with noble intentions. Are you one of those men?
Kind Regards,
M. G.

"Who is M. G?" Garrett asked.

"Probably one of the men who works for William. You'll find out when you get to Garfield," Rex said.

Garrett turned to the next page to read the response Rex had sent on his behalf.

Dear M. G.,
I'm delighted you wrote to me. I will answer your questions as best as I can. Over the last year, I have endured some losses. My beloved dog, Hutch, fell prey to a hungry coyote. My home was built in an unfortunate location in the direct line of a twister. I've lived in a

friend's barn while I wait to rebuild or find a home of my own. My projects have included structures in Chicago and nearby cities. I desire to find a trustworthy woman who can tolerate a dog or two. I'm generous and would do my best to make my wife happy if I should be chosen. I want to be the best husband and provider for the right woman. I can assure you I'm honest and sincere. What makes you say your town is unlike any other? Why did you choose to respond to me?

Sincerely,

Garrett Hanley

"Honest and sincere? I lost my dog to a coyote, my home to a twister, and I live in a barn? Who would believe such nonsense?"

"M. G. apparently believes every word. Besides, this is a true tale. I try to add some honesty to all my endeavors because I'm a trustworthy man when people don't take advantage of me. The unfortunate circumstances all happened to someone I know. I was correct to think I might find use of his story one day. Read on."

Dear Mr. Hanley,

I'm sorry to hear about your dog. I'm sure you must miss him. I cannot imagine how awful it was to have your home swallowed up by a twister. You have had some bad luck, but you sound like a resilient man. You will be an easy man to make happy if trust and tolerance of dogs are the main traits you want. One way our town is unique is we don't have many families who live here. We are close-knit and look out for one another. I have chosen to respond to you, specifically, because you are a Christian man, which indicates you're considerate of others, and owning a dog proves your generosity of spirit. To have succeeded in an expanded area, at your young age, indicates you're a hard worker. You are someone who I believe might be a wonderful asset to our community. If you're interested in an invitation to come here, indicate this in your next letter. I will send

you a train ticket. We would like you to be here on the first of October if possible. I assume your travels would originate in Chicago. Is that correct?
Kind Regards
M. G.

"A wonderful asset? I don't know what makes you think I can live up to whom they expect to meet."

"You'll find a way if you want to help your mama," Rex said. "Read the rest."

Dear M. G.,
I'm interested in your invitation to meet my potential wife. Your town sounds like a place where people are family to each other. I imagine having friends to count on is quite a comfort. I will get my affairs in order so I can arrive on the first of October. Yes, Chicago is where I will originate. I appreciate the train ticket. I will reimburse you when I am able. Where will my travels take me? I look forward to the potential future you have made possible for me. I will do my best not to disappoint.
Sincerely,
Garrett Hanley

"The first of October? That's impossible. I can't be ready to travel by then."

"You'll be ready."

Garrett clinched his teeth as he continued to read.

Dear Mr. Hanley,
Enclosed is your ticket, which will take you from Chicago to Hannibal, Missouri. No reimbursement is needed. I will pick you up at the train station when you arrive. This is not a guarantee you will be invited to stay nor a promise of a wife. This is merely a chance for the potential wives to meet you and for you to meet them. If you become betrothed to one of our special ladies, we will welcome you as a permanent resident. In the interim, living quarters will be provided to allow time

for courtship. Wait by the front of the depot, and I will find you. Wear a red shirt if possible. This might help me to locate you. Thank you for your interest.
Kind Regards,
M. G.

Garrett shook his head. "Remarkable, Rex. You even got them to buy the train ticket to transport the thief to their town. Can't you just let this one go? I don't see how I could possibly do this."

Rex pounded his fist again. "Absolutely not! This is what I have dreamed of for years. You *will* do whatever I say."

Garrett paced the room, deep in thought. He nodded and turned to Rex.

"You must put this absolution of any obligation to you in writing, as well as turn over the deed to my mother's property. You will completely and forever leave my mother and me alone if I do this."

Rex limped to Garrett and grabbed his arm. "Don't tell me what I must do. I decide how things unfold. Fortunately for you, I don't want your mother's property. You can have it. I see no reason to stay in touch after the job is completed, either."

Garrett stared at Rex until he released his grip.

"In writing. Signed, witnessed, and sealed before I leave on any train. Agreed?"

"Gladly. I'm certain you'll miss working with me, but I will have no need for your services after this. Now let's go over this perfect plan."

Chapter 3

Maggie hurried to the stable to retrieve her horse. Blaze was already saddled and waiting for her under the tree next to the barn. She had made a habit of riding out to her parent's gravesite every Saturday since her father had died.

Blaze greeted her with a whinny.

"Hello, my favorite friend," Maggie said. "What a glorious Saturday morning." She scratched his neck while he sniffed with anticipation trying to find the hand she held behind her back. He rubbed his nose against her arm trying to pull it forward. Maggie laughed as she made him wait for what they both knew she had for him.

"All right, Blaze, here you go." Maggie gave up the apple she'd been hiding, stepped onto the mounting block, and placed the small package of food, a container of water, and her Bible into Blaze's saddlebag. Then she gripped the pommel and settled into the saddle, thankful to be wearing pants, so she didn't have to ride sidesaddle. She planned to spend some quiet time with God today and had much to share with her earthly father too.

Maggie gathered the reins. "Let's ride for a while around Black Swan Lake before we visit Mama and Papa's gravesite. I'll let you decide how fast we go."

The horse nodded his head in agreement as he gently walked to the other side of the barn. When they reached the open field, Blaze picked up the pace to a brisk trot.

The sweet freedom of open air encircled Maggie as they roamed the huge, unrestricted acreage. The sun radiated a bright smile while the wind provided a cool breeze.

Blaze slowed down, ambling along as if he wanted to take in his surroundings. Maggie relaxed in the saddle. The trees swayed in the breeze, allowing the vibrant leaves to dance in delight. Fall was pushing out summer as its multi-colors covered the green grass.

Blaze moseyed beside the lake on the property. Two rabbits barely missed being stepped on when they hopped in front of his hooves.

Black Swan Lake covered eighteen acres, and was forty-five feet at its deepest. Hank was about the only one who fished the lake. With his daily catches of crappie, striped bass, and walleye, Annabelle served fish often for dinner at Mando.

"Let's take a break, Blazey boy. My legs could use a bit of stretching."

Blaze came to a stop next to a stump to allow Maggie to step down. They walked to the water's edge where Blaze took a long drink. Maggie pulled her Bible from the saddlebag, then sat on the bench Hank had built under her favorite sycamore tree. Blaze grazed on the grass, twitching his tail at flies trying to take rest on him.

Maggie turned the pages to the book of James. She read the first five verses to herself, and then slowly read verse six aloud. "But let him ask in faith, nothing wavering. For he that wavereth is like a wave of the sea driven with the wind and tossed."

These verses gave Maggie a sense of strength. God must want her to move forward with the plan to bring in potential grooms for the ladies of Garfield. She had wavered between doubt and confidence, never completely trusting God. Maggie bowed her head in repentance.

Dearest Lord, help me not to waver in doing your work. I'm convinced we have created a wonderful community, and we need to let others in. Unless you show me differently, I will pursue this endeavor to the fullest. Give me wisdom and discernment to choose the right gentlemen for our precious ladies. I want to honor you in this town, and I thank you for the opportunities you have given us. I love you so much. Thank you for all you do. Amen.

Maggie returned her Bible to the bag, then stood on the stump to climb into Blaze's saddle.

"All right, let's go spend some time with Mama and Papa."

Ten minutes later, they arrived at her parents' resting place. Maggie slid to the ground and retrieved the food and water from the saddlebag.

She pulled out some carrots and handed one to Blaze. "Here you go."

Blaze nodded his head in agreement as he chomped on the desired snack. Maggie gave him several more carrots, then she sat next to the headstone.

"Hello, Mama. I'm here again. I should be the one in the ground, not you. Your other babies knew you wouldn't be strong enough to give them life. I was stubborn and selfish, even before birth. I fought for my life without a care for you. Papa's heart remained yours until the day he died. How wonderful the world would have been with you in it."

Maggie moved to the other side of the stone to face her father's name. "Hello, Papa. I take the responsibilities you've left to me quite seriously. I will do my very best to continue your work to honor Mama. I don't feel competent to oversee the company or the town, but since you always had such confidence in me, I'll work hard to make you proud. We've come to a major decision regarding the dynamics of Garfield. The ladies want families, so we're planning to invite potential grooms to come here. I'm fearful of the plan, but I believe we must move forward. How I wish you were here to help me. If successful, perhaps some of the ladies will be able to have many years with their husbands, unlike you and Mama. Don't worry, Papa, I will never marry, as I've always told you. My purpose is overseeing Mando and Garfield."

A white-tailed buck led a doe and fawn from behind a big oak tree, strolling to the headstone, as if they were friends with Maggie's parents. The buck munched on grass until he saw Maggie.

"I won't hurt ..." Maggie was unable to finish her sentence before the graceful animals raced away out of sight.

"Thank you, Lord, for sending a family of deer. Perhaps you've given me a sign of confirmation to form families in Garfield. This encourages me to press on toward my goal of doing what's best for your town."

Maggie ate two biscuits filled with plum jelly and took a long drink of water while Blaze chomped the last few carrots.

The sun was moving down the horizon, waving goodbye with its slanting rays of orange. Maggie patted her parent's tombstone. "I need to go. I love you both and wish we were together now, but I look forward to eternity with you. Hope you're having lots of fun up there. I'll come talk to you again next week."

Maggie led Blaze to a stump, then climbed up into the saddle. "Ok, sweet friend, we'd best head back to the house."

Chapter 4

"Dear, look at what I found," Mr. Walker said, handing the *St. Louis Post-Dispatch* to his wife, pointing to an advertisement. "This might be the solution to our son's future. I have never heard of such a ridiculous thing—lonely spinsters begging men to marry them. Ludicrous." He laughed so hard he snorted.

Mrs. Walker read the entry that had brought so much entertainment to her husband. She looked up at him with a twinkle in her eye. "Although I will admit to a somewhat shocked reaction to women publicizing to marry, upon further thought, this might be the perfect endeavor for our son."

"Have you gone mad? I was joking!"

She scolded him with her eyes. "I take offense to your question."

"I would never desire to offend you, my dear, but I must point out the obvious. Jesse has shown no interest to become betrothed to anyone, nor does he appear to be ready to be a husband any time soon. I do not want him to go near any of these desperate women."

Mrs. Walker frowned. "I think you're underestimating the potential here. We should give this opportunity proper deliberation. I'm done with Jesse's shenanigans. You must be too. Twenty-three years old with no apparent desire to leave his carefree life. Burning down Mr. Haskell's barn was the last straw. You had to give Mr. Haskell enough money to build three barns to get Jesse out of trouble."

Mr. Walker shook his head. "Even if we want this, I'm certain Jesse will not. He would never agree to marry, let alone meet a wife in this manner. Getting him to write to those despairing women would be impossible. I think you should abandon this idea."

Undeterred, Mrs. Walker answered, "I will respond on his behalf. If Jesse is chosen, we will force his hand. Should he refuse, we merely invoke the consequence of no more financial support from us."

"What? Cut him off? That's extreme. Would this be fair?"

"Fair? Was it fair for him to burn down the barn, even if he says the fire was an accident? I think it's time for Jesse to recognize he's an adult.

"I cannot imagine a positive outcome, my dear. Disaster is around the corner. However, I will be supportive as I leave this in your capable hands."

Mrs. Walker was confident she could write a convincing enough letter to get Jesse chosen. At her desk, she pulled out a sheet of paper and dipped the fountain pin into the ink.

Dearest Ladies,
I was thrilled beyond measure when I read your advertisement in the St Louis Post-Dispatch. I couldn't help but think this is exactly the opportunity I need. As a Christian man, I too desire companionship and family life. I'm a recent graduate from the prestigious Transylvania College, having obtained my law degree. I would like to start a practice in a city which could use my services. I'm also a seasoned teacher who has tutored many fellow classmates. I have much knowledge and experiences to share. I could be a valuable citizen to any community. My family and friends would say I'm

an asset to know. Even children love me. I've not found anyone to share my life with here in St. Louis and desire to meet someone special. My mother would tell you I'm kind and considerate. I need a family of my own to be the man I'm meant to be. I'm willing to sacrifice and leave my loved ones in St. Louis if it means I will be matched to my ideal companion. Respond soon because I'm anxious for this chance to fulfill my life. I trust I've not appeared to be boastful. Since this letter is my only way to get your attention, I feel it is important to share my most outstanding qualities.

With Sincerest Gratitude,

Jesse Walker

Mrs. Walker read over the letter and nodded, confident the words represented Jesse's positive attributes. She handed the letter to her husband. "Please read this and tell me what you think."

Mr. Walker took the paper and read the words his wife had written. He set down the correspondence, shaking his head.

"I think this sounds like a young man who is well-thought-of by his mother. This letter should get the attention of many ladies because you have presented our son in an unmerited favorable light. You used your superb gift of embellishment, which is necessary if Jesse is to stand a chance. There is no way he can live up to the reputation you've dreamed up for him. My greatest joy would be to see Jesse become a man deserving of such desirable praise. Send the correspondence, then wait to see if they're interested in meeting our perfect son."

Mr. Walker chuckled. "Can you envision Jesse writing this letter? Oh, and what a scene he will make when he finds out what you've done. My, my! This could be quite entertaining."

"It doesn't matter what Jesse *wants*. This is what he

needs. We must pray our Jesse will be chosen."

Mr. Walker embraced his wife. He released his hold and lifted her chin.

"He'll be fine. Remember the Bible says if we rear a child in the way he should go, he will remember it. We've done our best to train Jesse to be a man of character. Now we must trust God to lead him to his full potential.

Chapter 5

Maggie had collected over thirty letters from potential suitors. Except for Garrett Hanley's, none of them compelled her to respond. She reluctantly opened the envelope from a Mr. Jesse Walker. Her heart leapt as she read the correspondence. She wanted to know more about this gentleman. Maggie replied right away.

> Dear Mr. Walker,
> Thank you for your interest in our advertisement. You seem to be a well-educated man with much to offer our town. I would like to ask you a few questions as I decide if you are a potential husband for one of our ladies. What do you desire in a wife? Do you currently have a law practice in St. Louis? How would your mother feel if you moved away, as it appears you are close? Do you have any siblings? When would you be available to travel?
> Sincerely,
> M. G.

Maggie received a reply a little over two weeks later.

> Dearest M.G.
> Thank you for your letter. I am an active seeker of knowledge, so I have learned much. The qualities I desire in a wife are companionship, along with intelligent conversations. Someone who can encourage me to use my talents. I need a woman who will be patient with me as I learn to be a husband. I do not currently have

a law practice but am anxious to get one started. My mother is also excited about this possibility, aware of our correspondences. I have not been blessed with siblings. I could be available to travel next month. You won't regret giving me a chance.

With a Heart of Anticipation,

Jesse Walker

Maggie was now certain she wanted to invite Jesse Walker to Garfield. If she could get her reply out right away, she might be able to coordinate Mr. Walker's arrival with Mr. Hanley's.

Dear Mr. Walker,

I would like to invite you to come to Hannibal, Missouri as a candidate for matrimony. Train schedules from St. Louis show you could arrive around three o'clock in the afternoon on the first of October. Would that be acceptable? I will arrange transportation to our nearby town. A room will be provided for the duration of any courtship. Train fare will be afforded if this is agreeable. We are delighted to get the opportunity to meet you.

Sincerely,

M. G.

Once again, Maggie received a letter from Mr. Walker within two weeks. She quickly opened the envelope.

Dearest M. G.

I am overjoyed to accept your invitation. There is no need to send a train ticket. I have the funds available. I will arrive in Hannibal at your desired time of three o'clock on the first of October. I am anxious to meet my bride. Thank you.

With My Deepest Happiness,

Jesse Walker

Relief came over Maggie as she realized there would be two gentlemen for the ladies to get to know. Perhaps her plan might work, after all. She sent her confirmation to Mr. Walker with haste.

> Dear Mr. Walker,
> I am delighted you have agreed to travel here. Your generous offer to purchase your train ticket is appreciated. However, we have rented a Pullman car for your comfort. Your fare has already been paid. Keep in mind this is not a guarantee you will be invited to stay in our town, just a chance to get acquainted. We are hopeful for a match. Thank you for your interest in our endeavor. Wear a red shirt to better identify yourself. Wait by the front of the depot. We'll find you.
> Sincerely,
> M. G.

After she sent her response, Maggie second-guessed herself. What had she done? Was it truly wise to invite strangers to Garfield? Knowing little about the gentlemen, Maggie hoped they would be what they claimed. Now too late to stop them, a burst of panic overcame her until she remembered what the Bible says about praying instead of being anxious.

Many had prayed about potential grooms for weeks now. Maggie needed to trust God for guidance and protection. He was faithful and always with her. Through this assurance, Maggie's anxiety receded.

Chapter 6

The porter reached for Garrett Hanley's bag as he boarded the train at Central Station in Chicago. Garrett kept a tight grip as he shook his head.

"No thanks. I might need some of the items in here. I'll keep the bag with me."

The porter nodded and Garrett stepped into the Pullman car. The luxury and comfort might make up for the extra time to route through St. Louis on the way to Hannibal. Garrett would have rather taken a more direct route, but the additional miles might be just what he needed to prepare his mind for what lay ahead.

Garrett sank down onto a plush bench in the back row, dropping his bag on the seat. He stretched his long legs under the table in front of him, then looked out the wide window. His bloodshot eyes stared back at him in the reflection. He should have shaved. He would need to present himself properly, with charm, to complete Rex's dirty job. Disgust at the man he saw forced him to look away.

Garrett's face heated with anger towards his father for causing him to be involved with a man like Rex Tillman. Willing himself to relax, Garrett closed his eyes. His thoughts turned to the immediate future.

Garrett buried his face in his hands.

I can do this. My only choice ... only choice ...

The train's whistle blew, causing Garrett to jump, realizing he'd dozed off. Another sleepless night.

Why did my father leave me in this predicament? I should not be here.

Garrett told himself he was a decent man. He didn't believe it.

"All aboard," the conductor yelled.

I need to get off. I can't do this.

Garrett was rising to his feet just as the train began to move.

Too late! Now I have no choice.

Garrett sat back down. He opened his bag to take out the letters from M. G.

I must do this for my freedom and for my mother. I'm not a bad person. Yes, you are, Garrett Hanley.

He reread the letters until he had memorized the information and thought of embellishments to add. Garrett returned the envelopes to his bag, then laid his head against the seat back.

"Would you like a meal, sir?"

The porter was placing a platter of food in front of him.

"Yes, thank you. I am hungry."

Garrett read the menu placed next to the meal. Hunter's soup, salmon with hollandaise sauce, sweet potatoes, green beans, plum pudding, and coffee. He ate every bite, unable to remember the last time he consumed such delicious food.

A full stomach added to Garrett's exhaustion. His body finally gave in to fatigue as he fell asleep, only to wake with a start when the porter touched his shoulder.

"Sir, I have your bed pulled down. Would you like to freshen up before you retire?"

Garrett could only convince one eye to open, making out a fuzzy image of a man.

"Ummm ... No ... just show me to the bed."

The porter led Garrett to the sleeper and shut the curtain.

A few hours later, Garrett awoke to squealing wheels.

The conductor shouted, "Next stop. St. Louis."

Chapter 7

"I'm confused. What are you talking about? I must be having a nightmare." Jesse's squinted eyes refused to open as the light poured in from the window.

"Your bags are already packed, Jesse," Mrs. Walker said. "Jack is ready to take you to the train station. Get dressed. Nine o'clock is fast approaching."

"Nine o'clock? Why are you in my room at this unreasonable hour? Talk to me when I get up after noon."

"Jesse Walker, it's time you made something of yourself," his mother declared. "Get up before you're carried to the car. I responded to that advertisement and you're going."

"You're not making sense. What advertisement? Just go away."

Jesse pulled the quilt over his head, which his father threw on the floor.

"Son, it pains me to do this, but your mother is right. We must help you become the man God wants you to be. You will get on a train to Hannibal, Missouri, to claim your wife."

"What? My wife? Have you gone mad? Absolutely not." Jesse put a pillow over his head.

Mr. Walker pulled Jesse up along with the pillow, holding firm as Mrs. Walker stepped across the room to stand directly in front of them.

"I replied on your behalf to an advertisement from ladies who want husbands. They will provide jobs and homes to the right men."

"I don't need a job. No. No. No. I won't go. This is more than ridiculous and it's too early in the day for a prank."

"This most certainly is not a prank, and, you absolutely have no choice. As of today, you will be responsible for yourself. Your father and I have cut you off from our money."

"Cut me off? You can't do that."

"Not only can we, but we have."

"Father, talk some sense into her. Let's discuss this as a family."

Mr. Walker looked down as he shook his head. "I'm sorry, Son. I must stand with your mother on this decision. We have truly done a disservice to you in allowing you to waste your intelligent mind with your frolicsome life style. You must go because you are no longer welcome to live here. Mr. Haskell's barn sealed your fate."

"You both know the burning of the barn was not intentional. Just bad luck. Let me show you my responsible self. I can move to my own residence right here in St Louis if you'd like. Your monetary assistance will only be needed until I can establish myself as a lawyer. It shouldn't take more than a couple of years."

"No, Jesse. Time has run out," his father said. "You are off to Hannibal today. Show us how mature you are by making excellent choices while you're there. Your future with our wealth is on shaky ground right now."

"You might be able to force me to go there, but you cannot make me marry anyone."

"All we expect from you is to have an open mind and to focus on your obligations as a responsible gentleman. If you truly give this a fair effort, we will re-evaluate your financial status. You must become accountable for your actions," Mr. Walker said.

"What do you mean by fair effort?"

"Several months, at least six, with a genuine courtship." Mr. Walker said.

"*Six months*?" Jesse grumbled.

"Yes, with a courtship. No exceptions," Mr. Walker said.

"I cannot promise to court or marry anyone, especially a less than classy woman who advertises in a newspaper for a man."

"And I cannot promise your financial future if you do not take this opportunity seriously," Mr. Walker said. "Besides, these ladies might surprise you with their merits. Don't be so quick to judge."

"We know you have much to offer this world," his mother assured Jesse. "We cannot sit back and watch you waste your talents on fun and games. We want you to be successful in life. Now, get dressed so you can go. Your valet has your clothes ready to wear. You will *not* miss that train."

The Walkers waited for Jesse in the parlor. He joined them a mere fifteen minutes later, less than well-groomed.

"Am I at least allowed to eat? I'm starving."

"Breakfast is waiting in the motorcar," Mrs. Walker said.

At the car, Mrs. Walker hugged her son. "We love you, Jesse. You will thank us for this one day."

Jesse mumbled his disagreement.

Mr. Walker reached out and shook Jesse's hand. "Make us proud, Son."

"I'm only going because I have no choice. But ... remember ... this is *not* a promise I will be married. This is unfair of you both."

"We pray for a wonderful outcome from this *very* fair adventure," Mrs. Walker said.

Jesse reluctantly got into the motorcar passenger seat. He used to be proud of the fact they were the only family in St Louis who owned a gasoline-powered Fisson Wagonette, which could hold up to six passengers. Today, he wished they didn't have such a luxury to get him to the train station on time. Horse and buggy would be better, and slower.

The family driver, Jack, put the car in motion. He pointed to the basket on the seat between them. "There's your food, sir."

"At least something is going right today," Jesse said as he devoured a sizable piece of meat. When he had swallowed the mouthful, he looked at Jack again. "Did you have anything to do with this trickery?"

Jack shook his head. "I only do what I'm told."

"You did get my bags, right?"

Jack pointed behind him. "They're in the back."

Jesse's curly black hair fell over his brown eyes. He liked his hair long, even though it was just one more reason for his mother to be irritated with him. Jesse pushed the curls back and pulled on a hat.

"Jack, why do you think my mother is so nonsensical in her treatment of me? Don't you agree I'm still a young man who needs to enjoy life before I'm forced to become a work slave?"

"You might have a point, sir."

"I have a valid point. What's wrong with a guy who wants to have a little fun?"

"Not wrong at all, sir."

"I've only been home for less than a year since I graduated at the top of my class at Transylvania University. Top of my class! Doesn't a guy get any credit for the hard work I've done to excel at my studies?"

"You've shown how smart you are."

"Honestly, Jack, if my parents wanted to send me away, why not let me explore places that would intrigue me? Like England or Canada? No. Hannibal, Missouri. Who goes to Hannibal? Who's even heard of Hannibal?

"I can see where you'd be upset."

"What young man in his right mind wouldn't be upset? My brain was made to take in the experiences of life while I'm still so full of curiosity. Besides, we both know my family has plenty of money. Why can't I enjoy it?"

"You should definitely be able to enjoy your life, sir."

"My father works way too hard, puts in too many hours. Doesn't have time to relax or enjoy life, ever. I don't want to live such a confined life."

"Hard work takes a lot out of a man, sir."

"I might admit some fun might have gone a little too far for my parents' taste, but they've always been able to afford to take care of the little mishaps."

"Yes, your parents have always supported you, sir."

You're a lucky man, Jack. You just get in a carriage or motorcar and take people places. You'll never have to worry about any big responsibilities like me. You're fortunate to have not been born into money."

"So lucky, sir."

"I need to take a nap. It's fine if you forget to wake me up when we get there."

"You deserve some rest, sir."

The motorcar stopped in front of Union Station in St. Louis. Jack got out and opened Jesse's door.

"We've arrived, sir," Jack said as he shook Jesse awake.

"Unfortunately, I can see we have," Jesse said, rubbing his eyes.

He slowly stepped out of the motorcar, and Jack handed his three bags to the porter.

"Best of luck to you, Mr. Walker."

"I'll need it. You might as well count on a return visit to this train station soon because I don't plan to be gone long. I *will not* marry some strange woman, either. I'll find a way to appease my parents so I can shorten my stay. Six months is a lifetime. Mother's plan is outlandish."

"Outlandish, indeed, sir."

"At least I'll have decent accommodations on this train since I'll be riding in the Pullman. No way I'd sit in a dirty hard seat in a crowded passenger car."

"You should never have to experience such an uncomfortable situation, sir. Take care."

Jesse watched Jack drive away, then boarded the Pullman car, taking a seat next to an unshaven man in a red shirt.

"Hi, I'm Jesse Walker."

"Garrett Hanley."

"Looks like red is the popular color today. Mind if I sit here?"

"Sure. Whatever."

"I'm off to somewhere crazy, and it would be nice to have someone to talk to."

Garrett shook his head. "Jesse Walker, it can't be any crazier than my destination."

Chapter 8

Maggie's mind was overwhelmed with a tussle of conflicting thoughts that refused to let her sleep. She watched twinkling stars in the darkness slowly fade away to the rising sun from her bedchamber window. Morning came much sooner than Maggie wanted. Lack of rest always gave her a headache and today was no different. She rubbed her throbbing temples.

What am I doing? I'm not ready for today. I need to find a way to stop those two strangers from arriving. This can't be a sound idea.

"God, can I talk to You? Will you intervene? If this is not what's best, block the way. If this is your will, give me peace. I trust you, Lord. Thank you for your faithfulness even when I make preposterous decisions. I doubt me, not you."

Maggie sat up and slid off the bed until her feet landed on the cool wood floor. She opened the window, taking in a long breath of chilly air as she continued talking to God.

"Oh Lord, I usually look forward to this time of year, when the trees are painted in their dazzling colors of reds and yellows, and cool weather has arrived. Today, I just feel dread."

Maggie watched the clouds dance above the lake, swirling into fog over the nearby misty grass. The pounding of a woodpecker added a beating drum to the singing birds nearby. Song birds are soothing, but the woodpecker wasn't helping her headache one bit.

"Dear God, I am blessed to live next to Black Swan Lake, so lovely and safe. I ask you to not allow any strangers to take away the serenity of our town."

After several minutes, Maggie reluctantly ambled from the window to the box Sophie Jenkins had sent. Inside was a new creation for Maggie to wear.

She donned the dark green skirt and crisp purple shirt. Maggie's uneasiness slipped away when she gazed at herself in the mirror. Professional. Businesswoman. Looking closer, she noticed the purple frogs embroidered throughout her skirt, bringing a smile to her face. Sassy. Fun. Maggie turned and walked down to the kitchen.

"Good morning, Emma, are you enjoying this cool weather today?" Emma had been working for William Garfield since Maggie was young, much more like a grandmother than an employee. There wasn't a need for so many staff members, but Maggie was glad she could provide jobs for eight people.

"Oh yes, dear. Who doesn't love fall? Breakfast is ready. I brewed some cinnamon ginger tea too."

"These eggs look delicious. Tea sounds wonderful—just what my headache needs. You're the best, Emma, always knowing what I like. Thank you. Please join me."

Emma poured them both a cup of tea, then sat down to eat with Maggie.

"I hope meeting the fellas goes well today. I'll be praying for you."

"Thank you. Prayers are much needed. Oh, Emma, what was I thinking inviting these gentlemen here? Will welcoming potential husbands to Garfield be wise?"

"You prayerfully considered the idea for a long while before telling the ladies. Remember feeling at peace about your plan?"

"Yes, but peace seems to come and go."

"Our Lord is a God of peace. Satan wants confusion. Perhaps these gentlemen will bring glory to our Savior, which the devil would not like. Don't let uncertainty take away your peace."

"Too late now, anyway. Mr. Garrett Hanley and Mr. Jesse Walker will be here today whether we're ready or not."

"I believe good will come of this. Trust God."

"Thank you, Emma. I adore you."

"I'm fairly fond of you too," Emma said with a smile.

After finishing breakfast, Maggie slipped into her waxed cotton duster, then grabbed the oversized leather handbag with work documents inside.

Maxwell Crawford was waiting outside to take Maggie to work. "Good morning, Maggie." He tipped his hat, helping her into the four-seater motorcar.

"Good morning, Uncle Max. You're certainly looking mighty debonair today. What type of hat are you wearing? Looks like a Bowler, but not exactly. I don't think I've seen you in one like that before."

"This is Aunt Catherine's take on a Bowler hat. She told me the hard black felt material, along with the narrow brim and rounded crown, have been credited with being much more durable than other hats. She added the blue trim and feather so I could show off her fashion sense. I could live without the extras, but you know Aunt Catherine. She sold me on this hat when she declared it would stay on my head, even when struck by a tree branch. I'm anxious to check the reliability of such a claim at some point."

"It suits you well, even with the feather. I certainly have the best-dressed driver around. Be careful with those trees. Your reliability test could be dangerous if the branches are too large or too low. One's head is important to the quality of life." Maggie snickered as she pictured Uncle Max challenging tree branches on his rides through the country.

Maxwell Crawford wasn't Maggie's blood uncle, nor was Catherine her real aunt, but the couple grew up in the same orphanage as her parents. Maggie had known them both her entire life, visiting each other often. They spent every holiday together, which made them seem like family. The Crawfords moved to Garfield from Kansas City shortly after Maggie's father died, so she wouldn't be alone. Uncle Max and Aunt Catherine wanted Maggie to have proper chaperones, but mostly family, nearby.

Max adored mechanical inventions, with a passion for motorcars, so being Maggie's driver was a perfect job for him. Max oversaw bringing in any motorcars he thought belonged in Garfield's small fleet, which Maggie was pleased to fund.

Max reached into the back seat to grab a box, handing it to Maggie. "Compliments of Aunt Catherine."

Maggie unwrapped the package and pulled out a green suede hat with little frogs hopping around the brim, along with a purple scarf.

Max laughed at the sight. "Hmmm ... Frogs."

Maggie opened her duster to show Max what she was wearing. "Aunt Catherine worked together with Sophie on this, obviously."

Max nodded. "Yes, quite obviously."

Maggie put on the hat and scarf. "Now my wardrobe is complete."

"Do you want to drive today?"

"No, no, no, not today. Let's save that lesson for a future tomorrow. I've got enough worries on my mind." Maggie looked straight ahead to avoid Max's eyes. "Besides, you know how much my sweet horse would get jealous. Blaze is sad enough to be left at home today."

Max shook his head and smiled. "I expected a similar answer. You win. I'll let you ride today. We're going to get you driving a motorcar one day soon. I don't know why you aren't more excited about this."

"Sounds perfect, Uncle Max. Tomorrow ... or so."

They both laughed as Max drove them down the hard packed clay road toward Mando Merchandising.

As they passed by Black Swan Lake, Maggie looked over at the white church with the steeple reaching for the sky. She loved seeing God's house come to life with her family of friends on Sundays. Garfield still didn't have a permanent pastor, so townsfolk took turns sharing Scripture lessons. They had been praying for the right pastor for a while now as they waited for God's timing

Max and Maggie greeted the folks on horseback as they rode past them. Most of them, like Maggie, had little to no interest in learning to maneuver a motorcar. Other than Max, only Mando Merchandising delivery drivers, using Garfield's Winton Motor Carriage Delivery Wagons, were operating vehicles.

The postmistress, Mildred Taylor, stood in front of the sky-blue post office, a bag of mail in her arms. Mildred, once an orphan keeper, had come to Garfield after the orphanage she supervised closed due to lack of funding. She lived in the back area of the building, which looked more like a home than a business with its window boxes filled with blooming petunias.

Max stopped as Mildred walked to the motorcar, placing the bag in the seat behind Maggie.

"These letters were missed yesterday when Daphne picked up mail. Thought you might need them before today's normal delivery."

"Thank you, Mildred. How is your day going so far?" Maggie said.

"Just finished tending to my garden. Pumpkins are about as big as the wheels on this car." Mildred cast a smug grin toward Max.

"Trying to dethrone me from Pumpkin Champion at the Harvest Festival, are you?" Max said with an ornery frown.

"Could be. I won't mention my sweet potatoes and squash. I've got to keep my competition in the dark."

"Challenge accepted. We need to get to Mando. See you later," Max said.

Across the street, Catherine's rosy pink shop, The Happy Hatter, vied with Sophie's pastel purple boutique, Sophie's Sensations, for the most colorful buildings on the block. Their hats and clothing were popular items in Mando's catalog. Catherine and Sophie were building a reputation with clients, receiving many orders for their goods. Maggie recently hired several more orphaned ladies to help meet demand.

"Good morning, dear ones," Catherine yelled as she stood in the doorway with an armful of hats.

Max stopped the car. "You work too hard, darling. How about if you take the day off so I can spoil you with a shopping trip to Hannibal?"

"Creating hats is not work, just a delightful way to pass time. Can't shop today. I have several orders to get out. Plus, I'm training the new ladies who got here last week. Thank you for the offer, love."

"Alright. I'll take you to dinner at the noon hour. You'll need a break by then."

"I accept."

Max and Maggie continued toward Mando.

The red brick Shoe Emporium next to Sophie's place had colorful painted shoes appearing to run across the building, thanks to Sophie's creative paintbrushes. Gladys Clark kept fashionable inventory to fit almost all sizes. Maggie no longer needed to order extra small shoes from New York to fit her dainty feet.

Hank and his crew of ladies were building a bookstore, already hard at work this morning. As soon as Max and

Maggie got close, Hank's Cocker Spaniel, Daisy, ran to greet them. Max reached down to rub his nose.

"Get on back over here, Daisy," Hank yelled. "Don't be bothering Max."

"No worries, Hank. Daisy and I are good friends who need to see each other occasionally."

Daisy ran to where Hank was standing.

"The store is coming along well, Hank. I can't wait to put lots of books in there," Maggie said.

"Should be ready in a couple of months."

"Very exciting. I appreciate all the hard work."

"Our pleasure," Hank said. "Still on for supper tonight?"

"Yes, the gentlemen arrive this afternoon. I'm so happy you can join us."

"Wouldn't miss it."

"We better get going so Maggie can get to Mando,' Max said. "See you tonight, Hank."

There was still plenty of room for more buildings in town. Annabelle wanted to open a Sweet Shop, and Maggie wanted to make that happen soon. A general store stood at the edge of town. Much of their stock came from Mando Merchandising.

"We don't have many shoppers who walk into our stores, thankfully, as everyone is quite busy creating items for catalog orders. If Garfield forms many families, and as we hire more workers, I imagine our town could become crowded," Maggie said.

"Yes, Aunt Catherine is quite thrilled to train more young ladies to make and sell hats."

Max and Maggie passed by houses, some were farms, while others had just a small yard to maintain. The ladies were offered several home plans to choose from, as well as furniture.

"All our diverse homes are quite lovely and colorful. Town folks seem to have varied tastes, which makes for a beautiful setting. Your father was smart to find an area like Garfield, with so many rocks and trees close by. I believe the rock quarry and sawmill will supply our town's needs for many years to come."

"He was the most intelligent man I've ever known."

Max cleared his throat.

"You come in a very close second." Maggie winked.

"Good enough."

Maggie wondered where a school might go for future children. Perhaps near the church. She felt overwhelmed again.

Max stopped the motorcar in front of Mando Merchandising.

"Thanks for escorting me, Uncle Max. I haven't taken a carriage into work since you've been here."

"My pleasure. I like spending time with you. This is a special day for a few of the ladies at Mando. I imagine they're a bit anxious."

"I don't know about Ruth, Sadie, and Annabelle, but my stomach has been in knots since last night. I hope I won't regret this decision."

"The two gentlemen are still scheduled to come at three o'clock, correct?"

"Yes, Mr. Garrett Hanley and Mr. Jesse Walker will be in Hannibal then. Are you still planning to escort me?"

"Absolutely, I'll be back here at Mando at two o'clock, which should get us to the train station on time. There's no way you'd be allowed to go alone. Besides, you refuse to drive a motorcar. Horse buggies would take too long, so we must go together. To be honest, I'm unsure about strange men coming here as well. I'll need to keep a very close eye on them."

"I can always count on you to look out for me and the other ladies. Of course, you know I *am* pretty good at taking care of myself.

"Yes, I'm aware. Just as your father wanted."

Max helped Maggie out of the motorcar, then drove away.

Maggie walked through the room where the announcement had taken place about bringing in potential husbands. She had to fight the feeling of panic as she entered the kitchen area where several of the ladies were enjoying breakfast. Many of the employees came in early so they could enjoy Annabelle's cooking.

"Good morning, my friends. What a glorious day." Maggie greeted them with a determined smile.

"Good morning." Their answer came in chorus.

"Yes, it is. The fall season is finally here," Ruth said. "You're beautiful, as usual, Maggie. Wait ... frogs ... Sophie?"

"Thank you, Ruth. Yes, frogs, created by Sophie. Don't you just love them?" Maggie said this with a wink as Ruth laughed.

"Oh, and Aunt Catherine made this with some of Sophie's material," Maggie removed her hat, holding it out for viewing.

"Those two make quite a duo," Ruth said.

"Yes, they do. Imagine how boring life would be without them," Maggie said.

She poured herself a cup of coffee with extra cream and a little sugar.

"Enjoy your day," Maggie said as she exited the room.

Chapter 9

The door to Maggie's office bolted open as Mr. Levi Jackson flew in like a hawk swooping down for its prey.

"What brain were you using when you decided to invite a bunch of strangers to come here without my knowledge? Have you lost all your senses or do you just like making reckless decisions?"

"What a pleasure to see you this morning, Mr. Jackson. Especially with such a warm and engaging demeanor."

The intruder ignored her sarcasm. "I won't allow it, Miss Garfield. Your father hired me to protect this town, and you have seriously altered my ability to do my job effectively."

"I own Garfield. I make decisions without you." Maggie leaned back in her chair and folded her arms in defiance.

"As a security agent from the prestigious Pinkerton National Detective Agency, I own Mr. Garfield's authority to govern those decisions which impact you and this town. In fact, I have a contract with his signature to back me up. You have proven to be a sound decision-maker up to this point. This is, by far, the most irresponsible venture you have ever gotten this town involved in."

Maggie took a deep breath to calm the rage building inside of her. "This is *not* irresponsible. Mr. Jackson, perhaps your disapproval is because, up to now, there has not been a need for any security measures. Garfield has no crime. You've been paid well to do almost nothing. Bringing in strangers might require you to leave your chair."

Levi's lips narrowed until he visibly calmed. "Miss Garfield, if you weren't a lady, I would use some choice words. Since you are unaware of my mission for your father, I will ignore your last comments."

"What mission? My father always made me aware of everything."

"Almost everything."

"Mr. Jackson, there is nothing my father would keep from me."

"Unless he was protecting you."

"Protecting me from what?"

"Not what ... who. Mr. Garfield told me to keep you abreast only if a threatening situation prevails."

"You cannot keep this information from me now that I'm aware my father thought I needed protecting."

Levi ignored her protest, appearing to be in deep thought. "Do you remember a man named Rex Tillman?"

Maggie thought for a moment. "Yes, I do recall a Mr. Tillman worked for my father when I was younger but left several years ago."

"Mr. Tillman was forced to leave when he tried to steal Mando Merchandising."

"Steal our company? Father would not have kept something of that magnitude from me."

"He sheltered you from this information. I'm here to make sure Garfield is safe from Mr. Tillman ... and now apparently, from strangers." Levi raised his voice again. "You cannot invite gentlemen here whom I have not checked out ahead of time. The plan must not proceed."

"You will need to lower your voice and settle down if we're going to resolve this matter."

"I am a little riled, which has caused me to be a bit loud, but with reason, Miss Garfield."

"Mr. Jackson, I've already placed the advertisements in the newspapers. In fact, I've been corresponding with two gentlemen for several weeks. They'll arrive in Hannibal today at three o'clock."

"Today? Three o'clock? That is only a few hours away. You truly have lost all your senses."

Levi paced around the room, shaking his head, mumbling his disbelief. "We need more time to prepare. These gentlemen must be stopped."

Maggie rose to her feet. "We cannot delay the gentlemen's arrival, Mr. Jackson. They're already on a train. Besides, this is too important for the ladies in this town. So, we just need to make sure we're ready for them."

"I do not agree with this craziness, but you've left me no choice. I will require temporary reinforcement. A few men must be hired to help watch over everyone here."

Maggie's fury returned. "Oh, so it's alright for you to bring in strangers to our town, but I can't?"

Levi glared at her. "Yes, it's completely appropriate to add staff to my security efforts since you've created an unstable environment. I will scrutinize any gentlemen coming here in the future ... *before* they are invited. As for those arriving today, I need their names and where they're coming from. I want to discover as much as I can about them."

Maggie gritted her teeth but tamped down her temper. "I can understand your concern, Mr. Jackson. However, I feel certain the gentlemen will prove to be upstanding."

"You cannot be certain until the records prove their characters. Their names?" Levi already had a pen in hand along with a pad of paper.

"Mr. Garrett Hanley is coming from Chicago, Illinois, and Mr. Jesse Walker is arriving from St. Louis, Missouri."

"I need to get going on this right away." Levi put the pad in his pocket and rose to his feet. "Miss Garfield, you *must* consult me before you do anything which will change the dynamics of this town. I cannot be blindsided by decisions affecting the community's security. Can we agree to work together?"

Maggie couldn't deny she understood his concerns. "I probably do need to inform you of important matters regarding Garfield. I'll try to remember in the future, as the safety of this town is vital to me, as well."

"*Probably*? You'll *try*? These are non-negotiable actions, young lady. You *must* inform me now, and in the future, no matter what."

"I will do my best to keep you aware of important decisions, Mr. Jackson. However, I expect the same from you. I certainly should have known Mr. Tillman is a concern." Maggie's words allowed no possibility of denial.

"Agreed. We can protect Garfield best if we work together. There's only one daily passenger stagecoach from Hannibal to Garfield, so will the gentlemen stay in Hannibal overnight? Obviously, they missed this morning's departure."

"Mr. Crawford will escort me in a motorcar to Hannibal. We will meet Mr. Hanley and Mr. Walker when they arrive, then bring the gentlemen to Garfield."

"What time do you plan to leave today?"

"Mr. Crawford will be here in time for a two o'clock departure."

Levi walked to the door, then turned to face Maggie. "I'll investigate these two gentlemen's lives right away. Oh, and I'll be out front at two o'clock to accompany you to the train station. Do not leave without me."

Maggie gritted her teeth as she watched Levi exit. *How dare he order me around?*

Chapter 10

Maggie paced her office, alternately castigating Levi Jackson's presumptuousness and herself for not standing up to him more. At length, she settled at her desk with paperwork.

Josephine Swanson, Maggie's secretary, knocked on her door. "Miss Garfield, I wanted to remind you of your meeting in a few minutes."

"Oh my, almost noon already? What would I do without you? Thank you, Josephine."

Maggie had told Ruth, Sadie, and Annabelle they would get together for dinner today to discuss the gentlemen's arrival.

Should I tell the ladies about Levi's concerns and intended investigations? Would this information cause them to not participate? What should I do, Lord?

Maggie hurried to the kitchen where all three ladies waited for her.

"I put together some chicken, potatoes, green beans, and sweet potato pie." Annabelle pointed to a table in the corner.

"Thank you so much, Annabelle. I do appreciate your servant's heart. My mouth waters in anticipation for your food. Let's eat, ladies."

Seated at the head of the table, Maggie prayed. "Heavenly Father, we're so grateful you're always with us. We pray for your guidance and protection. Prepare our hearts and minds as we seek your will in finding husbands for these sweet ladies. We trust them in your capable hands. Thank you for Annabelle's meal and for all you do for us. Amen."

"Amen," the ladies said in unison.

"Tell me something. How do you feel about Mr. Garrett Hanley and Mr. Jesse Walker arriving today? Maggie asked.

"I won't lie," Annabelle said. "A little anxious."

"There are only two of them and three of us," Ruth reminded them. "Since I'm still not sure I want to be married, I'll plan to be more of a chaperone, available for any group activities."

Maggie acknowledged her readiness to serve. "Thank you, Ruth. We might find these first two gentlemen aren't right for any of you. I think we should all meet them as we assess who might be well suited."

"I'm excited and nervous all at once," Sadie said. "You're the only one who has corresponded with them. Why did these men stand out to you?"

"Qualities they shared about themselves seemed in line with Garfield's values. I brought the letters with me, so each of you can read them. You might see something which appeals to you."

Maggie pulled out a package of three envelopes with a rubber band around them. "These are Mr. Garrett Hanley's letters."

She handed the letters to Annabelle.

"Read the one on top first to view them in order of receipt. After you finish reading a letter, pass it to the person to your right. We'll discuss them when you're all done."

The ladies silently read the letters one by one until finished.

"You are now privy to everything I know about Mr. Garrett Hanley. Do any qualities stand out for you?"

"He seems sad he lost his dog. People who love animals have caring hearts," Annabelle said.

"Good observation. Sadie, what are your thoughts?"

"I've never been to Chicago. He must have a lot of interesting experiences to share. I would enjoy learning more about a busy city."

Ruth spoke up next. "He's had a lot of hardships. How could one man have endured so much? I worry he's either embellishing or coming to us out of desperation."

"I think for now we must believe he's being truthful, Ruth, until he proves otherwise," Maggie said. "Perhaps he is coming here out of desperation, which might or might not be a bad thing. Sometimes despair can bring out strengths to help one persevere. Hard times push us to react negatively or respond positively. We'll find out more about him when he gets here before anyone accepts an offer of marriage."

"One thing concerns me," Ruth said. I wonder how reliable he is. He said his focus was on work. Yet he seems to be out of work. Otherwise, he probably wouldn't want to come here.

"I'm a bit confused about that part of his life, as well," Sadie agreed.

Maggie nodded. "This will be something we can explore as we observe his actions while he's getting to know us. So, from the letters alone, does Mr. Hanley appeal to any of you?"

"Three letters don't give us much, but I'll stay open to possibilities," Annabelle said.

"I'm willing to get to know him," Sadie said. "Let's look at Mr. Walker's letters, if you're ready to show them to us, Maggie."

"Yes. I have three letters from Mr. Walker, as well. I'll let you pass them around until you've read all of them. Mr. Walker seems excited about coming here, which intrigues me. He does not appear to have had a difficult past like Mr. Hanley."

Maggie handed out Jesse Walker's letters and waited while the ladies read them.

"What do you think about Mr. Walker?"

"He sounds somewhat arrogant," Annabelle said. "Kind of conceited if you ask me. He talks about how smart he is and how much schooling he has. I don't know what appealed to you, Maggie."

"Do you also remember reading he loved children and offered to buy his own train ticket to get here?" Maggie asked.

"His correspondence says children love *him*, which is also somewhat haughty. I do like he wanted to take care of his travel costs, but I'm still not sure about him," Annabelle said.

"I agree with Annabelle. He's overly proud of himself," Ruth said.

Maggie glanced through Jesse Walker's letters until she found what she was looking for.

"He did say, 'I trust I've not appeared to be boastful. Since this letter is my only way to get your attention, I feel it is important to share my most outstanding qualities.' We're judging him only on what he reveals in his letters. I think he seems more excited than arrogant."

"I suppose you could be right," Annabelle said.

"I noticed he has beautiful penmanship. Most of the boys I knew from the orphanage never cared much about neatness," Sadie said. "He does seem attached to his mother."

"I think all his schooling has impacted his penmanship for the better. Also, a man who loves his mother will probably adore his wife," Maggie said.

"Perhaps," Sadie agreed.

"He's from St. Louis. I don't know much about that place, so this could allow for interesting conversations," Ruth said.

"What if more than one of us wants to get to know either of them, Maggie?" Annabelle asked. "I wouldn't want to get into any kind of competition or hurt anyone."

"I think we, as a group, need to get to know them. We can find activities for all of us to do together so we can become acquainted. I don't anticipate anything romantic or individual, at first. We can see if any of you begin to form feelings for either of the gentlemen. When you're ready and comfortable, the courting can start. I'm sure we'll find a way to resolve issues from multiple matches for one gentleman, if that should happen. I'm already corresponding with others who might be potential candidates too. Let's get back to Mr. Walker. Does anything else stand out for you?"

"He wrote he graduated from Transylvania College with a law degree," Ruth said. "Is that a real place?"

"Yes, and quite credible too. Some of the graduates have been influential in Missouri and service to America. For example, have you heard of John Cabell Breckinridge?"

"He was Vice President to James Buchanan," Sadie said.

"That's right. Also, Benjamin Gratz Brown, the twentieth governor of Missouri is a graduate. And John Calvin McCoy is regarded as the father of a notable city in Missouri—Kansas City.

"Very impressive," Ruth said. "We don't have any college-educated folks living in Garfield. Maybe he could teach us some of what he's learned. He said he was a teacher, as well as a lawyer. Someone of his abilities would be a good addition to our community."

"Yes, I agree, Ruth, an excellent addition. As families are formed, we'll need schools for children, as well as teachers. Mr. Walker might help us with these efforts. Hannibal is too far to send our future children. My oh my, Garfield will need to change to meet the needs of a growing town," Maggie said.

"I've always wanted to know a well-educated man. I haven't experienced much of the world since only living in the orphanages and now Garfield," Sadie said.

"Maggie, other than the letters, do you know more about them? Are we relying only on what they've written?" Ruth asked.

Maggie pondered the questions. She decided they didn't need to know about Levi Jackson investigating the men. No need to cause any extra worry at this point. "As of now, yes, all we know of them is from their letters. We must trust God to bring the right kind of gentlemen."

"I just thought of this, Maggie. Are you planning to find a husband too?" Annabelle asked.

Maggie was taken aback by the question. "Oh heavens no. I'm very happy as an unattached woman. I don't have time for romance."

"You never know who might steal your heart. Best to stay open to the process," Annabelle said.

"Let's focus on you for now," Maggie said. "Mr. Hanley and Mr. Walker will arrive in Hannibal at three o'clock today. Plan to meet for supper at the restaurant at half-past six. That should give the gentlemen time to get settled and cleaned up. Having a meal with them will allow us a chance to get to know them. Does that work for you?"

"Yes, we'll be there," Ruth said. "I'm anxious to try what the newest cooks prepare."

"Thanks for the scrumptious dinner, Annabelle. I appreciate you ladies meeting with me. Bringing the gentlemen here is going to be beneficial for all of us." Maggie said.

I hope it's going to be beneficial and not end up making trouble for Garfield.

Chapter 11

Max was waiting for Maggie when she walked out to the six-passenger motorcar at two o'clock. "Are you sure about this, Maggie?"

"No, but let's go anyway." A nervous laugh escaped Maggie.

Levi Jackson joined them.

"We'll find out soon enough if these strangers are good for our town," Max said.

"If they cause any problems, I will not hesitate to escort them out of town," Levi said. "With a shotgun, if necessary."

"I'm glad you're accompanying us, Mr. Jackson. Will you follow or ride with us?" Max said.

"We should have two vehicles in case anything goes wrong. I'll take the time to introduce myself to the gentlemen upon arrival so they're aware of my existence right away. This should prevent any unwanted shenanigans. I'd prefer these men did not come, but will make sure Garfield is protected."

Levi returned to his motorcar.

"Uncle Max, what have I done?"

Max asked, "Maggie, did you pray about this?"

"Many times."

"Trust God to work it out."

"Thank you. I need to keep remembering that."

"Let's see if either of these men will measure up to our expectations for the women of Garfield."

"Yes, we need to do this," Maggie said as Max helped her into the motorcar.

"Let me say one last quick prayer before we leave," Max said.

"I would love that." Maggie closed her eyes and took his hand.

"Dearest Father. Help us to be gracious hosts to Mr. Walker and Mr. Hanley. We pray we will represent you lovingly. Guide the ladies' hearts, as well as the gentlemen's. Should there be any, expose the troubling characteristics of these strangers and give us all wisdom on how to handle them. Protect us and lead us as we meet our new friends. Most of all, help us to share your love with them. In Jesus's name we pray. Amen."

"Ready?" Levi called to them.

"As ready as we can be," Max shouted back.

In a little less than an hour, they were parked near the train depot in Hannibal.

"We're a few minutes early. Let's sit on the bench in front of the depot," Levi said.

Max took Maggie's hand as they followed Levi.

The train arrived on time. Max and Maggie stood, searching for the two strangers to disembark. They quickly saw who Garrett Hanley and Jesse Walker must be, the only two gentlemen who got off the train, and both wore red shirts. Maggie and Max waved them over and the men strode towards them.

Garrett reached his hand out to Max. "Hello, sir. I'm Garrett Hanley. You must be M. G. Glad to make your acquaintance."

Maggie laughed. "No, he isn't M. G."

"I'm Maxwell Crawford, Mr. Hanley." Max shook his hand. "This must be Mr. Walker?"

Max shook the other man's hand.

"Yes. The one and only, Jesse Walker."

"Mr. Crawford, do you know M. G.? He was supposed to meet us here," Garrett said.

"I'm Margaret Garfield, or as you know me, M. G."

Garrett lowered his gaze to see the small woman who had spoken. He took her hand in his to greet her. "My sincere honor to get to know you, Miss Garfield. I thought I was corresponding with a man."

"No, I'm not a man."

"I concur. You are not. What a pleasant surprise to meet such a lovely lady."

Maggie instantly felt warm as she looked up and into Garrett's hazel eyes. She thought he was handsome, despite his unshaven face. Weakened knees suddenly didn't want to hold Maggie up, causing her to weave. Garrett must have felt her losing her balance because he grasped both her hands.

"Are you alright, ma'am?" Garrett asked.

"Umm—Oh sure … Yes … Just got a little dizzy there. Thank you. I'm not sure what came over me. Probably the heat."

Maggie wanted to hide.

Max frowned. "The temperature cannot be more than fifty-five degrees out here. Are you sure you're well? Do you need to sit?'

"No. No, I'm fine, Maggie assured him. Pulling her hands from Garrett's, she turned to the other man standing there.

"Hello, Mr. Walker."

"Hello, Miss—I'm sorry, what was your name?" Jesse said. His overgrown black curls fell over his forehead when he looked down at her.

"Miss Margaret Garfield." Maggie was surprised to see such long hair on the well-educated gentleman.

Jesse scowled. "Eee Gads! Are those frogs on your clothing?"

"Mr. Walker. I apologize if my frogs offend you."

Jesse looked her over again. "The frogs don't offend me too much—as long as I don't have to be the one wearing them."

Max moved in front of Maggie, between her and Jesse.

"You, Mr. Walker, are out of line to make such disrespectful comments. I will not tolerate your rudeness," Max said.

"What was your name again—Clawfield, was it?" Jesse asked.

"Crawford. Maxwell Crawford. I believe you owe Miss Garfield an apology for your impolite comments about her lovely wardrobe."

Levi now stood next to Maggie. "I agree with Mr. Crawford. I'm Levi Jackson. I, as well as Mr. Crawford, will be watching your every move. I oversee the safety of this lady. Apologize now."

"No offense intended," Jesse said. "I just didn't expect the frogs. Speaking of frogs, I'm hungry. Is there somewhere to eat around here?"

"I brought some ham and cheese sandwiches. And, we'll have supper at half-past six." Maggie said.

"Sounds perfect to me. I appreciate you being so kind to us, ma'am. Thank you," Garrett said.

Garrett's smile warmed Maggie's heart. Sort of overheated it. *What in the world is happening to me? I never react this way to anyone, especially a gentleman, and certainly not a stranger.*

"Ham? Did you bring any other meat? I'm more of a beef man myself," Jesse said.

Maggie wanted to leave the ungrateful man at the station. Her face grew warm with impatience. Maybe the ladies were right. He did seem arrogant.

"The ham is sugar cured and quite delicious. I brought an ample amount. I think you will be satisfied." She was irritated but managed to add, "I will keep your admiration of beef in mind for future."

"Walker, don't be disrespectful. Show your gratitude for Miss Garfield's kindness to us," Garrett said. "Should we get on with our journey, Mr. Crawford?"

"Yes, let's go." Max's words were gracious, his glare at Jesse was not.

Before Maggie could take Max's outstretched arm, Garrett hooked his hand around her arm and started walking.

Maggie's knees wobbled again. *Why aren't my legs working properly today? I feel like I'm going to fall again.*

Garrett held on tight. "Perhaps you should see a doctor about your wavering balance, Miss Garfield."

"My balance is just fine."

Garrett looked at Max. "Which way to the carriage, Mr. Crawford?"

"No carriage today. We'll travel by motorcar."

"I've not been in a motorcar. Should be a fun way to travel. I can escort Miss Garfield. She seems to need a little extra assistance this afternoon."

"I'm not helpless, Mr. Hanley."

"Just the same, I am happy to accompany you," Garrett said. "Alright with you, Mr. Jackson?"

Levi thoughtfully observed Garrett. "Yes, if Miss Garfield approves. Just remember I'll be right behind you."

"May I walk with you to our ride, Miss Garfield?" Garrett asked.

Maggie couldn't help but get caught up in those hazel eyes, which now appeared green. "Yes. Thank you, Mr. Hanley." She forced herself to look straight ahead.

Max redirected his scowl to Garrett and then led the way to the motorcar.

"We're going in this? Got one just like it back home," Jesse said, as he stepped up to get onto the front seat. "I never expected to see one here. To be honest, this model is a bit bulky for my taste."

Max grabbed his arm and pointed to the back seat. "The front is for Miss Garfield. You sit there on the middle bench behind me."

"Ok, whatever, old man." Jesse tossed his bags onto the back seat and climbed in.

Levi glared at Jesse. He opened his mouth to speak, but Maggie beat him to it.

"Mr. Crawford is not an old man. You will speak to him with the esteem he deserves, Mr. Walker."

"Certainly, no disrespect meant." Jesse grinned. "Make sure that food makes its way back here to me."

Max took Maggie's arm and helped her into the motorcar, then turned to Garrett. In a voice of thinly disguised steel, Max said, "You better be nothing but a gentleman to her or you will answer to me. Miss Garfield is a very special lady, and I don't take kindly to anyone who upsets her. Understand?"

"Yes, sir. I will treat her like I would my own sister. You can trust me. I'm grateful for the opportunity Miss Garfield has provided me."

"As long as we understand each other."

"We do, Mr. Crawford."

Garrett sat next to Jesse and leaned back in the seat as far as he could, his knees pressed tightly against the back of Maggie's seat. The pressure of his knees behind her caused goosebumps on Maggie's arms.

Standing next to the motorcar, Levi said, "I too hold Miss Garfield in high regard and will be scrutinizing both of you very closely. Remember I'm watching." Levi hurried to his motorcar.

Max handed the basket of food to Garrett.

"Thank you, Mr. Crawford." Garrett opened the basket and held it out to Jesse. "Walker, help yourself."

Jesse grabbed a sandwich and took a bite. "You're right about the ham, Miss Garfield. This isn't too bad for not being beef."

Maggie rolled her eyes as she continued to face forward.

Garrett took out a sandwich and began eating it. "Delicious, Miss. Garfield."

"I'm delighted you're both satisfied with what I brought."

The motorcars moved onto the road to take the passengers on their way to Garfield. Maggie was glad to be sitting so she didn't have to worry about her legs holding her upright.

Maggie turned to look at Jesse. "Why did you want to come here, Mr. Walker?"

With his mouth full, Jesse replied, "I didn't want to make this journey. My mother and father made me do it."

Maggie frowned. "So, you were forced to do this? Your letters implied you were quite excited about the opportunity."

Jesse swallowed to make a little room for his tongue to move. "My mother answered the advertisement. She thinks I need to settle down. I had no choice, but I guess she thinks she knows best. We'll see."

"Mr. Walker, if you don't want to be here, you can get right back on the train. I thought I was corresponding with *you*.

"Calm down, Miss Garfield. I'm open to the process. My mother wrote the letters, but everything she wrote about me was true. She didn't mean to deceive you. She knew I would never respond on my own. I'm willing to see what you have to offer me."

"And I look forward to finding out what you have to offer *us*, Mr. Walker." Maggie gritted her teeth. Margaret Eloise Garfield would not allow this upstart's arrogance to upset her. "What qualities would appeal to you in a potential wife?"

"I can't say I've given it much thought. I'm still a young man with much life to experience. I've often thought waiting until at least twenty-eight or so before being saddled with a wife might be best. Hand me another sandwich, Hanley."

"Mr. Walker, I think perhaps you need a few years of maturing before we should introduce you to any of the wonderful ladies here," Max said. "You might be best suited to take the first train back in the morning."

"No. The endeavor can't be abandoned quite yet. My parents are requiring me to tough it out for a while. My priority is to appease my mother. However, I won't settle for just anyone."

"Nor will anyone settle for you," Maggie said as her face grew hot.

To get her mind off Jesse, she turned to Garrett. "Why did you respond to our advertisement, Mr. Hanley?"

"A new life."

"Was the old one always so bad?"

"Not all of it, Miss Garfield. What made you feel the need to invite gentlemen here?"

"Several of the ladies in Garfield want families. We needed to bring in quality gentlemen to make that happen. Are you a quality man, Mr. Hanley?"

"Yes, I'd like to think I am."

"I saw honorable characteristics in both of you from your letters," Maggie said. "I'm hopeful my initial thoughts match reality."

"I'm confident we'll both show ourselves as having been judged correctly," Garrett said. "By the way, where is our final destination?"

"Garfield," Maggie said.

Jesse frowned. "Let's not get too far out in the plains. I hoped we would stay closer to Hannibal. Populated cities provide less boredom."

Maggie was about to tell Jesse he could get out now and walk back to Hannibal when Garrett intervened.

"Is Mando Merchandising located there? I've ordered a few items from that company."

Maggie was glad for the diversion. She took in a deep breath to compose herself.

"Yes. My father was the founder of Mando Merchandising as well as the town of Garfield."

"Amazing. I can't wait to meet him," Garrett said.

"I wish you could have met him. Sadly, he passed away about a year ago," Maggie said as a lump formed in her throat. She still couldn't believe he was gone.

"I'm so sorry for your loss, Miss Garfield. I expect he found an intelligent man to run the company."

"My father must not have seen the need for an intelligent gentleman. He left the job to me."

Garrett chuckled. "There is no way a perceptive businessman like Mr. Garfield would allow such a thing. The company must be huge, with numerous employees. A woman isn't qualified to do something of such magnitude, especially in the business world."

Maggie turned to face Garrett. "Most closed-minded people would agree with you, Mr. Hanley. Many would say a man might have been the better choice. However, my father asked me to be the one to step into his shoes. Thankfully, the company is doing well under my watch. I plan to spend my life trying to make my father proud."

"Do you mean to tell me there are no men around here who would want to run Mando Merchandising for Mr. Garfield? I would think many fine businessmen would be chomping at the bits for such an incredible leadership role."

"I'm certain there are plenty of gentlemen who would have been more than elated to have been offered such an opportunity. However, my father trained and prepared me to be ready for this position. He purposely built the company and town with women in mind. In fact, the employees are almost all women. It seems most men have the same attitude as yours about females in business. Unfortunately, many ladies don't have opportunities to be self-sufficient. The women we employ have helped not only to keep Mando Merchandising running efficiently, but to be very profitable. In addition, they have helped to form a nice town."

"The employees are women? It just doesn't make sense to have a woman oversee so much, and certainly not to be the majority workforce," Garrett said. "Females are not able to work as hard as men, which will cause reduced production. Your father must have been a gambling man to roll the dice on women. My experience indicates a man is needed to keep things going long term."

Max chimed in. "You're out of line, young man. William never gambled. He only made the soundest of decisions. The women employed at Mando Merchandising are excellent at what they do, equally or more productive than men. As for Miss Garfield, she is a wise businesswoman. We have yet to see if she is wise about choosing you to come here."

"My apologies, sir. No disrespect meant. Surely, you can understand my shock at this unusual situation, Mr. Crawford. You too had to come to terms with the idea, I can imagine."

"I have known Miss Garfield her entire life and grew up with her father. Both have proven incredibly gifted when it comes to business." Max paused. "You, young man, are not qualified to judge either of them."

"You're right, Mr. Crawford. I have no right."

Maggie turned forward in her seat and stared straight ahead. She fumed in silence at the attitude of men until the motorcar came to a stop.

Doubts overwhelmed Maggie as she stared at Home Sweet Home Boardinghouse, knowing Mr. Crawford and Mr. Walker would be taking up residence for an infinite number of days. There was a marvelous diner attached to the boardinghouse aptly named Slumber and Vittles, since those staying as boarders ate their meals there. The restaurant also served many noontime meals to workers, such as delivery drivers and postal employees.

"This is where you'll stay. Staff members are expecting you. Plan to be at the restaurant next door for supper at half past six," Max said.

Garrett opened the door and stepped out. "This is a beautiful town. Clever construction for the diner to be a one-story duplicate of the stone boardinghouse, shows how they're connected. I saw the rock quarry on the way into town. Using local material is always best, cost wise.

"We have a reliable crew in charge of building this town. They use our resources wisely," Maggie said, refusing to look at Garrett.

"I apologize, Miss Garfield. Sometimes my curiosity can come across as judgment. I might need some time to wrap my head around the idea of a successful company being run by women."

"Spending time in Garfield might cause you to view many things in a different way. Or, even prompt you to leave. We shall see," Maggie looked away. Even though she was angry at Garrett's comments, she didn't want him to see her react emotionally. Neither Garrett nor Jesse was helping to lessen her apprehension of bringing in strangers. Instead, her fears were growing. For the first time, she was glad Levi Jackson was here.

Chapter 12

"Ladies, I'd like you to meet Garrett Hanley and Jesse Walker," Maggie said as the group sat down at the round supper table at the Slumber and Vittles restaurant.

"Delighted to make your acquaintance," Garrett said.

Jesse bit into the buttered roll in front of him.

"Aren't you delighted, too, Mr. Walker?" Garrett asked as he tapped Jesse's arm.

"Sure. Can someone pass the jam?"

Maggie pressed on, ignoring Jesse's lackadaisical involvement.

"I'll just go in the order of where everyone is seated, beginning to my immediate left," Maggie said. "This is Miss Annabelle Stoddard.

Annabelle stood and said, "Hello, Mr. Hanley and Mr. Walker. I'm certain getting to know you both will be a pleasure."

Annabelle was a bit taller than Maggie, and rounder. She wore a lavender dress which was probably lovely if not hidden under a flour-covered bright orange apron.

Annabelle grimaced as she looked down at her apparel. "Oh, my, what a mess. Pardon my appearance. I seem to have forgotten about my apron."

"Wonderful to meet you, Miss Stoddard," Garrett said. "The pleasure is mine to have an opportunity to know you. I think your apron is nice and well worth wearing to keep your beautiful dress from potential soiling."

Annabelle laughed as she pulled the garment over her head. In the process, she caught some hairpins in the material, which caused several strands of long brown hair to fall over her right shoulder. She appeared to turn white. Upon close examination, one could see some of the white on her face was caused by the falling flour from her apron.

"Thank you, Mr. Hanley. Leaving my apron on might have been a better choice, as I'm certain to be much more of a mess now than I was before. I'm quite embarrassed."

"No need to feel embarrassed Miss Stoddard. You still look lovely."

Garrett's kindness toward Annabelle impressed Maggie. She was glad to see he had a sensitive side. She felt herself warming to his charm again.

"Annabelle, perhaps you should step away for a few minutes and freshen up in the powder room ... if that would make you feel better," Maggie said.

"A very sound idea. Excuse me." Annabelle hurried away.

Maggie gazed at Garrett. He had shaven his whiskers. She wondered why he would ever let anything cover that handsome face. Garrett's red bow tie stood out from the dullness of his worn grey suit. Tattered clothes or not, dashing described him this evening.

"Will we eat soon?" Jesse asked, barely looking up from another roll.

Jesse's words brought Maggie back to the reason they were meeting for supper. She looked at him and saw a man very different from Garrett. Immaculately outfitted in what appeared to be fine attire—black suit, bright white shirt, and black silk tie. He dressed the part of a grown man, but his face showed a youthful carelessness.

His long black curls were slicked back, hanging over his shoulders.

"Yes, shortly, Mr. Walker," Maggie assured him. "I'm certain you want to get to know everyone before settling down to supper. Meet Hank Rothstadt, who is an excellent carpenter. Mr. Hanley, the two of you will probably have much in common to discuss."

"From the looks of Garfield, Mr. Rothstadt can teach me a thing or two about construction. I hope we can converse soon," Garrett said.

"Anytime," Hank said.

"Next, is Miss Ruth Calvin. She helps to manage the employees at Mando Merchandising."

Ruth smiled at Garrett and Jesse, "Hello, gentlemen. I'm eager to learn more about both of you."

Ruth's green dress made her brown hair and eyes seem darker, appearing somewhat powerful. She was quite pretty, even though she didn't seem to realize this fact.

"Hello, Miss Calvin. I look forward to getting acquainted with you as well," Garrett said. "Must be difficult for a young woman like you to manage so many employees and the day-to-day activities of the business. Do you have a male mentor who helps you make decisions?"

All the warm feelings Maggie was having for Garrett disappeared instantly. She turned to tell him how irritating his comment was. Ruth beat her to it.

"I will have you know I am fully capable of managing the employees at our company and making any needed decisions, Mr. Hanley. I take aim at a question so full of attitude. I have a brain which functions very well."

Ruth's glare demanded an apology.

"No disrespect meant, Miss Calvin. Just trying to understand the peculiar dynamics here. I apologize if I have come across as anything else. You must admit, though, it is odd to leave a successful company in the hands of women. Men are groomed to be business leaders. The women I know are mothers and wives. They have the fine job of running the home front, and most do a remarkable job. Certainly, this is what I've observed throughout my lifetime."

"Mr. Hanley, I suggest you keep these wonderings to yourself until you can fully grasp the competencies of women in the professional world outside the home." Maggie's tone left no misunderstanding. "I can assure you Miss Calvin is extremely capable of managing her responsibilities efficiently and effectively without having a man's mind to fall back on."

"There's no need to get so riled up," Garrett said as he folded his arms. "This is a prime example of why women should not be the decision-makers, which running a business requires. Females are too emotional."

The women at the table shouted their disapproval of Garrett's statements. Maggie whistled, bringing instant silence.

Maggie glared at Garrett. "Mr. Hanley, your welcome is wearing thin the more you speak."

"Now, ladies, calm down," said Garrett. "I merely shared the opinion of most business-minded people, but certainly don't want a mutiny on my hands. You'll likely enlighten me on how this town functions in due time."

Maggie took in a deep breath to calm herself. *Mr. Hanley is just as arrogant as Mr. Walker. I don't know which is worse, self-centered, or male haughtiness. Lord, clearly show me if these gentlemen are good for Garfield. I need your wisdom.*

Jesse took the last bite of his roll and showed no intention of joining the conversation. Garrett elbowed him. "Where are your manners, Mr. Walker? Greet Miss Calvin properly."

"Hello, Miss Calvin," Jesse said as he continued to chew. "We need to eat soon. I'm famished."

Maggie ignored him.

"Moving along, next to Ruth, we have Miss Sadie Stoddard. She authors much of Mando's catalog. Oh, and she is Annabelle Stoddard's sister."

"Hello, Mr. Walker and Mr. Hanley. I hope you had nice travels as you made your way to Garfield," Sadie said.

Jesse dropped the third roll he was buttering, his gaze fixed on Sadie.

"Hello, Miss Stoddard. You are quite lovely," Jesse said.

Sadie turned a light shade of pink. "Thank you, Mr. Walker, for those kind words."

"Wonderful to meet you, Miss Stoddard," said Garrett.

"You as well, Mr. Hanley," Sadie looked at Garrett and smiled.

Jesse's eyes stayed fixated on Sadie. "I've published a few articles here and there. Perhaps we can discuss our writing experience."

"That would be nice, Mr. Walker. Yes, let's do compare some time."

"As you must be anxious to move on, Mr. Walker, so we can eat, I'd like to introduce you to the lovely lady next to Miss Stoddard. Gentleman, meet—"

"I'm certain you have many talents, Miss Stoddard, in addition to your writing," Jesse interrupted.

Sadie blushed again.

"All the ladies bring some wonderful talents and contributions to help make Garfield a lovely place to live," Max said. "We're proud of them all. The one I'm most proud of is sitting next to me. To finish out our introductions, this is my lovely wife, Catherine Crawford. I'm so sorry, fellas, but this one is already spoken for." Max put his arm around Catherine and kissed her on the forehead.

"Hello, gentlemen," Catherine said.

"And you know Mr. Crawford," Maggie said.

Jesse sat next to Max and then Garrett. Maggie and Max wanted the men between them so they could be privy to all conversations tonight. Maggie wished she had thought differently because she didn't particularly want to be next to Garrett right now. He made her uncomfortable on so many levels.

"In addition, you are already acquainted with me," Maggie said. "You have now met everyone here."

"Except for me, Miss Garfield." Levi got up from the table next to them. "Don't ever forget I will always be close by."

"Thank you, Mr. Jackson. I didn't mean to leave you out," Maggie said. In truth, she hadn't noticed him.

Annabelle returned to the table. She had done a satisfactory job of getting her hair back in place and flour off her face. "I apologize if I kept you awaiting supper for my return."

"We've just finished introductions, so you didn't keep us waiting at all," Maggie said.

"Oh perfect, perhaps we should order our meals," Annabelle said.

Hank helped Annabelle into her chair.

"Excuse me, Miss ... uh ... oh I'm so bad with names ... what was your name again?" Jesse asked as he looked at Catherine.

"I am Mrs. Maxwell Crawford."

"Mrs. Crawford, would you do me the kind favor of switching seats with me?" Jesse asked. "I would enjoy dining next to Miss Sadie Stoddard so we can discuss our writing and other interests."

Catherine looked at Sadie. "Would that be satisfactory with you, Sadie?"

"Oh, well, I guess, yes," Sadie said.

Maggie looked at Sadie to try to read her expressions. She did not want her to be in an uncomfortable situation.

Sadie must have seen the slight panic on Maggie's face because she nodded her head and mouthed, *"I'm fine."*

Jesse seated Catherine in his chair and, with a smile, sat down next to Sadie.

Maggie raised her hand to let the staff know they were ready to be served. After the orders were taken and the food arrived, Max announced he would pray before they ate.

"Dear God, we thank you for all the wonderful blessings you have brought to us. We ask for your guidance as new relationships are on the horizon. Help each of the potential couples to think with their heads, and not just their hearts. Give them all wisdom and discernment. Thank you for this delicious meal you have provided. Use it to nourish our bodies. Amen."

"Amen," several in the group said.

"Let's eat," Jesse said.

Max and Maggie shook their heads at him. The others followed Jesse's lead as they picked up their forks.

Garrett looked at Maggie. "Perhaps I could visit you on the job to see what you do in a typical day at Mando Merchandising. I would enjoy seeing the inside of such a successful company."

"I don't have typical days, Mr. Hanley. Every day brings new challenges as well as rewards. My focus varies based on the needs as they arise." Maggie hesitated and then said, "Besides, it might be hard for you to see competent women successfully working in the business world."

"The idea intrigues me. I would find it educational, I'm sure. Perhaps you can prove me wrong about the abilities of females."

"My position is not to prove you wrong, rather you are responsible to open your mind. However, I might allow you to see a bit of how we operate if you agree to my terms."

"What terms might those be?"

"You must leave your comments about women's supposed inabilities out of any discussions while you're there. Can you possibly refrain?"

Garrett ignored her sarcasm and flashed a grin. "I will practice for hours tonight before I go to sleep."

Maggie swallowed a sigh. Why did she find him so charming and maddening at the same time? She thought of her schedule. "Come to Mando tomorrow afternoon at around three o'clock."

"I'll be there. You'll see I can behave quite well when needed."

"I'll be there too," Levi announced. "You'll have a brief tour but will not be allowed access to all areas of Mando. *I* will decide how long you stay."

Maggie frowned at Levi. How dare he make decisions about *her* business.

Chapter 13

Rex Tillman read the telegram from Garrett one more time just to make sure he hadn't imagined it. This was the best news he had received in a long time. How had he not known about this?

> Garfield dead. Maggie running the business. Need more time. Stay put until you hear from me.

William Garfield was gone. Rex was excited beyond measure, as well as irritated no one had informed him.

For now, Rex would celebrate. He had saved a prized possession to partake in when he took over Mando Merchandising. William's death was reason enough to consume the reward now. Martinez-Ybor, a premier cigar maker, had given Rex one of his personal cigars while in Florida last year. Rex's mouth salivated as he put the cigar under his nose. He let himself get caught up in the aroma of a privileged life.

Rex struck a match and lit the cigar. He drew in a puff that lingered in his mouth. He slowly blew out the smoke that loitered in front of him until the cloud disappeared. He laughed out loud. "This is for you, William Garfield—cursed friend of mine. My next celebration will be when I finally own what you kept from me for all these years."

Rex was building his empire, with ownership of two of the three companies he wanted. He obtained Jackson Shipping two years ago, giving Rex proprietorship to the major passageways on the Mississippi. Ships had to pay hefty fees for right-of-way.

Of course, acquiring Jackson Shipping did necessitate a bit of sacrifice on the part of the original owner, Levi Jackson, when he foolishly refused to hand over the company to Rex. Levi was yelling something about getting the authorities involved when Rex's men grabbed him, put something smelly under his nose and dragged him away. Rex was never happier to see anyone leave a room. When Levi awoke, he was forced to sign over his company after the pain of losing a toe and half a pinkie finger. Rex realized just how cowardly Levi was when he gave up the company so quickly. Apparently, quite pain intolerant.

Rex attained his next conquest, Hanley Construction, about six months previously. He grinned at how easy it had been to force James to sign away the company to him. The man was an excellent carpenter, but easily fooled.

An unexpected bonus to owning Hanley Construction was retention of Garrett Hanley—a workhorse and very accommodating to Rex's business needs. Customers liked Garrett and trusted him as the unfortunate son of James. He had become a valuable asset.

Even more valuable was Rex's lawyer, Lester Grover. Although somewhat questionable in his 'legal' procedures, Lester could be counted on to secure transactions that were ironclad in Rex's favor. Lester was paid well for his indiscretions, which kept him silent.

James had been working with Lester—at Rex's suggestion—to get paperwork done to transfer ownership of Hanley Construction to Garrett. Rex was in the room to witness James finalizing the deal. The ink was already dry when James got up to walk out. He couldn't wait to get home to his wife so they could pack for their two-year trip around the world for their twenty-fifth wedding anniversary. Unfortunately for James, the documents he endorsed were not the ones he had looked over so thoroughly and accepted. Instead, he had signed Rex's replacement papers, giving full ownership of the company to Rex, along with all his assets. James never made it home to his wife. Instead, he was led away and vanished to an unknown location.

The time was finally right for Rex to go after the company he wanted more than anything, Mando Merchandising. He would have acted sooner if he had known William had died more than a year ago.

William was dumber than Rex thought, hiring all those women. Rex laughed out loud as he thought of little Maggie running the place. She was young when he saw her last, maybe nine or ten years old. Rex couldn't imagine her as a grown woman. He was certain she wouldn't remember him. Regardless of how much she had matured, she would be no match against Rex.

He read the telegram again. "Stay put until you hear from me." Who did Garrett Hanley think he was to tell him to stay put? Nobody told Rex Tillman what to do. He would go to Garfield as soon as possible to take care of the job Garrett was incapable of completing. Rex wasn't comfortable leaving his fate in Garrett's hands any longer. Besides, with William no longer a barrier, he didn't see a need for Garrett's services. Maybe Rex would send him off to be with his worthless father.

Chapter 14

Garrett walked to the livery stable across the street from Home Sweet Home Boardinghouse. Maggie Garfield said he could get a horse and buggy there to visit Mando Merchandising today. Garrett opened the door and tried to find someone who worked there. He was about to give up when he noticed a man crouched, cleaning the shoe of one of the horses.

"Hello, sir. I'm Garrett Hanley. I'd like to rent one of your horses today."

Hank stood. He must have been at least six inches taller than Garrett and thirty pounds lighter. Garrett instantly remembered this man's unique moustache, with the waxed handlebar curving several times above his lips.

"Hank Rothstadt. We met last night."

"Yes. I didn't recognize you from behind. Do you have a horse available, or maybe a buggy?"

"I don't have any say in who takes one of these horses, but there's no charge to borrow any of them. I just try to keep them watered and fed. All the folks around here look after them, anyone who can stop by. The horses end up with a little more food than they need, but at least they're not neglected. The buggies are taken on a first-come basis, so help yourself to what you find. Miss Garfield keeps them here for us to use anytime."

"Thank you. It sounds like Miss Garfield is quite generous to all."

"Oh yes. There's no one else like her, other than her father, but he's gone now. Look around and see what might suit you. I can help you get the horse hitched up."

Garrett strolled about the barn and rubbed the noses of a few of the horses. When he walked around one of the corners, he saw something which piqued his interest, a motorbike.

"Do you know how to drive one of those?" Hank asked.

Garrett felt a pang of sadness with the innocent question. He used to have several motorbikes in Chicago that he rode to various construction sites. Rex kept Garrett away from the bikes once he took over the company. His father had known Garrett was fond of them, so he would buy new models each year. Garrett didn't realize his father had been building the fleet for Rex. Anger enveloped Garrett as he thought about how little his father must have cared about him.

Hank saw the change in Garrett's demeanor. "I didn't mean to make you feel bad if you can't drive one. I was just going to offer it up instead of a horse if you wanted a bike today."

Garrett forced himself to clear his mind of Rex and his father. "No. Yes. Thank you, Hank. Yes. Yes, I can drive a motorbike. I've owned a few in the past. I would appreciate riding this one."

"Fairly rare to find someone who knows how to run one around here. I'm sure the bike is ready to go. Mr. Crawford looks after all the mechanical things. Take it for as long as you need."

Garrett pushed the motorbike to the entrance, got on, and started the engine.

"Thank you for your help today, Hank. I appreciate your time."

Garrett drove off towards Mando Merchandising. He couldn't help but think Hank was a good man, just like the rest of the kind people in this town, the very ones he must deceive. Garrett was angry with himself until he thought of his mother. He would do anything to keep her safe, and away from Rex Tillman.

Chapter 15

Josephine knocked on Maggie's door.

"Miss Garfield, there's a Mr. Garrett Hanley here to see you. I think he's one of the men who responded to the advertisement. Pardon me for noticing, but he's quite handsome. Should I send him in?"

Why did I agree to let Garrett come to Mando Merchandising? Why am I so nervous? Why do I care what he thinks? What is wrong with me? No time now to answer all these questions.

Maggie looked at the time, one-forty-five. "Wait, he's early. No. Don't send him in. I'm not quite ready. Oh, send him in."

"I'm confused. Am I supposed to bring him to you or not?"

"Yes. I'll see him now."

Josephine left and returned too quickly with Garrett. "Miss Garfield, here is Mr. Hanley. Let me know if you need anything while he's here."

"Thank you, Josephine. I will."

"You're here well ahead of your scheduled time, Mr. Hanley. Did we not agree on three o'clock?"

"Oh my, I apologize. I thought we had said two o'clock. I don't like being late. Should I come back?"

"I don't have anything pressing right now. You can stay. I am curious, though, what really brings you here, Mr. Hanley? Are you trying to take over my company?" Maggie grinned.

"No, I'm not here with any dastardly intentions. I have no desire to take anything from anyone, especially a well-established business like yours. I'm merely curious about this unique town and the operations of Mando Merchandising."

"I was obviously being playful with that question. But you seem reactive in your response. Tell me the real reason you wanted to come to Garfield, Mr. Hanley."

"A need to start over with my life, work, absolutely everything. I lost my company to a man I foolishly trusted. Perhaps Garfield can help me gain back some dignity."

Maggie gazed into Garrett's eyes. "I can't imagine what pain you've gone through. I remember reading about losing your dog and home but had no idea about a business."

"The death of my dog, Hutch, was quite painful. He was an amazing companion. I still miss the little guy. Guess most people can't relate to loving an animal so much."

"I've always liked animals and admire people who take care of them. I'm very sorry for your loss."

"Thank you. I had three great years with him." Garrett said. "Enough about me. What can you tell me about your company?"

"Who was this man who took everything from you?" Maggie asked.

"My father."

Maggie's mouth opened wide. "Your father? Did I hear you correctly?"

"Yes. He disappeared about six months ago, taking every penny with him. Left my mother and me with nothing. Like your father, he'd been preparing me to take over his company. Unlike your father, he was a selfish liar."

"What a horrible situation. I've only known a loving father who would never take anything from me. He was the best man I've ever known. Can't imagine a father stealing from his own family. Perhaps there is more to the situation than you know. Things are not always as they appear."

"A small part of me hangs on to hope that my father is somehow innocent. Considering the circumstances, I can't imagine a good outcome. He was a stellar provider before disappearing. One day I'll find him. The man needs to pay for what he's done to my mother."

"Has he tried to contact you since leaving?" Maggie asked.

"No. He broke my mother's heart."

"Maybe I can help find your father. I have the resources and staff." Maggie patted Garrett's hand and then held on to it. "Would you let me try?"

Levi walked in the room glaring at Garrett. "You came early—even earlier than I had anticipated."

Garrett pulled his hand away from Maggie.

"What's been going on here? Why were you holding Miss Garfield's hand?"

Levi moved directly in front of Garrett as he waited for a response.

Maggie's admiration of Levi Jackson was not growing any stronger. "Mr. Jackson, nothing inappropriate is going on here. Just an innocent gesture and nothing more."

"Why are you here so much earlier than the agreed upon arrival, Mr. Hanley?" Levi asked.

"Just got a little confused about the time. Thought we were meeting at two o'clock, Mr. Jackson."

"These types of actions do not help your case in proving you are a man of character and honesty. Any more stunts like this and you will be forced to leave."

"An honest mistake. No need for concern. I'll be careful not to alarm you again."

"Just the same, your every move will be scrutinized. Better not be planning to cause trouble because I will find out before it happens."

"I have no desire to cause any problems. I'm glad Miss Garfield has you to look after her."

"That makes one of us," Maggie mumbled under her breath.

"Did you say something, Miss Garfield?" Levi asked.

"No."

Levi looked back at Garrett. "As long as we understand each other. I'm here to supervise the tour, which is not a sound idea, but let's get this over with."

"We can talk more later, Mr. Hanley," Maggie said. "Shall we proceed, Mr. Jackson?"

Garrett frowned when Maggie moved from behind her desk. "Pants?"

"Yes, Mr. Hanley, I do wear pants from time to time. I can maneuver around Mando more easily compared to when I'm in a dress." Maggie kept her voice deceptively sweet despite Garrett's obvious disapproval. "Are you able to be seen with me today, or should we call this meeting over?"

"You should know ladies are made for dresses. A woman wearing male attire is strange."

"These pants are not male attire. They were made specifically for me by Miss Sophie Jenkins. She does not create clothing for gentlemen."

Levi stepped forward, "Are you saying Miss Garfield is not a lady because she wears pants? That is quite offensive."

"No, I would never insult Miss Garfield by saying she is not a lady. Quite the contrary, she is unquestionably feminine." Garrett laughed. "You, Mr. Jackson, must agree pants are an inappropriate choice for any woman, unless you're Annie Oakley, I guess."

"Mr. Hanley, apparently, you did not practice enough last night, having already broken your promise to keep arrogant opinions about women under wraps." Maggie spoke through gritted teeth. "Perhaps we should cancel this opportunity to see ladies quite adeptly doing their jobs. I have more productive things to do today than listen to your sentiments."

"Miss Garfield, truly, you are beautiful in all the attire I've seen you wear, including today. In fact, I've never met a more fascinating woman. I didn't mean to offend you."

Maggie's face heated at Garrett's sentiments. She was about to forgive him when he interrupted her thoughts.

"You must realize anyone seeing you in pants for the first time would have the same reaction."

Maggie knew he was right. She had endured comments among the townsfolk regarding her choices in attire, but couldn't recall getting annoyed with any of them. For some reason, Garrett's opinion seemed to matter.

"I've been the center of discussion on occasion due to my uncommon, but delightful, apparel decisions. However, this is not for you to debate."

Maggie walked to the doorway. "Come on, gentlemen."

Chapter 16

"Many of the items sold through our catalog are purchased in bulk and stored here. Some are locally made, like Mrs. Crawford's hats and Miss Stoddard's clothing," Maggie said.

"How is merchandise transported here and orders filled?" Garrett asked.

"We use Railway Mail Service, have our own railcars and stagecoaches. Steamboats on the Mississippi River bring in merchandise too. Mr. Crawford has even procured a delivery truck from Alexander Winton, who is in the business of creating various motorized vehicles. Mr. Winton has seen horses treated poorly or left to die when no longer able to work efficiently. His love for horses brought on his passion to create other means of transportation. Mr. Crawford has a few inventor friends involved in motorized endeavors."

"Impressive to see what goes on inside Mando Merchandising. Your father knew how to build a fortune."

"Monetary rewards were secondary. Father's main business focus was to help farmers get products at reasonable prices. Nearly sixty-five percent of the American population live in rural areas. In the past, farmers would spend a day or more traveling to towns for mail and supplies at inflated rates. Mando Merchandising purchases or creates products in bulk, keeping costs low. We pass on the savings to customers. In addition to our distribution methods, access to Rural Free Delivery service has helped us get products to farmers' homes."

"Thank you for showing me around, Miss Garfield. Quite enlightening to see such large inventory of so many different products. You and your father have created something special here," Garrett said as he, Maggie, and Levi walked into her office. "I am more than impressed."

Maggie was feeling better about Garrett. Once they got past his views on her pants, he was quite enthusiastic about every aspect of the company. True to his promise, Garrett made no offensive comments about women during the excursion through the warehouse even though several wore pants. Maggie expected him to accuse her of corrupting her employees.

"From what you told me earlier, you and your father had a successful business for several years. Seems you had something to be proud of, as well," Maggie said.

"Yes, we were doing quite satisfactorily in the construction industry. After losing the company, I felt more like a failure than proud."

"You didn't fail, just trusted the wrong person."

Levi stood tall from his spot against the wall, listening to Garrett's every word.

"Today has been enlightening. Seems to have awoken some of my ambition lost along the way. Perhaps I'll get the opportunity to build something here in Garfield."

"Perhaps indeed. Should you become the husband of one of our ladies, we would welcome your abilities. There are many future buildings to construct. Your expertise would be an excellent fit for our town."

Garrett rose to his feet. "Thank you for your time. I've overstayed my welcome."

Maggie touched his arm. A warm tingle rolled all the way from her hand to her neck. "My offer still stands to help find your father."

Maggie tensed when Garrett slipped his arm around her shoulder drawing her to him. "Thank you."

Levi was at her side in a flash. He jerked Garrett across the room.

Maggie leaned on the side of the desk to keep from sliding to the floor. She had liked Garrett's arm around her and admitted regret to herself at Levi's prompt action. Maggie remembered Garrett wasn't here for her but was a potential husband for Ruth, Sadie, or Annabelle. She must avoid further affection between them.

"Mr. Hanley. I do not tolerate inappropriate behavior with Miss Garfield. You are done here today. I am in agreement you have overstayed at this point. Time to leave the building." Levi gripped Garrett's arm, leading him to the door.

"I apologize, Mr. Jackson. Miss Garfield's kind offer might have caused me to overreact."

Garrett looked back at Maggie. "Forgive me, Miss Garfield. I meant no disrespect."

"This behavior absolutely will not happen again." Levi stared at Maggie. "And, Miss Garfield, you will not make any offers to locate anyone without my involvement."

Maggie contained her fury.

"If Mr. Hanley wants our help, you would be the one to oversee finding his father. These are the kinds of services your firm provides, correct? Let's save that discussion for a future time as it is irrelevant now."

"Yes, future," said Levi. "Or never."

Maggie continued to hold her anger at bay.

Levi pushed Garrett closer to the door. "Good day, Mr. Hanley."

"Thank you again, Miss Garfield," Garrett said. "Have a wonderful afternoon. You, too, Mr. Jackson."

Levi glared out the window until he saw Garrett leave the building.

"Miss Garfield, I don't have information yet on Mr. Hanley's character. Therefore, it is not a sound decision to have him return here for any more tours."

"No need to fret, Mr. Jackson. I believe Mr. Hanley is a fine man who is dealing with many difficulties. Your worries are likely in vain."

"You will not pursue any searches for missing fathers. I am still investigating these strangers' pasts. Do we agree?"

"I wouldn't know how to begin. To leave you in charge of such matters is beneficial to all."

"Do you have the correspondences you received from Mr. Hanley?"

"Yes, why?"

"I'd like to see them. In fact, share any letters you've received from Mr. Jesse Walker too. I've been remiss not having asked for these before now."

Maggie took two bundled packs of letters from a desk drawer, handing them to Levi. "I don't think there's anything alarming in them."

"I'll be the one who decides what is alarming or not. I need to take these with me to look them over thoroughly."

"Read them." Maggie nodded her dismissal. She'd had enough of his interference for one day.

Chapter 17

Max drove towards Mando Merchandising with a planned arrival of four o'clock to escort Maggie home. Seeing Garrett Hanley on the side of the road disturbed him.

"Good afternoon, Mr. Hanley. What brings you out this way?"

"Hello, Mr. Crawford. I borrowed a motorbike to visit Miss Garfield and Mr. Jackson at work today. Upon my departure, I couldn't get the bike's engine to start up. I'm well skilled at driving them, but a complete idiot about mechanics."

Max laughed, somewhat relieved at the explanation. "I'm not surprised you had a problem. No one rides the motorbike except me, so I haven't been diligent with the maintenance. Folks around here prefer the horses. Where is the bike?"

"Outside Mando Merchandising."

"I'm going there now. Get in and I'll drive you back. Let's see if we can get the bike running. If not, I'll take you to the boardinghouse after we pick up Miss Garfield."

"I would appreciate that, sir."

At Mando, Max looked the bike over for several minutes and nodded.

"I see the problem, an easy fix. A few tools will be required. Do you need the use of the bike today, or can I take care of it tomorrow?"

"No hurry on my part, Mr. Crawford. In fact, I can walk back to the boardinghouse. There's no need to put you out."

"The air is brisk, and the walk to town is a bit lengthy. I'd be happy to drive you as soon as Miss Garfield ends her workday."

"Miss Garfield is done," Maggie said. "I've been standing here watching you for a few minutes."

"I didn't see my girl come out," Max said.

"I know how you are when working on any of the vehicles. Almost impossible to get your attention. Why is the motorbike here?"

"I rode the bike today," Garrett said. "With Hank's blessing. The bike wouldn't start up again when I left Mando Merchandising."

Maggie frowned. "You've been here a while, since our meeting ended over an hour ago. Why didn't you come back inside to let me know you needed help?"

Max interrupted. "Mr. Hanley was walking home when I found him. We came back here to see if I could get the bike working. I can't, so the bike is out of service until tomorrow. I told him we could get him back to the boardinghouse."

"Yes, Uncle Max, we need to be kind to our guests." Maggie smiled across her shoulder as Max helped her into the motorcar, with Garrett taking the back seat. Maggie could feel his long legs nestled in behind her seat which warmed her back.

"Miss Garfield, working all day in such a hectic environment must exhaust you. I'm sure you need some recovery time from trying to do the job of your father. Perhaps we should take you home first."

Once again, Maggie's warmth toward the man disappeared. "Mr. Hanley, I am perfectly capable of filling my father's shoes. I am not so weak I need recovery time. Honestly, I wonder why you feel the necessity to share your unmerited concerns of my being born a woman."

"To your credit, Miss Garfield, I concede a woman has much domestic proficiency, far outdoing men. I admire the qualities of females. However, doing the job of a man, even as competently as you, must be draining. As is well understood, women have quite different God-given skills than men, and vice-versa."

"Mr. Hanley, are you saying women are only proficient at domestic chores, and lack enough endurance to run a company or step into their father's shoes without needing extra rest and recovery time?" Maggie asked.

"All I'm saying is gentlemen and ladies are made differently. This is not an insult, only pointing out the facts. Women are the weaker sex."

Maggie looked at Max. "Are you in a hurry to get home?"

"No. I can take you anywhere you want to go, Maggie. Perhaps we should take Mr. Hanley to the boardinghouse first."

"Oh, I would very much like Mr. Hanley to accompany us. Would you take us to Orchard's Corner?"

Uncle Max laughed. "I can. Does Mr. Hanley know what Orchard's Corner is?"

"No, I don't." Garrett spoke for himself. "What is it?"

"Let's keep Orchard's Corner a secret, Uncle Max." Turning to Garrett, Maggie said, "You will join us in the activities, right, Mr. Hanley?"

"Oh, most definitely. I obviously have nowhere to go except a small room. Besides, I would enjoy some fresh produce."

"Orchard's Corner, it is," Max said, with a sinister laugh.

"Am I sure I want to go? What are you getting me into?"

"You'll see," Maggie said. "Trust me when I tell you this will be a fun experience for all of us."

Thirty-five minutes later, with little conversation having taken place, they arrived at Orchard's Corner.

"This doesn't look much like an orchard to me. I doubt we'll walk away with many apples today."

"No apples here. Look closer," Max said.

Garrett surveyed the surroundings including several targets.

"A shooting range? This is no place for a wo—"

"I wouldn't finish that sentence, if I were you, Mr. Hanley," Max interrupted with a smile.

"I was just going to say this is no place for a woman, *or man*, without a gun." Garrett said.

"Lucky for you, we have plenty of guns," Max said.

Max unlocked the door of a small building and took out a Colt 45 revolver and a box of ammunition.

Garrett took the weapon from Max and looked it over. "A gorgeous pistol. I've never seen one quite this fancy. Who's going to be shooting?"

"All of us," Max said.

"Even Miss Garfield?"

"Yes," Maggie and Max said in unison.

Garrett shook his head. "Oh no. I don't want to take any chances of someone getting hurt. Miss Garfield, trying to prove your abilities with a pistol is too dangerous."

"Mr. Hanley, I assure you there is no need to worry about me handling a gun. Your life is not in danger."

"I've seen her with many guns. You're safe," Max said.

"So, we're going to take turns with only one gun?" Garrett asked, looking a bit pale.

"One is enough," Maggie said. "Are you ready for the contest to begin?"

"Contest?" Garrett raised his eyebrows.

"Yes, with no prize other than pride of winning. Your competition will be a man, *and a woman.* If you are agreeable." Maggie's tone showed her doubt.

"Can *you* shoot a gun?"

"I guess you'll find out."

Max marked the course. "We're only counting bull's-eyes for points."

"You go first, Uncle Max."

Max shot at the targets, hitting four bull's-eyes out of six. He came very close to the rest, hitting the target every time.

"Nice shooting," Maggie said. "You shoot now, Mr. Hanley. I'll go last."

Max handed Garrett the bullets. Garrett loaded the gun, then shot at the targets, hitting five bull's-eyes, having barely missed the last one.

"Impressive. Ok, Margaret Garfield. You're up," Uncle Max said.

Garrett backed up. Maggie ignored him.

Maggie aimed and quickly shot at the targets. Six bull's-eyes out of six.

Garrett closed his gaping mouth. "Can you hit all six again? Or were you just lucky?"

Maggie loaded the gun, shot six more times, hitting six more bull's-eyes.

"Amazing," Garrett said.

"Mr. Hanley, my shooting ability is just one of the reasons why I, a woman, know I can handle anything I set my mind to, including running a company. I am perfectly capable of taking care of myself ... *without* the need for extra rest."

"I'm seeing more evidence of that claim every time we're together."

"Let's get everyone home now," Uncle Max said. "I'd like to take my lovely wife out for supper."

They put the Colt 45 away and returned to the motorcar.

Chapter 18

"Look around us, Maggie. There's a lot of open space between here and town. Besides, you seem to be feeling quite self-assured right now. Would you like to drive us home?" Max opened the driver's door and waited.

Maggie stood firm, somewhat paralyzed. She pleaded with her eyes to get Max to relent. She didn't want to fail in front of Garrett. For some reason his opinion mattered. This awareness unnerved her. "Uncle Max, I will take a turn when it's just the two of us."

Max smiled and kept the door open. "This is the most remote part of Garfield, so there shouldn't be anything you can hit or run into."

"I don't think this is a good idea," Garrett said. "I know she can shoot, but operating vehicles is very difficult. Motorcars are so new, and Miss Garfield does not seem to be skilled in driving them. Come on, Mr. Crawford, you take us home."

That's all she needed—more demeaning words from him. Maggie stepped forward and slid into the driver's seat.

"Mr. Hanley, you're exasperating in your opinions of women. I will be happy to drive, Uncle Max." Maggie said, with confidence. "Get in, both of you."

Garrett reluctantly climbed into the back seat. Max chuckled as he cranked the car. Then walked around to the passenger's side and stepped in.

"Stay right next to her, Mr. Crawford, in case you need to take over. I'd like to get to the boardinghouse without injury," Garrett said.

After a few jolts and a bit of bobbling, Maggie got the motorcar moving down the road. Feeling surprisingly comfortable, she picked up speed.

Hmmmm ... Sweet Freedom. This isn't so bad, quite fun, in fact. I can do this, maybe even drive myself to work tomorrow. Garrett Hanley will see what women are made of.

Maggie began whistling a tune.

I wonder where else I might drive this car in the next few days. Maybe as far as Hannibal to get a few new books to read. Getting lost in captivating stories is always a joy.

"Maggie, watch out for Bertha!" Max yelled.

Maggie's mind lost all thoughts of books as she swerved, barely missing the cow.

The motorcar started down a long hill, picking up speed with every passing second.

"You're going too fast! Pull the brake!" Max reached over to pull the lever but got caught in strings attached to Maggie's reticule.

"The tree, the tree!" screamed Max, just before a branch stole his hat, the very one Aunt Catherine had said was designed to withstand any trees it might encounter.

Maggie and Max held on tight and weathered the impact of the collision as they remained in their seats. Garrett's tall body had been no match for the branch. He was thrown from the car and landed hard on the ground. He didn't move.

"Oh no! Uncle Max, I've killed him!"

They got out of the car and rushed to where Garrett lay, his head on a rock. Maggie lifted his head into her arms, watching his hair turn red from the flowing blood.

Max felt his pulse.

"He's alive," Max said. "We need to get his wound wrapped quickly."

Maggie pulled off her scarf and bound it around Garrett's head. Her heart ached as she looked at his limp body. "Maybe Mr. Hanley should have been wearing one of Aunt Catherine's Bowler hats. Might have protected him from that boulder."

"Keep holding his head. I'll check on the motorcar to see if it's drivable."

Maggie pulled the scarf tighter and pleaded to God. *Lord, don't let my stubbornness and pride cause Garrett to die. Help us to get him to the doctor on time. I promise to never operate a vehicle again.*

Max was able to get the mostly unscathed car started and moved away from the tree.

They lifted Garrett as gently as possible, struggling to pull him into the car. Maggie sat on the back seat. After much effort, Max was able to lay Garrett next to Maggie. She laid his head on her lap, holding on tightly.

"I'll stay back here to keep the pressure on his wound," Maggie said, looking down at Garrett's face. So handsome. So annoying.

Max drove them to town. Fortunately, Dr. Emma Gibson was in her office. The doctor walked confidently to the motorcar with her black bag in hand to evaluate Garrett. Dr. Gibson had been in town for only a few months. Although knowledgeable about the latest remedies and illnesses, the doctor was struggling to acquire patients willing to allow a woman to doctor them in Kansas City, so Maggie asked her to come to Garfield.

Max opened the car door and Dr. Gibson stepped in.

"Has he been unconscious since this happened? What *did* happen?" Dr. Gibson asked.

"He has not been awake since being thrown from the motorcar," Maggie said.

Dr. Gibson looked at her with disbelief. "You weren't driving, were you?"

"I wish I could say no, but, yes, I was the driver," Maggie said, embarrassment coloring her confession.

"I can hear details later, but—you really should stay away from operating vehicles."

"I might have to agree."

The doctor looked over Garrett for any other cuts or injuries. "Who is this young man?"

"Mr. Garrett Hanley from Chicago. One of the gentlemen who came here to find a wife," Maggie said.

"Let's take him inside," Dr. Gibson said. "Can you help me get him out of the car?"

"He's a muscular fellow, but I think we can manage." Max said.

Maggie pulled herself out from under Garrett and laid his head down on the seat, then hurried around the motorcar. Max picked him up under his arms, carefully supporting his head, while Maggie and Dr. Gibson each took hold of one of Garrett's legs. They were able to get him out of the car and onto the bed in the doctor's office after several minutes. Right now, the office was one of the bedrooms in Dr. Gibson's house. Maggie wanted to have better accommodations built for her soon.

While Dr. Gibson tended to Garrett, Maggie went to the basin and washed the blood from her arms and hands, using a wet towel to wipe her dress.

Fresh blood started to flow when Dr. Gibson removed the scarf from Garrett's head.

"You did well to wrap his wound. Probably saved his life and certainly kept him from losing too much blood. However, I don't think your scarf is salvageable."

Maggie was glad to hear she had done at least something right, not caring about the condition of a scarf.

Dr. Gibson cleaned and stitched the laceration with quick precision. She covered the wound with a bandage, before using smelling salts to awaken Garrett.

Maggie watched as Garrett turned away from the smell and opened his eyes.

"Why is everything so blurry? Who is this woman that's trying to poison me?"

"Mr. Hanley, this is Dr. Gibson. She's taking care of you," Maggie said.

"Why does my head hurt so bad? And ... why do I need a doctor?"

"You needed stitches after your unfortunate fall out of the motorcar."

"I fell out of a motorcar? What? Wait ... I remember now ... you drove us into a giant tree. I told you a woman shouldn't drive a car."

"I'm inclined to believe you are correct." Maggie said. "This time."

"My head feels like nails are being hammered into it. Can you do anything for the pain, Doctor? Oh no, wait ... did you say *she* is a doctor? Where is the real doctor? Make her leave me alone. I want to see a qualified physician now."

The doctor kept her voice steady. "You are free to go find a male doctor while you deal with your horrible headache in your unstable condition. The nearest one is about twenty miles from here. I can remove the stitches if you'd like to bleed to death on your way to a 'qualified physician.' Or, you can allow me to provide some medicine to relieve much of the discomfort in your head. Your decision, Mr. Hanley."

"Unfortunately for me, you make a sound argument. I'm at your mercy." Garrett was grimacing from the pain.

"I have no desire to bleed to death or do anything to worsen my current situation. You win. I guess a woman will have to do. What can you provide for my pain? I'll take anything."

"Thank you for such a lovely endorsement, Mr. Hanley. If I weren't a devoted doctor who puts the welfare of her patients first, I would walk away and leave you to deal with your discomfort. However, I have prepared some laudanum tea. Drink it and you should receive some relief."

Garrett sipped the warm beverage and was surprised by how pleasant it tasted. "This is delicious. Are you sure it's medicine?"

"I like to add some spices to take away any bitterness. Kind of a woman's touch," Dr. Gibson said.

Garrett stroked the back his head. All he found were bandages.

"How many stitches did you give me, Dr. Gibson? I need to know just how dangerous my ride with Miss Garfield turned out to be."

"The laceration is about four inches long. I used twenty-two stitches to close the wound. You have two sizable knots which will be quite sore for a couple of days. One is to the right of the cut with the other just above your temple. All should heal without incident," Dr. Gibson said.

"Miss Garfield, you've certainly gotten your revenge for any unwelcome comments. I'll be sure to tame my tongue from now on ... especially with Dr. Gibson joining forces."

"Mr. Hanley, I certainly did not wish to bring any harm to you. Although I do believe you deserve some sort of reprimand for your ridiculous ideas about women, I would never throw you out of a motorcar for the purpose of implementing punishment. In fact, I feel quite badly for causing you harm. As for taming your tongue, I'm not sure you have the ability. Since you're now showing signs of life, perhaps we should get out of here."

"Are you planning to drive when we leave here?" Garrett asked.

Max hid a grin at the horror on Garrett's face. "I'll drive. I'd like to make it home safely to my dear Catherine."

Maggie glared at both men. "No need to worry. I have no desire ever to drive a motorcar again."

"Good," said Dr. Gibson and Garrett in unison.

Maggie frowned but kept her mouth shut.

Dr. Gibson put together a package with bandages so Garrett's wounds could be changed daily. She included laudanum for pain, along with spices and instructions for making the tea. "I will be out to see Mr. Hanley to remove the stitches in one week. He should rest as much as possible. I'm assuming he's staying at the boardinghouse."

"Yes, Mr. Hanley has taken up residence at the boardinghouse. Thank you, Dr. Gibson. You are a wonderful addition to our community," Maggie said.

The three of them helped Garrett into the car. Then Max hurriedly got into the driver's seat.

"You don't need to rush past me. I told you I don't want to drive." Maggie frowned as she sat next to Garrett, wanting to be near him in case he needed anything.

"Uncle Max, I'm not sure Mr. Hanley should stay at the boardinghouse alone tonight. With the enormous house father built for me, there is plenty of room for ..."

"Oh no." Max interrupted. "He is not staying with you. I won't allow it, not for your reputation or safety."

"You didn't let me finish. I have plenty of room for him as well as you and Aunt Catherine. Do you think you two could stay with me for a few days, along with Mr. Hanley?"

"I'll have to check with my wife when I get home. She might be agreeable, but we'll need to find someone who can run The Happy Hatter for a day or two."

"I still possess the ability to make decisions even with a wounded head. Staying at the boardinghouse is best for me." Garrett took a long breath. "I won't put anyone out, especially to the point of rearranging schedules. I'll be fine in my own room. All I might need is to brew a cup of tea if needed. I truly just want to rest."

Maggie frowned at him for a moment as she assessed his desired arrangement, surprised to feel a little hurt and rejected.

"You should stay wherever you feel most comfortable. I do want to make sure you're settled for tonight, which is the least I can do after harming you. We'll want to look in on you again in the morning on our way to the warehouse. Would that be acceptable?"

"I can agree to those terms. Thank you, Miss Garfield. Oh, and thank *you*, Mr. Crawford, for driving."

Impossible man.

As they were getting Garrett into his room, Jesse came in to see what had happened. Shortly afterwards, Annabelle, Ruth, and Sadie showed up. Annabelle brought chicken and dumplings, cornbread, and apple pie. Word traveled fast in the small town of Garfield when any new incidents took place.

"You have plenty of helpful people, so I'll go home to my lovely wife now. Are you ready to leave, Maggie? Or should I come back for you?"

"Yes, I too would like to go. Mr. Hanley seems to be well cared for. Thanks, everyone, for coming. Don't stay too long. Mr. Hanley needs rest, doctor's orders. Uncle Max and I will be back in the morning."

Maggie paused as she looked at Garrett. "I'll leave word with the staff to contact me if you need anything, Mr. Hanley. I am enormously sorry this happened."

"You are forgiven. I'm certain I shall recover," Garrett said with a smile.

His smile ... those hazel eyes ...

Chapter 19

Levi sipped coffee and stared at the letters from Garrett Hanley and Jesse Walker spread on the table in front of him, along with the investigator's reports for both men.

Levi first read every word of Garrett's report.

> Subject: Garrett David Hanley, Male, Born March 14, 1874, Age: 24

> Lives with mother, Martha Jean Hanley, Age 44, in Chicago, Illinois. Garrett Hanley's father, James David Hanley, Age 48, vanished six months ago. James Hanley's location is unknown and there has been no death reported. Prior to his disappearance, James Hanley sold his company to Rexton Arthur Tillman, Age 42.

Levi gasped. "Rex Tillman! No! Garrett Hanley has ties to this horrible man. I knew these strangers would be trouble!"

Levi's valet, Carson, stepped into the room, "Is everything alright? Mr. Jackson, did you say Rex Tillman?"

"Yes ... Yes, I did. He's on the move, Carson. My worst fears have come true."

"I hoped we'd never have to see him, again."

"Yes, my sentiments too."

"Can I bring you anything, Mr. Jackson?"

"More coffee. Hot and strong. I need to look over some more information.

Carson set the coffee at Levi's elbow, then left him alone to read the rest of the report.

> Garrett Hanley has continued to work for Hanley Construction. Known to work long hours and appears to have little wealth. No siblings. Unmarried. No offspring. No criminal records. Current location might be Hannibal, Missouri.

Levi paced the room.

After several minutes, he sat down and opened the first envelope.

"Mr. Garrett Hanley, let's see what you wrote about yourself."

After reading the correspondence, Levi pounded his fist on the table, knocking his cup to the floor.

Carson looked in, saw the mess, and returned with a broom and mop.

"An honest living? Doubtful. Kind and considerate? Not if he's a friend of Tillman's. Rex must be the force behind Garrett writing this letter. Garrett responding to the advertisement is not just a coincidence. There is something evil afoot, and I'm sure a battle is about to begin."

"Are you talking to me, Mr. Jackson?"

"No ... No ... Just to myself, Carson."

"A fresh cup of coffee is on the table. Or is there a safer place?"

"I'll be careful. News of Tillman has me riled up."

"Understandable, sir. That man ruined your life."

William Garfield and Levi had worked together to keep Rex away. William promised to help Levi get Jackson Shipping back. Unfortunately, he died before they could complete the mission. The main reason William hired Levi was to protect Maggie from Rex. He would make sure this obligation was honored.

Levi moved on to the second envelope and pulled out the letter.

He trembled with anger when he read the words.

Levi shouted, "This is *my* story. *I* lost *my* dog, Hutch, to a coyote. A twister took *my* home. *I* lived in a barn. This thief has stolen my identity. Garrett Hanley is absolutely conspiring with Rex Tillman. Who else could have provided the facts of my life to him? Why would Hanley partner with a rogue like Tillman? I knew bringing in strangers was going to create unnecessary havoc for Garfield. I did not think this would cause *me* hardship."

Carson stepped into the room again. "Am I needed, sir?"

"No. No. Thank you, Carson. My anger cannot be contained, so I might be a bit loud for a while. I'll call you by name if I need you."

Still in a state of stunned shock, Levi read the final letter.

He snorted. "Friends to count on? Hanley would never be able to count on Tillman for anything except deceit."

Levi contemplated the details he was now privy to concerning Garrett Hanley. He remembered Maggie wanted to help Garrett find his father. "Tillman must be behind the man's disappearance."

Levi held up his partial pinky finger. He wished he had been stronger when Rex and his gang confronted him.

An overwhelming spirit of power came over him. For the first time, Rex Tillman was coming within reach. Perhaps the time was near to get Jackson Shipping back.

Levi pulled his thoughts away from Garrett and turned to Jesse Walker's information. For all he knew, the two strangers could be partners. He opened the report.

Subject: Jesse Paul Walker, Male, Born January 8, 1875,
Age: 23
Lives with his father, Jonathan Bernard Walker, Age 48,
and his mother, Wilma Geraldine Walker, Age 43, in

St. Louis, Missouri. Parents are wealthy. Jesse Walker obtained a law degree from Transylvania College last year, graduating at the top of his class. No known employment. Jesse Walker has traveled extensively to places outside of the country. No siblings. Unmarried. No offspring. Jesse Walker has been known by many as the instigator of minor pranks with no arrests. Jesse Walker was caught burning down a barn, but charges were not filed when his parents compensated the barn owner for the damages. Current location might be Hannibal, Missouri.

Levi realized St. Louis was not far from Chicago, with easy access by train service between the two destinations. He would need to investigate the possibility of Garrett and Jesse being acquainted prior to arriving in Garfield.

Levi read the correspondence, muttering throughout.

"This man is quite fond of himself. So far, I am not. A lawyer? Maybe he represents Tillman or Hanley in some way."

Levi didn't feel he had gained much insight about Jesse based on the first two correspondences. He read the final letter.

"Sounds like Jesse Walker has access to family money. Hope none of that wealth is tied to Tillman."

Carson appeared again. "Mr. Maxwell Crawford is here to see you. Should I ask him in?"

"I wasn't expecting a visit, but yes, he's welcome."

Carson held open the door for Max, then left.

"What brings you here, Mr. Crawford?"

"I let Miss Garfield drive today …

Levi interrupted, "Oh no … is Hank Rothstadt's horse alive? Was she alone?"

"This time, she hit a tree. Garrett Hanley was thrown out of the motorcar. Ended up with a substantial gash to his head, requiring twenty-two stitches. He'll be bedridden for a few days at the boardinghouse. I just wanted to make sure you're aware."

"Is Miss Garfield injured? Wait, what was she doing alone driving Hanley?"

"She wasn't alone. I was with them. And, yes, we're both fine although she's feeling guilty right now. I have a hunch she'll want to spend more time with Mr. Hanley to help him recover. I plan to stay close by."

Panic ran through Levi. "I want to make sure Miss Garfield is not alone with that man. Where did this incident happen?"

"We were returning from Orchard's Corner. Miss Garfield challenged Mr. Hanley to a shooting contest, and you might be able to guess who won."

"Mr. Hanley had a gun with him?" Levi asked.

"No. We loaned him a pistol. He was almost as accurate a shooter as Miss Garfield."

Levi shook his head. "Why on earth would you hand a gun to a stranger? How did you not think about the danger in that? What if Mr. Hanley had decided to shoot both of you? He has not proven himself to be trustworthy."

"I would never want to put Miss Garfield in danger. I'm ashamed this thought never occurred to me."

Max dropped into a chair. "I have failed Maggie Garfield."

"Fortunately, there was no harm this time. I trust you'll be much more careful in the future. We need to proceed with caution regarding these strangers. In that regard, Pinkerton Agency is sending three men who will arrive tomorrow. Mr. Garfield provided ample funds to bring in reinforcement if ever needed. Now is the time. These agents are skilled in security and detective work."

"I like the idea of extra protection. I'll make better choices regarding these strangers. You have my word. I'm glad we have a man like you, Mr. Jackson. William made a wise choice."

Levi considered informing Max about Garrett's connection to Tillman but decided to wait until he had talked to the Pinkerton agents.

"Thank you for the confidence. I won't let anything happen to Miss Garfield. That's a promise. Keep your eyes open for anything out of the ordinary. You might want to carry your pistol for now."

Chapter 20

Maggie and Max walked up the stairs towards Garrett's room. As they rounded the corner, they saw a well-dressed man in a black suit sitting between Garrett and Jesse's two rooms. Max pushed Maggie behind him when he realized the man was armed. Max pulled out his pistol just as Levi came out of the room.

"Watch out. He has a gun," Max yelled as he aimed at the stranger.

Levi moved in front of the man and waved his hands. "No. No. Stop. He's one of the gentlemen I've hired to help with security. Meet Chester Davis."

Max put his gun away, relieved but still shaken. "I wasn't aware that your men had arrived."

Levi nodded. "Yes, I apologize, Mr. Crawford. They got here this morning. I haven't had time to discuss this with you, yet. Two other men, Ernie McGuire and Rich Dodson, are here as well. They're watching Mando Merchandising right now."

Maggie looked annoyed. "Why are those gentlemen at Mando? I thought you wanted to keep watch over Mr. Hanley and Mr. Walker, not those who work for me."

"The men are getting to know the town and how we operate. I assure you they will not interfere with your workers, Miss Garfield."

"They had better not."

Levi jerked his thumb toward the door. "I imagine you've come to check on Mr. Hanley. He's awake if you'd like to go inside. I'll be right outside the door."

Maggie wanted to talk more about this security business but didn't have time now. She walked into Garrett's room with Max right behind her.

"I hope Mr. Walker and the ladies didn't stay too late last night so you were able to get some sleep," Maggie said as she and Max sat next to Garrett's bed. His scruffy hair was sticking out around his bandages. Maggie wondered how he could look so handsome even when in such a disheveled state.

"I'm not sure when they left. I fell asleep during Miss Stoddard's step by step guidelines to making dumplings. I remember her warning us of the very important step of allowing dough to have proper time to rest. The next thing I recollect is hearing the door shut. My pounding head woke me up early this morning."

"Oh, no, someone should have been here to help you," Maggie said.

"I was fine. There was a cup of laudanum tea sitting next to my bed. I drank it and went back to sleep. Had another cup waiting for me when I awoke again. I suppose you left instructions for someone here at the boardinghouse."

"I do feel responsible since I almost killed you."

"You make an excellent argument, but I was never anywhere near death."

"Can we order you some breakfast," Max asked.

"No, I'm not hungry. I just want to sleep."

"Since Dr. Gibson said rest is best, we'll take leave now, but will be back with dinner at noontime," said Maggie. "I know the boarding house would bring you dinner from the restaurant, but Miss Stoddard has insisted you will get well faster with some of her soup."

"Soup sounds nice," Garrett's voice trailed off.

Max opened the door for Maggie.

"You look lovely today, Miss Garfield. I like you in blue," Garrett said with one eye closed.

Max cleared his throat.

"Oh, you look nice too, Mr. Crawford," Garrett said with a smile as he dozed off to sleep.

Max shook his head as he took a snickering Maggie by the arm.

Maggie and Max returned to the boardinghouse at noon, along with Annabelle. Chester Davis still kept watch outside the rooms. Max handed Chester a basketful of food.

"We brought you dinner—vegetable soup and cornbread. Miss Stoddard is an incredible cook, so I hope you enjoy it," Maggie said.

"Thank you, ma'am. It smells delightful," Chester said.

Maggie, Max, and Annabelle went into Garrett's room where they made sure he ate all his vegetable soup and bread.

Jesse came in without knocking. "Something smells good. What did you bring? Is there any left?"

"Vegetable soup. Eat whatever you want. There's plenty," Annabelle said.

"Did you know there's an armed guy sitting outside this room?" Jesse asked. "He checked me for a weapon before letting me in."

"Yes, Mr. Chester Davis has joined Mr. Jackson's security staff since we might invite several potential husbands to our town. Mr. Jackson wants to ensure Garfield remains a safe place to live," Max said. "You'll have no worries if you don't do anything to cause them to question your character. Mr. Davis has been here all morning, so I'm surprised you didn't see him earlier."

"I just got out of bed. It's barely past noon."

Maggie frowned. *Jesse just left his bed?*

Jesse was already eating and seemed to have lost interest in any explanation of the man sitting outside. Apparently, food was the only thing to captivate his attention. Other than Sadie.

"Annabelle needs to get back to oversee the kitchen at Mando, so we'd best go. Some of us will bring you supper this evening, Mr. Hanley," Maggie said.

"Miss Garfield, I don't mean to sound ungrateful, but I could use rest tonight. The housekeepers check on me and they've offered to get meals from the restaurant. Perhaps you could ask my new friends of Garfield to stay away for a couple of days."

"Yes. Rest is what you need right now. I'll make sure you have no visitors. Perhaps we should go, Uncle Max."

"Miss Garfield, would you like to come by for supper day after tomorrow? I'm sure to be rejuvenated by then."

"Yes, I can be here."

"Maggie, I promised to take Aunt Catherine to supper in Hannibal on that night. We'll need to make sure you have a proper chaperone," Max said.

"Uncle Max, I don't need a chaperone. Mr. Hanley is just a friend, and besides, he's laid up in bed with a headful of stitches."

"*I* see the need to keep your reputation, so you *will* have a chaperone."

"I can chaperone," Jesse said, "Bring Miss Sadie Stoddard along as an additional chaperone. I believe she would like to get to know me better."

"Miss Stoddard has not indicated one way or the other, although you appear to have some interest in her, Mr. Walker," Maggie said.

"Yes, I do. Isn't it why you brought me here? How will we know of our compatibility if we don't spend time together?"

"You make a sound point, Mr. Walker. I will ask Miss Stoddard. Up to her if she wants to attend. I will also invite Miss Calvin and Miss Annabelle Stoddard. They need to get to know both of you gentlemen as well. Let's not forget about our armed friend right outside the door. I think we'll be well chaperoned. Do you agree, Uncle Max?"

"Yes, that will be appropriate."

"Are you able to attend, Annabelle?" Maggie asked.

Annabelle shook her head. "I have a commitment for that evening, Maggie. I don't think Ruth will be available, either. She and I are meeting with Sophie Jenkins at her shop for a fitting for new dresses. This might take hours."

Maggie was pleasantly surprised to hear Annabelle and Ruth were planning to wear Sophie's creations. They tended to dress more conservatively. Maggie hadn't known them to purchase garments from Sophie in the past and was anxious to see what they had chosen.

"Sounds like a wonderful outing," Maggie said. "So, if Miss Sadie Stoddard agrees, we'll be here at six o'clock. Will that time be suitable, gentlemen?"

"Yes. Should I order meals for us?" Jesse said.

"Let's decide on supper after Miss Stoddard and I arrive, if she is able to accompany me," Maggie said. "Is there anything else I can get for you, Mr. Hanley, before we go?"

"All needs have been taken care of and more," Garrett said. "Thank you. And since we're friends, may we use given names?"

"If the two of you can be so informal to use your given names, then the rest of us should also," Jesse said.

"We've known each other for a few days and been through some trials together. Using our given names will be acceptable at this point," Max said. "If it is satisfactory with Miss Garfield and Miss Annabelle Stoddard."

"Agreed," Annabelle said.

"Garrett and Jesse, we'll see you for supper in two days," Maggie said.

"Make sure you bring Sadie ... er ... Miss Stoddard," Jesse reminded her.

"She *is* still Miss Stoddard until she says otherwise," Max said.

"Right. Miss Stoddard. I'm eager to see her again. Meanwhile, I'll keep an eye on old Garrett here."

"Wonderful, Jesse. Good to know you'll be available," Maggie said.

"Be very convincing with Miss Stoddard. I'm counting on spending some time with her."

"I'll do my best," Maggie assured him.

Maggie doubted Jesse was the kind of man Sadie would be interested to know better. He was much too self-absorbed from what she had observed so far. Her matchmaking experiment was not off to a stellar start.

Chapter 21

The Crawfords delivered Maggie and Sadie to Home Sweet Home Boardinghouse at precisely six o'clock. With Maggie's insistence, Max did not go inside.

"We'll be back here at nine o'clock to escort you home," Max said.

"I can procure a carriage. Just enjoy your night with Aunt Catherine."

"Aunt Catherine and I will be riding through town at that time anyway, so expect us to be waiting for you."

"All right, since you can't be convinced otherwise." Maggie smiled, then turned to the silent Sadie.

"I'm so happy you were able to come tonight, Sadie. I hope you don't feel obligated to be here."

"This will be a wonderful way to spend an evening. Truth be told, Mr. Walker intrigues me."

"So, you do have some interest? Pay attention to Mr. Walker's actions as you're getting to know him. Be discerning. I want nothing but the best for you."

"Being in his company will show me more. I want to be open to whatever plans God has for me."

"His way is always best."

They nodded to Mr. Davis and knocked on Garrett's door.

Jesse appeared, his gaze going straight to Sadie. "You are a vision of loveliness, Miss Stoddard."

"Thank you, Mr. Walker. Having supper with you and Mr. Hanley this evening will be very nice," Sadie said. "May we enter?"

"Yes, most definitely," Jesse said.

"Come in, ladies. You look lovely as well, Maggie," Garrett said.

Sadie frowned. "Maggie?"

Maggie nodded. "Yes, I have given Garrett and Jesse permission to use my given name since we've become friends."

"If Maggie is comfortable with first names, you can use mine, as well," Sadie said.

"I hoped we could get a little less formal, Sadie. Call me Jesse, as I would like to think we have become friends."

"Yes, we seem to be getting along nicely."

"How are you feeling, Garrett?" Maggie asked.

"Much better. No pain this afternoon. I've even been able to get up without my head whirling. I might heal from your attempt to kill me," Garrett said with a laugh.

Maggie gasped. "That truly isn't funny. You could very well have been harmed much worse than you were."

"Thankfully, I wasn't. Are you ladies hungry?"

"I don't know about them, but I'm famished," Jesse said.

Maggie couldn't stop herself from rolling her eyes. "When are you *not* hungry, Jesse?"

Jesse grinned. "Hmmm ... I can always eat. Food doesn't stay with me long."

"Yes, I'm ready to eat, as well," Sadie agreed.

"I'm disappointed Miss Ruth Calvin and Miss Annabelle Stoddard could not attend this evening," Maggie said.

"I like the small group tonight since I'm still recovering. In fact, the present company is perfect."

"Just the same, next time we'll make sure to include them," Maggie said.

"Let's get on with the meal. The choices tonight are roast beef or pork chops. Which would you prefer, Sadie?" Jesse said.

"Pork chops would be lovely."

"Pork chops for you and roast beef for me. I'll go down and put in our requests to the restaurant. Be right back."

Garrett spoke as Jesse opened the door. "Oh, Jesse ... what about Maggie and I? We'd like to eat as well. Would you be so kind as to ask what we want before you go?"

Jesse turned to face Garrett. "Almost forgot you were here. My mistake. Roast beef or pork chops?"

"Maggie, what is your preference?" Garrett asked.

"I think pork chops sound wonderful."

"And I would like roast beef. Thank you, Jesse," Garrett said.

Jesse went next door to the restaurant for the meals. When he returned shortly thereafter, the four of them sat down at a small table.

Jesse had a forkful of beef in his hand when Maggie interrupted, "Should we say grace before we begin?"

Jesse felt all eyes on him so he put down his fork. "Sure, go ahead. Hanley?"

Maggie noted Garrett's pinched mouth when he reluctantly said, "Yes, I can say grace."

Garrett cleared his throat. "Dear God. Thank you for this meal you've provided. Bless our time in Garfield. Amen."

"Amen," the rest of them echoed.

Maggie wondered if Garrett was fully committed to living here permanently after she heard his prayer. Referring to "our time in Garfield" sounded temporary. She felt a little ping in her heart as she thought of the possibility of him leaving. Maggie reminded herself Garrett was not here for her. If he didn't match well with any of the other ladies, Garrett would have no choice but to leave.

Sadie and Jesse were engrossed in conversation with each other. Maggie was somewhat happy that there might be a successful match.

My risky plan to find husbands could truly work. I'm still worried Jesse might not be the man portrayed in his mother's correspondence. Trusting you, God.

"I believe they've forgotten we're here," Garrett said as he leaned a little closer to Maggie.

"Yes, it does appear so. My heart smiles to see the two of them get along so well."

"Does your heart smile that you and I get along well too?"

"I'm happy you're becoming friends with *all* the ladies." Maggie hesitated. "You were brought here to meet Miss Calvin, Annabelle, and Sadie. I have inadvertently monopolized your time, leaving them little chance to get to know you. I must step back so you can explore any potential with one of them."

Maggie looked at Sadie and Jesse. "You might have already missed your chance with Sadie."

Garrett touched her hand laying on the table. "What if I see potential with someone else? How would you feel if I were to tell you I'm interested in courting you?"

"Oh, no, Garrett, that is not possible." Maggie tried to calm her rapidly beating heart. "I did not place the advertisement so *I* could find a husband. Miss Calvin, Annabelle, and Sadie are the ones who might wish to be betrothed. I will never become a wife. This endeavor is for them, not me."

Maggie tried to pull her hand away, but Garrett held on.

"Of course, you'll marry. Why say such an outlandish thing?"

"I would rather not discuss my reasons. This is a non-negotiable part of my life. You came here as a potential groom for these remarkable ladies, not me."

"You care so much about those living in Garfield. Do you ever think of yourself?"

"Oh, yes. I struggle with my own self-centered desires constantly. Putting other's needs above my own is what God wants. I fall short most of the time. Thankfully, we have a forgiving and loving God."

Garrett smiled. "I've never met a lady like you, Maggie. You make me want to be a better man. Sometimes we don't see things the same, but the way you stand up for what you believe in is one of the qualities I admire most. You're such a fiercely strong lady."

"What? Did I just hear you say a lady can be fiercely strong? Garrett Hanley, could you be changing your mind about women's abilities?"

"Not all ladies, but certainly Maggie Garfield is strong. You do have a way of forcing me to see things differently, so there might be hope."

Maggie looked down and closed her eyes. *Dear Heavenly Father, guide Garrett's heart and clearly show him if Annabelle or Ruth would be a suitable match for him. Thank you for never failing us.*

Maggie opened her eyes and pulled her hand away. "When you're back on your feet, spend some time getting to know the other ladies. One of them might be a perfect match for you."

"Were you praying?"

Maggie nodded.

"I want to be the man you thought you brought here."

Maggie smiled. "I do, as well. I'm counting on it."

"Maggie?"

"Yes, Garrett?"

Garrett hesitated. "How do you have so much faith? God took your mother, then left you to be alone in this world when your father died. How can you not be angry with him?"

Maggie frowned. "God never lets me down. Blaming him for situations which make us angry or sad is wrong. He's my comfort and the only Father I have now. Unfortunately, life is hard. More than likely, we'll be disappointed at times, and possibly treated unfairly by others. Without God, life would be unbearable and difficult. He gives me hope and security. I'll see my earthly father and mother when I die. This is comforting. Life on earth is short. Eternal life with God is forever."

"God let down my mother. How could he allow my father to walk away from her?"

"There might still be hope with your father, Garrett. Perhaps there are circumstances beyond his control. Maybe contacting you is impossible for some reason. From what you've shared, he truly loves you and your mother. Something must have happened that he couldn't overcome. Don't blame God. Instead, ask for his help and wisdom. Allow him to guide your decisions. Life will be much less difficult if you do."

Garrett stared into Maggie's eyes. "You're quite a lady—your faith encourages me. I hope to have that same steadfast belief again one day."

"God never leaves us. We're the ones who pull away from him."

Chapter 22

Rex was giddy as he looked over his plans one last time before putting them in his briefcase.

He glanced at the telegram he had received a few days before from Garrett. *Garfield dead. Maggie running the business. Need more time. Stay put until you hear from me.*

Rex felt renewed excitement along with fury. He was thrilled William would not get in his way, gut angry at Garrett's demanding words. Who was Garrett Hanley to tell him to stay put? No one told Rex Tillman what to do.

He should have known not to send Garrett to do a man's job. Wanting more time proved his incompetence. Garrett would likely make a blunder of the situation, just like his father had done. Rex needed to take over and get Garrett out of the way.

Rex walked down the stairs of his twenty-six-room mansion. Soon he'd have a home three times this size—the least he deserved as the king of his soon-to-be three empires. Rex entered the parlor where his secretary, Arthur, was putting paperwork and supplies into his briefcase.

"Is everything ready?" Rex asked.

"I was just adding the last items."

Rex's valet, Grayson, entered the room.

"Make sure my bags get into the motorcar. I'll leave in fifteen minutes."

"Yes, sir."

"Don't let anyone in this house while I'm gone, Grayson."

"All the rules will be strictly followed, sir."

Grayson left the parlor to load the motorcar.

"Arthur, my location will be confidential. You know where to reach me, but no one else. Handle my affairs to perfection while I'm gone."

"I will take care of everything, sir."

Rex walked down the hallway to exit the mansion. "Goodbye, measly little house. I have outgrown you."

His evil laughter followed Rex out the door.

Chapter 23

Eight days had passed since the accident. Garrett was completely back to normal—other than a few bruises. The stitches came out when Dr. Gibson came to see him that morning.

Garrett hadn't had a headache for two days. A pain-free head, along with being stuck in a small room, allowed Garrett much time to think about what he'd agreed to do for Rex. Guilt had made him feel much worse than any of the pain he'd experienced from his wounds.

I won't hurt Maggie. There must be a way to take care of my mother without causing Maggie any harm, Garrett thought, then shouted, "Do you hear me, Rex Tillman? I won't do your despicable deed. As of this moment, I gladly give up living a double life. No more deception on my part. Somebody needs to stop you, and that somebody might be me."

Garrett's proclamation brought peace that he hadn't felt since his father left, assuring him this was the right decision. *As of this moment, Rex Tillman will no longer control me.*

Garrett knew he must keep Rex away from Garfield. He decided to send another telegram reminding Rex not to come until summoned.

Garrett thought about how Maggie had been by to check on him each day, always accompanied by Ruth or

Annabelle. She said few words and kept her distance from him, which was probably best for now. Garrett needed time to get rid of Rex. Romance would get in the way. His focus was on Maggie's safety right now, not on trying to win her heart.

Garrett walked out of his room and down the stairs. Standing on the porch, he took in a long breath. Cool air filled his lungs. There wasn't a cloud in the sky. The sun was warming up the crisp air, inviting Garrett to venture out. He'd secured the use of the motorbike earlier and couldn't wait to go for a ride. Thankfully, Max had the bike running efficiently again. Garrett sauntered over to the motorbike where Rich Dodson joined him.

"So, you're my designated babysitter today, huh, Mr. Dodson?"

"Yes, it's my turn. Anywhere you go in Garfield, I'll be nearby in my motorcar. Just remember that. Where are you heading?"

"No need to worry. I simply wanted to get outside since I haven't seen daylight in over a week. I just plan to go for a long ride. I might even venture out of town for a bit, possibly to Hannibal later."

Rich stared at him. "What you do in Hannibal is your business. What you do in Garfield is mine."

"I know how important Maggie's safety is to everyone in Garfield. I won't give you any reason to worry."

"Definitely in your best interest to keep that promise."

Garrett headed west along the road leading out of town, with Rich following a short distance behind. Going as fast as the bike would allow, Garrett was free for the first time in many months, albeit with an agent following him.

A large lake came into view surrounded by mature oak, evergreens, and sycamore trees. A few willow trees were weeping over into the grass.

Garrett saw a handful of houses around the water. One very sizeable yellow house with a wraparound porch stood out. Garrett wondered who lived there. Then, he was sure he knew.

This must be Maggie Garfield's home. She would be the only one here who could afford such an extravagant dwelling. Mr. Garfield had taken care of Maggie grandly when he was alive. He certainly made sure she would continue to be quite comfortable without him. I wonder how it would feel to live in a mansion. Thanks to my father, I'll never know.

Garrett didn't want to intrude on Maggie's personal space, so he kept his distance from the house. He noticed a limestone church with a small steeple near the lake. Garrett rode to it, and after some hesitation, got off the bike, walking to the building. Over six months had passed since he'd been in a church—the same amount of time his father had been gone.

Garrett gazed at the wooden door with the words, *Welcome Friends*. Garrett was not a welcome friend. In fact, he'd been an enemy. Realizing this unnerved him.

Garrett put his hand on the door but couldn't bring himself to open it. Instead, he turned around and walked away.

God, I know I haven't reached out to you in a long time. Not sure you're still there. Even if you don't care about me anymore, I hope you'll hear my prayer for Maggie Garfield's sake. Clear my mind and help me devise a way to get out of this mess with Rex without harming Maggie. I'm not an evil man. Guide my steps to do what's right. God, if you do hear me, I'd also be forever grateful if you would lead my father back home.

Garrett wasn't sure why he had felt the urge to pray, even more perplexed to have included his father.

Truthfully, Garrett wasn't convinced he wanted to find his father or God. How could he trust a Heavenly Father when an earthly father is so unreliable?

Think, Garrett, think. How can I outwit Rex and get him out of my life, as well as my mother's and Maggie's?

Garrett walked to the edge of the lake and stared out over the water. A drake and a female mallard swam directly in front of him, looking like they were bonded for life. The drake was in full color, looking handsome and proud to have found a mate. Like all drakes, this male would stick by the female's side, seeming to be inseparable, at least until mating season was over. Then he would leave this poor mallard to take on the full responsibility for their offspring. Garrett felt irritated at the thought. A drake was as reliable as his own father had been. His mother had trusted him to stay by her side. Garrett would never understand how his father would leave his family as if they never meant anything to him.

Garrett forced himself to stop thinking of his father before his resentment could take lead over his thoughts, pushing aside any feelings of abandonment.

There was a slight breeze, rustling the trees enough for them to boast of their colorful foliage, as if waving at the world to take notice. Several leaves floated to the ground, giving beautiful color to browning grass. Garrett loved the splendor of fall, feeling a little envious of the fortunate people living by such an enchanting lake. One day soon, he hoped to have a peaceful life again. Perhaps here. Getting out of Rex's web of devastation was necessary to make that happen.

After a good hour of contemplating the situation, Garrett heard the trotting of a horse's hooves. He saw a woman riding towards him. Realizing the rider was Maggie, a smile come over his face.

"What brings you out here?"

Maggie pointed to the yellow house. "I live there. My horse, Blaze, and I ride as often as possible. Cows and trees are easier to avoid on a horse."

"Sticking with horses might be best for all of our safety." Garrett grinned.

Maggie nodded. "I hate to admit that but must concur. Happy to see you outside of the boardinghouse. Does this mean your injuries are healing well?"

Garrett stood up and brushed dust off his pants. "Yes, no more headaches. I was growing tired of the walls in my room. I needed to get outside. Fresh air is better than medicine. The little time I've been out here has made me feel like a new man. Would you care to share this beautiful day with me?"

"Spending time with you alone out here wouldn't be appropriate."

Garrett pointed up to Rich. "We're hardly alone."

"Thanks for the invitation, but I'm on my way to an important appointment. Enjoy your day."

Before Garrett could say anything else, Blaze trotted away with Maggie.

Garrett took in his surroundings one more time, then returned to the motorbike, swiftly driving away. As promised, Rich only followed him to the outskirts of Garfield.

Chapter 24

Rex Tillman arrived in Hannibal, pulling up to John Madison's mansion. John owned several banks throughout the Midwest. Rex had charmed his way into Madison's life when he deposited most of James Hanley's money into John's bank in Chicago. Rex made it a point to take John to supper anytime he was Chicago, forming a close friendship. John invited Rex to stay at his home if he ever came to Hannibal. Unaware, John was providing the perfect place for Rex to hide.

John wasn't in Hannibal, but assured Rex the staff was expecting him. Rex was proud of his skills of building trust. The unsuspecting souls always made it so easy to betray them.

Rex admired the tall pillars and the huge porch. The white house with black shutters was gigantic and even more elegant than he imagined. He walked up the stairs and banged on the door with the brass knocker.

A tall man in a tuxedo answered. "Hello, you must be Mr. Tillman. We have been expecting you. I'm Remington, Mr. Madison's butler."

Rex didn't have much respect for the help. They were way beneath him, after all. He charmed them anyway, which usually motivated them to want to do more for him.

"Hi there, Remington. Yes, I'm Rex Tillman. Thank you for having me. I won't wear out my welcome, but I might be here several days."

"Mr. Madison wants you to stay as long as you'd like. He's out of town for at least two weeks, but left instructions to take care of your every need."

"If it isn't too much trouble, I could use a warm bath and a thick steak. I've had a long trip."

"Yes, sir. I will have the tub in the room next to your bedchamber filled right away. A meal can be ready when you choose to dine."

"Thank you for your kindness, my dear man. I will do my best to be an easy guest. Oh, I'd like to eat alone in my room, if possible."

"Whatever you need, Mr. Tillman. I will show you to your bedchamber now."

After Remington left, Rex gazed around his room, admiring John's taste in mahogany furniture. He pressed on the fully stuffed feather mattress. Not too hard, nor too soft. Should be comfortable for a few nights. Rex strolled to a window that provided a breathtaking view of the Mississippi river, which he owned several passages along. Hannibal wasn't one of them. He made a mental note to check into obtaining a passage once he completed his business in Garfield.

A knock on the door startled Rex. He reached for the pistol in his holster. "Who's there?"

"Your bath is ready, sir," Remington said from the other side.

Rex put the gun back in the holster and opened the door. "Yes. Thank you, Remington. I need to relax before supper."

"I can have your food sent up in an hour, sir."

"Make it forty-five minutes," Rex said.

"Yes, sir. Is there anything else I can get for you?"

"Not now. Thank you."

Rex took a long bath, requiring Remington to add hot water three times, before putting on a clean suit. He stood in front of the mirror to admire himself. Rex still liked what he saw even though he wasn't a tall man, nor had much hair, and perhaps carried a few extra pounds.

"You are a very clever and fine-looking man, Rex Tillman," he said aloud as he sank into the leather davenport, dozing off to sleep.

Rex jumped when he heard a bell ring. A small door opened in the wall. He quickly grabbed his pistol and aimed until realizing he'd been about to shoot his supper. Rex was pleasantly surprised to have his food delivered by such a delightful contraption, making a mental note to add one in his own future mansion.

After his belly was more than full, Rex laid out his strategies on the table and viewed them with as much admiration as he would have for a priceless painting.

"I'm a brilliant man," Rex said while laughing hysterically.

If things went according to plan, and there was no reason to believe otherwise, Rex would be the owner of Mando Merchandising by next week.

He pulled out a cigar from the container John had left on the table, a hand-rolled H Upmann brand, one of Cuba's best. "Mmmmm ... very nice."

After a few puffs, Rex emptied the box of the remaining smokes. He put them in his bag for his future enjoyment. "I'm certain you would want me to have these, John. Oh, and these too." He stashed two vases and a gold elephant statue in his bag.

Rex pulled out his pocket watch. Half past one o'clock. The men he had hired would be here soon. He sat back down and finished smoking his cigar.

Chapter 25

Garrett parked the motorbike near the train station in Hannibal, then walked inside. No one occupied the telegrapher's desk.

He went back outside. After looking around, he noticed the station agent who had assisted him when he arrived three weeks before.

"Hello, sir. I hope you can help me." Garrett said.

"I remember you. Mr. Hanley from Chicago, wasn't it? Where are you heading? Back home?"

"No, not going anywhere by train today. Impressive to have you remember my name. I need to send a telegram, but I don't see an available agent."

"He's only here until noon. Hannibal Hotel is about a mile west of here. They can telegraph your message and send it on to Western Union."

"You've been quite helpful. Thank you, sir. What's your name?"

"Geoffrey Mayfield. You can call me Jeff."

"You can call me Garrett. Thanks again."

Garrett got back on the motorbike and drove to the Hannibal Hotel, where a young desk clerk greeted him.

"Good day, sir. I'd like to send a very urgent telegram," Garrett said.

The clerk shook his head. "The telegrapher is out today. If you can't wait until tomorrow, check with Woodson Hotel next to the river. Just go east about three miles."

Garrett thanked him before leaving. He was getting frustrated, but drove onward toward Woodson Hotel.

Along the way, Garrett noticed the most incredible home he had ever seen. He was sure the house situated on a cliff had a view of the entire city, as well as the Mississippi. Garrett always enjoyed beautiful craftsmanship. Hanley Construction had never built a house this enormous. Garrett stopped within a few hundred feet of the property. He was sure the home had to be at least twenty-five thousand square feet.

Who might live there? Someone extremely wealthy, no doubt. I wonder if I might know him?

Garrett got off the motorbike and walked in the direction of the house. He saw a gentleman come out the front door, excited about the possibility of meeting him. Maybe Garrett could talk him into sharing some specifics of this spectacular home, or if lucky, perhaps provide a quick tour.

He stopped in his tracks, instinctively falling to the ground. His body reacted quicker than his mind because he couldn't comprehend what he had seen. Garrett lifted his head to peek at the gentleman who was standing on the porch.

Garrett's mind was racing, as well as his heart. *I know that limp. Rex Tillman! Was he able to buy a house of this magnitude? My father's company wouldn't have been enough to pay for this. Perhaps Rex's shipping business was more profitable than I realized.*

Sour bile rose in Garrett's throat as he watched Rex limp down the steps and into the backseat of a motorcar. Garrett ran back to the bike, making sure to stay hidden while waiting for the car to depart, then slowly followed. Keeping a sizable distance from the vehicle, Garrett stayed close to trees lining the road.

He didn't like the direction Rex was heading, worried he was going to Garfield. Now Garrett wished Rich Dodson had still been following him. Mr. Dodson was sure to be watching for anyone coming into Garfield. At least, Garrett hoped so.

Fury almost choked him. Rex was an evil man who never seemed satisfied with the riches he acquired, not caring who got hurt in his path of destruction.

The car stopped on a hill overlooking Garfield. Garrett got off the motorbike, tramping through tall weeds to get as close as he could to Rex's vehicle. Three other men were with him, all at least twice the size of Rex, which wasn't really saying much since he was exceptionally short. Rex wore what appeared to be an expensive tailored suit, probably purchased with Hanley Construction's profits. The other men were dressed in ill-fitting suits with too-short pants and jackets unable to be buttoned. Garrett doubted any of the three had ever been in suits before today. Rex's exuberance made his words audible to Garrett.

"There she is, boys," Rex said as he pointed straight ahead. "Mando Merchandising. And she will soon be mine."

Rex was practically drooling as he surveyed the landscape surrounding the building.

"William Garfield has been busy. This town has grown since I left. I'm looking forward to owning all his good fortune," Rex said with an eerie laugh.

"Are we going after the girl now, Boss?" The biggest one asked. "I'm ready to get the job done."

"No, you fool. We aren't going to do anything in the daylight. We'll go to her house in three nights, as planned, and kidnap her when everyone is asleep. We'll need the time to get everything ready. Just have some patience. I've been waiting over ten years. Surely you can wait a few days."

"Whatever you say, Boss," the biggest man said.

"I say let's go back to Hannibal and get prepared for our fabulous adventure," Rex said as he limped towards the car.

Garrett couldn't believe what he heard. *Apparently, Rex doesn't need me to marry anyone, after all. He must have decided to take matters into his own hands after learning William Garfield was dead. I hate myself for providing that information.*

Garrett needed to find Levi Jackson as soon as possible to let him know of the new situation. Everyone needed to be ready for Rex and his hired thugs. Garrett would not allow Rex to get anywhere close to Maggie Garfield. And he knew Mr. Jackson would feel the same way.

Garrett waited until the men were out of sight, then he ran to the motorbike and rode as fast as he could into Garfield. Just as he hoped, Rich pulled up behind him as soon as he got into town. Garrett stopped the bike and let Rich drive up next to him.

"You must take me to see Levi Jackson. I have an extremely urgent matter that involves Miss Garfield's safety. Will you lead me there?"

Rich got out of the motorcar and walked up to Garrett. He pulled out his gun and aimed it at Garrett.

"Wait. What are you doing? I'm not planning to cause any trouble."

Rich's hand didn't move. "I need to make sure you're not armed before I take you to Mr. Jackson."

Garrett got off the bike and held up his arms. "You can look me over, but hurry. I assure you I have no weapons. We need to go now."

Rich frisked Garrett, unable to locate any firearms. He put his gun away and got back into the motorcar.

"Follow me. You better not be thinking of causing any trouble or you'll be sorry."

Garrett shook his head in disgust. "I'm trying to prevent trouble, not cause any."

Garrett stayed close as they drove down the road. All the dust flying off Rich's tires made keeping his eyes open a difficult task. Garrett finally found the correct distance to be able to see and breathe.

Chapter 26

A knock on the door pulled Levi Jackson away from his thoughts.

"Rich Dodson and Garrett Hanley are here to see you. Should I let them in?" Carson said.

"Hanley too? Not sure what would merit his visit. Yes, I'll see them."

Carson retrieved the unexpected guests.

"Hello, Rich. Why are you here, Mr. Hanley?" Levi said.

"I have an urgent matter to discuss. If you'll invite me in, I can explain."

Garrett heard a click as he realized Rich's cocked gun was pointed at his back. "In light of this unannounced visit, you might feel the need for pistols. However, rest assured I'm not here to create trouble."

Levi frowned. "What kind of urgent matter?"

"Miss Garfield's safety."

"Miss Garfield's safety? Is she in danger?"

"She's safe at the moment but might not be three nights from now."

"Explain."

"I have information which will help us keep Miss Garfield from harm. Can we talk without a gun poked into my back?"

Levi looked at Rich. "Go ahead and leave, Rich. You've had a long day. I can handle Mr. Hanley."

Rich kept his gun on Garrett. "I'll stay. Mr. Hanley hasn't proven himself trustworthy yet."

"All right, Rich, hold on to your gun, but keep it off Mr. Hanley for now. Follow me. We'll sit in the parlor."

Levi led them into the room.

"Talk to me, Mr. Hanley. What's going on with Miss Garfield?"

"No. This is extremely confidential. I insist we speak in private. Mr. Dodson must leave."

"I'll decide who stays or leaves my home. The team is kept abreast of all matters of security. Rich is welcome. Speak, Mr. Hanley."

"Call me Garrett. I believe we might spend quite a bit of time together over the next few days."

"I doubt there's a need for us to keep company, but you can use my given name as well. Now back to Miss Garfield."

"Let me start by saying I came to this town under false pretenses. There is a repulsive man who sent me here to help him steal Mando Merchandising."

Levi stood up, reaching for his gun, as did Rich.

"Hold on. I wouldn't be here talking to you if I intended to steal anything. I need to rid my life of this man, but not at the expense of others."

Levi lowered his gun and motioned for Rich to do the same.

"What is this man's name?" Levi asked.

"Rex Tillman, the most ruthless man you will ever meet," Garrett said as he tightened his fists. "He came close to Garfield today."

Levi tightened his own fists. "How close?"

"Just before coming here, I followed him to the hill overlooking town. Rex and three burly men discussed plans to kidnap Miss Garfield three nights from now."

"Kidnap Miss Garfield? How do you know this?"

"I got close enough to hear Rex's conversation but managed to remain unseen. I clearly heard their plans, while staying hidden until the men drove away. Then I came here."

"How did you happen to come across Rex Tillman before following him? Have you been in his company since arriving as a guest in Garfield?"

"No, I have not seen Rex until today. I spotted him while in Hannibal quite by accident. I didn't expect to see Rex so close to Garfield, which alarmed me. I decided to follow him to make sure he wasn't on his way here. That's when I overheard Rex's plan."

"Do you know where Tillman is now?"

"On the way back to Hannibal. At least, that's the direction they were heading."

"Tillman is a horrible, dangerous man." Levi turned to Rich. "Find Ernie and Chester. We need twenty-four-hour surveillance for Miss Garfield. No strangers are to be allowed near Mando Merchandising or Miss Garfield's home. Coordinate that now. Immediately. I can take care of Garrett."

Rich left quickly.

"Obviously, you know of Rex Tillman," Garrett said.

"Yes, I'm aware of him. Explain more to me about your association with Tillman." Levi's heart was beating so fast he thought it might come right out of his chest.

"I'm not here by choice, nor do I desire to have any association with Rex. My father had been transitioning his company, Hanley Construction, to me so he could travel with my mother. But instead, he sold the company to Rex, who claims my father emptied his bank account, taking much more than the agreed upon price. Money must have meant more to my father than I realized because he took off after the sale, leaving my mother with nothing. Even her home was deeded to Rex. We thought my father was an honorable man until the day he chose to disappear."

"Let's move on from your father for a moment. What is *your* association with Tillman?" Levi said.

"Rex is a vindictive man, especially if you take something from him. According to Rex, my father double-crossed him, which caused my mother and I to be Rex's targets of retribution. To make matters worse, Rex has an eye for my mother. I would do anything to protect her. Rex promised to leave her alone if I agreed to work for him. Big mistake to work for the devil."

Levi leaned forward and glared at Garrett. "Regardless of your ill-fated situation with Tillman, you're obviously a dishonest man. You responded to an advertisement for a husband, willing to bring harm to innocent ladies. Let me share a little bit about me with you. A coyote killed *my* dog, Hutch. A twister destroyed *my* home, and *I* lived in a barn for a while."

Garrett's mouth gaped. When able to speak, he said, "That was *you*?"

"Yes, and apparently those same tragic events happened to you as well, at least according to your correspondence with Miss Garfield."

Garrett shook his head vehemently. "No, as you have already ascertained, none of those horrible situations happened to me. Rex wrote those letters, claiming to be me. I didn't know about the advertisement until after Miss Garfield offered an invitation. Mr. Jackson, did these things truly happen to you?"

"I'm that unfortunate man."

"How do you know Rex? I had the impression you were a law-abiding gentleman who would never associate with the likes of him."

"We've had some regrettable business deals. Tillman is the master of manipulation. He'll appear to be your best friend while secretly cutting your throat."

A terrible thought crossed Garrett's mind. "My father must have been made from the same cloth. He deceived my mother and me into believing he was a decent man." Garrett paused and looked down. "I was becoming just like them."

Levi shook his head. "You get to decide what kind of man you want to be. Follow in their footsteps or not—your choice."

Garrett looked up at Levi with a renewed sense of strength. "You're right, Levi. I want to be a better man than both of them. My father's bad decisions will not rule my life."

Levi paced the room in deep contemplation. After several minutes, he looked at Garrett. "I wouldn't be too quick to judge your father based on information you received from Tillman. If anything was stolen from anyone, Tillman likely committed the crime, not the other way around."

Garrett put his head in his hands and rubbed his temples. "I'm an even worse human being than I thought. How could I have not considered my father to be a victim?"

"Where is your father now?" Levi asked.

"I don't know. Rex led me to believe he was living a grand life as a wealthy bachelor. Perhaps instead of being angry with my father, I should fear for his safety. I just don't know."

"That explains the offer Miss Garfield made to you the day we were in her office about helping to find your father. You might be right to worry about him."

Levi stared at Garrett for a long moment in silence. "Do you know anything about a shipping company Rex owns?"

"Jackson Shipping. The way Rex ran that company was what impressed my father to partner with him. Why do you ask?"

"That was my shipping company until Rex stole it."

Garrett was flabbergasted. "Stolen? I know your name is Jackson but didn't make the connection."

"I'm missing part of a finger to prove how dastardly Rex can be, and a toe as well." Levi showed his hand to Garrett. "He had a man torture me into turning over ownership. I should have been braver. That's why I'm in the security business—I don't want Rex to hurt anyone else."

"Nor do I. Levi, we must stop this man. Rex has ruined too many lives. We can't let him go on. You and I have both been deceived by him in life-changing ways. I will do anything in my power to protect Miss Garfield and rid our lives of Rex."

Levi was silent for several minutes. "My gut instinct tells me you're a changed man who can be trusted. If we join forces, we might be able to stop Tillman's destruction."

Garrett stood up and held out his hand. "I would be honored to join forces with you."

Levi could see the sincerity in Garrett's face. Teaming up with him might be what could finally take out Rex. He shook Garrett's hand, hoping his instincts were not deceiving him.

"Who knows, we may be able to get our companies back and locate your father as well. For now, we must focus on Miss Garfield's safety."

Levi unlocked a cabinet and took out a pistol, along with bullets, which he handed to Garrett.

"You may need these. Go back to Hannibal and check on Tillman. Notify me immediately if he heads towards Garfield."

Garrett took the weapon and nodded. "You can count on me. Nothing will give me more pleasure than to take down Rex Tillman."

"I must meet with Miss Garfield and Mr. Crawford right away. They need to be aware of Tillman's presence." Levi grabbed Garrett's arm. "Don't prove me wrong about your character. Miss Garfield's life might depend on it ... as well as yours."

Garrett nodded and clenched his fists. "I won't let you down."

Chapter 27

Garrett had been back and forth between Garfield and Hannibal, keeping a close watch on Rex for the past three days. Now late afternoon, he was finally back in Garfield to prepare for battle.

Levi, Chester, Ernie, Rich, and Garrett were to stay on guard at Maggie's house all night. Garrett had not seen Maggie in almost a week. His heart was racing as he arrived at her house.

The home was even more beautiful up close. The bright yellow color suited Maggie well, bold and strong, yet as warm as the sun. Garrett sauntered up the stairs of the full wraparound porch and looked out at the stunning view of the lake. He sat down in one of the many rocking chairs and took in the scenery.

Garrett heard the rambling of an approaching motorcar. He pulled out his pistol and hid around the corner of the house. Maggie's sweet voice sang to Garrett's ears as she and Max came up the walkway. He put his pistol away and strolled to the stairs to greet them. Maggie was wearing black pants with a matching coat. Garrett saw some red spots on the material, finally realizing they were little ladybugs embroidered throughout. Maggie's blouse was red and black to match the spots of ladybugs. She seemed to have a fondness for wearing critters on her clothing.

"Hello, Maggie and Max. I was just taking in the magnificent view of the lake. You're extremely lucky to live in a place this splendid."

Maggie smiled, and all thoughts of ladybugs left Garrett's mind. She was even more beautiful today than the last time he had seen her.

"I don't know about luck, but I'm very blessed," Maggie said. "Nice to see you again, Garrett. I wish this meeting was under more ideal circumstances. I'm still finding it hard to believe my father associated with a man like Rex Tillman. Even harder to imagine anyone would try to steal Mando Merchandising."

Garrett wanted to tell her he had missed her, but she appeared to be losing her balance. He grabbed her arms.

"Are you all right, Maggie? You don't seem quite steady."

"Perhaps I just need to sit for a moment."

Max put his arm around her waist as he and Garrett led her to a rocking chair.

Max frowned. "I must insist you see Dr. Gibson, Maggie. Your wooziness is happening too often, and the weather is far from hot."

Maggie shook her head. "I'm fine. Perfectly steady now. I probably need a bite to eat. As usual, today got busy, and I missed my noontime meal. Not to mention the uneasiness of knowing I'm supposed to be kidnapped tonight."

Max and Garrett sat down in the chairs on either side of Maggie.

Garrett said, "Another prime example of what I've been trying to make you realize, Maggie. This lurking danger is too much for a lady to handle. I'm certain you're weak from worrying about Rex Tillman. There will be five strong men staying here tonight. I hope knowing this will help to keep you stable by easing any worry."

Maggie stood up, looking fully recovered and reenergized.

"We're going to have a contentious night if these narrow-minded conversations continue, Mr. Hanley. You exasperate me. I am *not* debilitated in any way. I *am* concerned about tonight. Any woman, *or man*, would be stressed, given the situation. My health is fine. Did you not hear me say I haven't eaten in several hours?"

Garrett stood up in front of Maggie. "I was merely trying to ease your worry by letting you know you will be well protected tonight. Women are just too sensitive. Makes it quite hard to try to be gallant in our efforts."

Maggie crossed her arms and was about to blister Garrett's ears, when Max got up and stood between them.

"You're wasting valuable time arguing," Max reprimanded them. "You should channel your worked-up energy in a more positive way—like preparing for tonight. I'm leaving now. Go inside to speak with Mr. Jackson."

"Yes, come into the house," Levi said as he strolled up to them. "We have Miss Garfield covered, Mr. Crawford."

"Even though I have every confidence in you, Mr. Jackson, I would much rather Miss Garfield was not here tonight. Are you certain I can't persuade you to allow her to stay at my house?"

"She will be much safer here. We won't let her out of sight. Go home. We'll contact you when Rex is no longer a threat."

Max stood firm as he stared at Levi.

"Trust me, Mr. Crawford. I will not, under any circumstances, allow Miss Garfield to be harmed by that disgusting man, Tillman. I would take a bullet for her. You have my word."

Max looked at Maggie and Levi. "William wouldn't have hired you if he didn't have every faith in you. I must leave my Maggie in your capable hands."

"You'll be kept informed of all happenings. Stay with Mrs. Crawford and try to relax."

Max approached Maggie and gave her the tightest hug she had ever received from him.

"Uncle Max, you are squeezing the air out of me. Don't worry. I'm well protected, completely safe."

Max pulled away as Maggie saw a tear running down his cheek. She felt an ache in her heart, grasping the blessing of just how much he cared. She too felt a tear roll out of her eye.

"If you want me to stay, I will."

"Uncle Max, Aunt Catherine must be waiting for you to escort her home from The Happy Hatter. She'll continue to work into the night if you don't show up. Moreover, look at all the gentlemen here to defend me. Besides, I've always done well taking care of myself."

"I'll go ... for now ... but will be right back here in the morning."

Reluctantly, Max left to go home to Catherine. The rest of the group went into Maggie's house.

Chapter 28

After supper, the Pinkerton men went to their posts surrounding Maggie's home, allowing full views of all windows and doors. Maggie would sleep in the parlor tonight, with Garrett and Emma remaining in the room with her. They agreed staying in her bedchamber would be inappropriate. Maggie highly doubted she'd be doing any sleeping, anyway, knowing a kidnapper could be nearby.

Before settling into the parlor, Garrett stood guard in the hallway near Maggie's bedchamber, while Emma helped her bathe and change into fresh clothing. When she was ready, Garrett walked the ladies down to the parlor.

Pillows and blankets had been placed on two davenports for the ladies. Garrett would keep watch over them, along with a loaded gun, in case Rex got past the men outside.

Maggie sat down in an armchair, with Garrett in the chair directly across from her.

"I want to pen a few letters," Emma said, as she settled down to a desk nearby.

"You might have much to write about if Rex Tillman shows up," Maggie said.

"Oh my. That's a frightening thought. Let's not make light of such a serious situation."

Maggie nodded, then looked at Garrett.

"I appreciate your willingness to give up valuable personal time to be here. I sincerely hope our time together will only include unprejudiced conversation, otherwise, silence might be best. There's enough stress and tension around here already without adding to the pot."

Garrett laughed.

"Laughing at me, Mr. Hanley, might be construed as impolite. I was not making a riposte." Maggie's words barely escaped her tightened lips. "You're the most exasperating man I have ever met."

"I was not laughing at you. I just reacted to your correct assessment of how our conversations can take a turn in the opposite direction of where intended. No doubt, there are times of misunderstanding. I have no desire to upset you, nor would I want to make light of your opinions. In fact, I find you quite fascinating and capable."

Maggie watched as he pushed his hands through his hair. Several strands fell out of place and landed over his forehead. Warmth invaded her insides as she reflected on his comments.

"Perhaps I *can* be quick to judge. I'll try to be less hasty in my reactions."

"Let's start the evening with a clean slate, concentrating on staying safe. We should try to keep our minds focused on what's going on around us, not arguing with each other."

"Agreed, Garrett. Besides, as the night grows darker, my apprehension of an impending kidnapping is growing. I need you on my side. I must admit to being glad you're here."

"We're making some progress since you're referring to me as Garrett again. I *am* on your side. Mr. Jackson's men and I will keep you safe."

"Garrett, why *are* you here tonight? You're not a part of any security team. Why put your life in danger?"

"Rex Tillman's devastation must end. I want to stop him as much or more than Levi Jackson does. I might as well make something known. Rex is the man who bought Father's construction company, claiming my father took more money than they agreed on. However, I'm becoming convinced Rex somehow stole the company from Father and forced Father to leave. This explanation seems to make sense. Father was consistently a generous and kind man until he disappeared."

"Rex Tillman owns your father's company? In light of what we're learning about him, you must be correct in your assessment. A man doesn't change overnight, especially a father."

"Exactly. I want to protect you and perhaps learn what happened to my father in the process."

"Do you think he's hiding from Mr. Tillman somewhere?"

Garrett nodded. "Hiding is a real possibility. Your idea is way better than something I hadn't contemplated until recently. Is Father's even alive? If Rex would kidnap someone, who's to say he wouldn't kill a man."

Maggie gasped. "No, no. Don't think that way. Your father is out there somewhere, and we *will* find him. You're risking your life for me tonight, and for that, I must help you locate him."

"No, Maggie. I cannot allow you to get involved or be in harm's way again. I'll find him if he's still alive."

"Mr. Jackson would help you."

"Let's concentrate on you for now."

"For tonight, but, then, we will find your father."

"One day," Garrett said. "One day, indeed."

Chapter 29

The day was finally here for the scheduled kidnapping of Maggie Garfield. Rex had never been this excited about anything. Wearing a black tuxedo for the occasion, he wanted to look his best for the greatest night of his life. Once Maggie was caught, Mando Merchandising would be his.

Foolish William. How dare he think he could treat me the way he did. William Garfield should have known he would never get away with double-crossing me.

Rex's thoughts were interrupted when he heard the now familiar bell indicating the kitchen had sent up something delectable to eat. He opened the door in the wall to retrieve his supper. A juicy steak, cooked to perfection, along with potatoes and asparagus. Dessert today was an apple dumpling. He quickly devoured the entire meal.

A full belly made Rex tired. He took off his jacket and stretched out on the davenport. He didn't intend to but fell asleep. A knock on the door awoke him. Sitting up, he looked down at his stopwatch, 10:57. Rex had slept for almost two hours. The nap was a good thing since he'd likely have a long night ahead of him. Rex opened the door.

"I'm sorry to interrupt, Mr. Tillman, but there are some rather large gentlemen waiting out front in a motorcar for you," Remington said.

"Excellent. Let them know I will be down momentarily."

Rex put on his jacket and grabbed his gun. Even with a bum leg, he made quick time of getting down the stairs and into the motorcar.

"Let's go, boys. A most excellent excursion awaits us. We're about to have some fun," Rex said.

Chapter 30

"Maggie, you did not indicate to me you were well-versed in the ways of playing poker when challenged to a two-handed match," Garrett said. "I will admit not wanting to introduce you to a gentleman's game, but now see you are already fully acquainted. Was Mr. Garfield aware of your familiarity to poker?"

Maggie laughed. "Know? He taught me to play. Furthermore, Father did not believe poker was only a gentleman's game, but rather an enjoyable way to pass time. We always played for candy, just like tonight."

"I do wonder how you've been able to maintain such a trim figure, since I'm quite certain you must have won a healthy number of sweets over the years."

Maggie pursed her lips. "A gentleman should know it is not appropriate to comment on a lady's physique, Mr. Hanley. I would take offense, and do somewhat, but am trying to honor our truce. As for the sizeable amount of candy that might have been won, I've always shared any earnings with others. Hence, not overindulging in my winnings."

Garrett put his hand over his heart. "My apologies. Referring to me as 'Mr. Hanley' again is not good. I'll try to avoid any other comments which might cause me to be in your bad graces."

"I'm not sure you're able, but I appreciate the effort."

"I'll do my best."

Garrett had been checking his pocket watch quite often throughout the night. There was still no sign of Rex. He walked over to the window and opened the drapes. The sun was just starting to come up over the lake, providing a breathtaking view.

Maggie joined him at the window. "Oh my. What time is it? Uncle Max will be here soon."

Garrett nodded. "Close to seven o'clock. We've been up all night."

"Did we miss a kidnapping?" Maggie asked.

Garrett peered around the grounds to see if anything was amiss, seeing Levi talking to Chester, Ernie, and Rich. He opened the window to hear what they were saying. The men immediate looked up at Garrett.

"We're coming in," Levi shouted.

Garrett gave him a thumb's up.

"The men must have been able to intercede since there's no sign of Rex Tillman," Garrett said. "I'm interested to hear what happened."

Levi and the other men walked into the parlor and sat down, shoulders drooping and bags under their eyes.

"Did anyone come here during the night? Was there a confrontation?" Maggie asked.

Levi shook his head. "No one showed up. Garrett, are you sure about which night?"

"Absolutely certain. They spoke of their plan each day I observed them. No way would Rex give up on his scheme. Something, or someone, must have gotten in his way."

"I never saw anyone. Rich thought he heard something at around midnight. We investigated but didn't find anything unusual. Probably just a jack rabbit or some other critter," Levi said.

Garrett walked around the room, then stopped in front of Levi. "Rex must have altered his plans. Maybe he saw you or the others guarding the house. I'm confident he's still in pursuit. This is not over."

"You're likely correct, Garrett," Levi said, "We need to continue staying close to Miss Garfield."

Levi looked at Maggie. "You should remain here today. Too risky to go to Mando."

"Oh, no. Uncle Max will be here soon, and I have work to get done. I can't hide in fear."

"With no sleep, how will you make it through the day, especially with tending to be weak when tired," Garrett said.

Maggie glared at him. Would this man never learn? "Weak? I need to freshen up. Somehow, I'll find a way to toughen up and make it through the day, Mr. Hanley."

"I'm merely thinking of times when you've been a bit dizzy—almost falling when you were exhausted or overwhelmed."

Maggie rolled her eyes. "As usual, you're exasperating."

"What did I say?"

Maggie ignored him as she poured water into the washbasin, immersing a cloth to wipe her face.

Emma and the staff members entered with trays full of breakfast.

"We assumed you might all be hungry," Emma said, as the staff set the plates on the table. "Let me know if you need anything else. Hope you enjoy what we've brought."

The grateful men thanked them. The help left as the men sat down to eat.

Garrett stood up and pulled out the chair next to him when Maggie joined them at the table.

"Let's pray before your breakfast is gone," Maggie said. "There's a lot to be thankful for. After all, we did make it through a kidnapping."

The men sat their forks down, all with sheepish expressions.

"We apologize, Miss Garfield. Go ahead and pray," Levi said.

They all bowed their heads as Maggie prayed. "Precious Heavenly Father, thank you for safety and protection. Help us never to take for granted the goodness you bestow upon us. Give us wisdom on how to deal with Mr. Tillman. Use this food to replenish us so we might do your will. Amen."

"Amen," the others said.

Maggie and the men lingered over the meal until half past seven, then gathered on the porch. Maggie expected to see Max waiting for her, but he was not there. Overcome with panic, Maggie grabbed Levi's arms, trying to pull him off the porch and towards his motorcar.

Through tears, she yelled, "Uncle Max is not here. He is *never ever* late, always early. I lost track of time. We need to check on him and Aunt Catherine. Mr. Tillman must have them."

"Now, Miss Garfield, calm down. Mr. Tillman would have no reason to go after the Crawfords. They don't own Mando Merchandising. Mr. Crawford might have had a restless night causing him to run behind," Levi said.

"No. Something terrible has happened. Uncle Max and Aunt Catherine are in trouble. I remember Mr. Tillman joining us when Uncle Max and Aunt Crawford came for holidays. He would be aware of how close I am to them. What if he's using them to get to me? We must go now." Maggie ran to the motorcar.

The men looked at each other and then followed her.

"Miss Garfield, stay here with Garrett. Your safety is priority," Levi said.

Maggie shook her head and got into Levi's motorcar. "I either go with you or on my own. Your decision. Uncle

Max and Aunt Catherine are my family. They must be in danger. We need to hurry."

Levi reluctantly stepped into his vehicle, along with Garrett. He knew Maggie was not going to back down or listen to reason.

Chester, Rich, and Ernie piled into another car.

A short time later at the Crawford's home, Levi grasped Maggie's shoulders. "You will stay here with Garrett out of harm's way. As soon as we determine the house is safe, I'll allow you in. Miss Garfield, don't make my job harder."

Maggie grudgingly stayed put. She and Garrett got back into the motorcar, holding on to pistols. After what seemed like an eternity, the men came out, looking concerned.

Levi strolled over to Maggie. "The Crawfords are not here. Rex has them. He left a note, along with an envelope with several documents."

"I knew it!" Maggie said through tears. "We need to get to them, fast. Give Mr. Tillman anything he wants. Let's go."

"We will find the Crawfords. I can assure you. But we won't give Rex what he wants. Here, read the note," Levi said.

> My Dearest Miss Garfield. I'm Rex Tillman. You might or might not remember me, but I have come for what your father owes me. Your beloved Mr. and Mrs. Crawford would not be involved if access to your home had not been blocked.
>
> If you want to see Mr. and Mrs. Crawford again, you will sign the papers in the envelope to grant me the company I helped your daddy build from nothing. Leave the signed papers here at their house. Once I have retrieved them, I will gladly hand over these two people you seem to care about. Don't cross me, or they will suffer. You have until dusk to complete the task.

Maggie could not stop the tears from flowing down her cheeks as she trembled. Garrett learned over and held her tight.

"Wait! I know where Rex took Max and Catherine," Garrett said.

"How do you know, Garrett? Where?" Levi asked.

"I feel certain they must be in the mansion in Hannibal. Rex doesn't know I saw him there."

Maggie looked up. "Mr. Jackson, we must go now."

Levi shook his head. "No way you …"

Maggie interrupted, "My Uncle Max and Aunt Catherine need help. You know I won't stay behind. Come on. We're wasting precious time."

"She'll be safer with us than staying here alone," Garrett said.

"Let's go," said Levi.

They drove away as Garrett kept his arm around Maggie. She knew it wasn't proper, but was scared and shivering. Maggie longed for her father's hug as she laid her head against Garrett.

Chapter 31

"There's the place," Garrett said, pointing to the huge house.

"What? He's staying at John Madison's mansion?" Levi asked.

"John Madison? My father has had business dealings with him for a few years. I know Mr. Madison is well respected," Garrett said. "I was unaware of the owner, but Rex seems to find plenty of victims to fall for his schemes."

"Mr. Madison is my banker and a very honorable man. At least I thought he was. Why would he be in partnership with Rex Tillman?" Maggie said.

"Likely he is a trustworthy man," Garrett said. "My guess is Mr. Madison is clueless. Tillman is a charmer when it comes to gaining the trust of others. Mr. Madison is likely out of town. I imagine he travels between his banks regularly. Rex probably conned Mr. Madison into allowing him to stay there."

"Mr. Madison is a possible victim," Levi said. "He might have been kidnapped, as well. We might have more to deal with than we realize. I need to find out if Mr. Madison is missing or truly on a business trip. I highly doubt he's involved in Tillman's evil activities."

Levi and Chester stopped their motorcars where they could be hidden behind some tall brush. "We better not get any closer with the vehicles. Let's go by foot the rest of the way."

Levi grabbed Maggie's arm when she started out of the motorcar. "Stay here. Remember, Tillman wanted to kidnap you first. With any opening, he would snatch you. We'll have a hard enough time freeing the people inside. We don't need to contend with rescuing you as well right now. Remain with Garrett. The rest of us can handle Rex."

Levi stood firm with his hand still on Maggie's arm. "You stay or we'll all stay, leaving the Crawfords in harm's way. Don't delay my efforts to get into the house."

Maggie couldn't allow Uncle Max and Aunt Catherine to be in there any longer without help, so she grudgingly agreed. "You win. I'll wait here."

The Pinkerton men made their way toward the mansion while Garrett and Maggie found a tree to hide behind, with a clear view of the front of the house.

Before long, Maggie and Garrett saw Levi and Rich sneak to the back of the house. Chester and Ernie stayed in front.

"They must have found a way to enter through a back door or window. I'm sure they'll get to Max and Catherine very soon," Garrett said.

Maggie didn't seem any less worried, so Garrett reached out and held her hand. She smiled at him, tightening her grip.

They waited, keeping their eyes focused on the house. And they waited. And they waited. Almost an hour went by.

"They need our help. We both have our pistols. Let's go check on them," Maggie said.

"First, we need a plan."

"There's no time for a plan. I just need to get Uncle Max and Aunt Catherine to safety. Maybe Mr. Madison needs to be rescued now too. Or, even worse, Mr. Jackson and his men."

"This is going against my better judgment, but I know I won't be able to convince you to wait here. Come on."

They managed to make their way to the livery stable next to the mansion.

"Look. Four men are coming out of the house," Garrett whispered. "The short guy limping is Rex Tillman."

"I remember him. Oh, they're leaving," Maggie whispered.

Rex and his men made their way off the porch, got into the motorcar, then drove away.

"At least they didn't have Max and Catherine with them. Hopefully, that means they're still safely inside," Garrett said.

"Oh, Garrett, what if they're not? We've got to get into that house right now."

"Have you seen Chester Davis and Ernie McGuire? Maybe we should find them first."

"No. They might have followed Mr. Tillman. Let's go."

Maggie pulled Garrett by the arm in the direction of the mansion. Reaching the backdoor, Garrett turned the unlocked handle.

"Rex is such an arrogant man, so sure of himself that he didn't even bother to try to keep anyone out," Garrett said.

Maggie and Garrett stepped into the kitchen. No one seemed to be around, including servants. The gigantic house overwhelmed them with silence, as they made their way through the hallway.

They walked up the stairs, searching the rooms on the second floor, disappointed at finding no one. The third level held many more empty rooms, causing Maggie and Garrett to increase the speed of their search.

Finally, the bedroom on the east corner held Max and Catherine, tied to chairs but appearing unharmed. Handkerchiefs in their mouths kept them from speaking. Maggie ran to Catherine and untied her, while Garrett got Max out of his bindings.

Maggie embraced them both. "I'm sorry, Uncle Max. I didn't mean to put you and Aunt Catherine in harm's way. Are you hurt?"

"The cause of our predicament is not your fault. We're fine, just a little unnerved. I'm overjoyed to see you're safe. I've been so worried that Rex Tillman got to you."

Garrett inspected the room to see if anyone else was there. "Have you seen Levi or his agents?"

Max shook his head. "There's been no sign of anyone since Rex left us in this room. Is Levi in the house?"

"Mr. Jackson and the others came in well over an hour ago looking for you," Maggie said. "They must be here somewhere. We need to find them."

Garrett helped Max and Catherine stand up. Max grabbed Catherine's hand.

"I'm stiff from sitting," Catherine said.

"Me, too," Max said.

They walked a few steps until straightened. Then they stood next to Maggie.

"We need to minimize the risks as much as we can," Garrett said, as he handed Max a pistol. "Just a precaution."

Garrett looked directly at Maggie. "Because you're Rex's target, we need to get you out of this house before he comes back. Let's move along quickly as we try to find Levi and the others."

"We'll stick together. But, if you see or hear anything, run for cover," Max said.

Right away, in the adjoining room, they came across a tall man dressed in a black suit. He was tied up in a closet, the door standing ajar. Garrett aimed his gun at the man while Max untied him.

"Who are you?" Garrett asked.

"Mr. James Madison's butler, Remington. I've been in here since late last night. The rest of the staff is in the attic," the man said. "Mr. Tillman has been busy collecting items from Mr. Madison's home, of which he was a trusted guest, and I appear to be included in what he plans to steal."

Remington stood up after Garrett put his gun down.

"Where is Mr. Madison?" Garrett asked.

"Out of town on business," Remington said. "He instructed me to make Mr. Tillman as comfortable as possible. Mr. Madison must have been unaware of the kind of man he had invited into his home."

Garrett nodded. "Just as we suspected, John Madison is not in Rex's company. I think Remington is correct in Mr. Madison's obliviousness of Tillman's true character."

"You should not be so quick to judge the generosity of my dear friend Mr. Madison," Rex said, standing in the doorway. "Especially you, Garrett Hanley."

Rex had somehow managed to grab Catherine, and now had his pistol pointed directly at her. "Drop your guns immediately, or I will shoot her."

Garrett and Max put their guns on the floor.

"Now, gently kick the weapons toward me," Rex said.

Max and Garrett thrust the guns Rex's way.

Garrett was relieved and worried at the same time when he realized Maggie was no longer in the room. Angry with himself for not keeping track of her, Garrett hoped she had found a safe hiding place.

Garrett gazed at Max, who looked terrified as he helplessly watched Catherine.

"As for my new treasures, I'm merely gathering the items Mr. Madison would no doubt want me to have," Rex said. "Remington, staff should never speak unkindly of their employer. You are way out of line."

"Yes, sir," Remington said with a shaky voice.

"I'm uninterested in retaining any of you, except my new butler, Remington," Rex said. "I will trade all of you, including Mrs. Crawford, for one Maggie Garfield. Just tell me where she is so I can send my men to retrieve her. There is a matter of some important papers to sign."

Garrett shook his head. "We cannot do that."

"Cannot or will not?" Rex said. "Mr. Crawford, if you want your dear wife to see daylight again, you will hand Maggie Garfield over to me."

"We cannot and will not," Garrett said. "We were under the assumption you had kidnapped her since we don't know where she is."

"Don't play games with me, Hanley. I don't have her, but I'm confident you know her whereabouts. Maggie will gladly come with me to save her cherished Mrs. Crawford. Tell me where she is. *Now*."

A shot rang out. Rex's gun flew out of his hand.

Maggie appeared from behind a curtain, keeping her pistol aimed at Rex. Max raced to Catherine to pull her into his arms.

Garrett swiftly moved next to Rex. He wasted no time in tying Rex's hands behind him with the ropes which had been used on the Crawfords.

"There's no need to be rough with me, Hanley," Rex said. "And whoever you are, young lady, you could have shot my hand off. That was very careless of you."

"I assure you if I intended to remove a limb, it would be gone," Maggie said. "I only wanted that gun out of your possession. I guess you don't remember me—Maggie Garfield."

"Ahhh! We are way overdue to spend time in each other's presence, Miss Maggie Garfield," Rex said as he looked her up and down. "You have grown into a fine-looking young lady."

Chills ran down Maggie's spine.

Garrett was livid. "You will be wise to refrain from noticing anything about Miss Garfield's beauty."

"You're a wicked terrible man, Mr. Tillman," Maggie said. "Your hand was spared only because Uncle Max and Aunt Catherine appear to be unharmed."

Rex glared at her as he shrugged to get Garrett's arms off his shoulders. "Let go of me, Hanley. You, of all people, should be helping me right now. Does Miss Garfield know you're an imposter working for me?"

Maggie, Max, and Catherine glared at Garrett with frowns.

"Explain yourself, Garrett," Max said. "What's he talking about?"

Garrett was trying to find the words to say when they all heard footsteps coming down the hall. In walked Rex's partners, all aiming their guns.

"Put your pistol down, Miss, or there'll be much blood spread about the room," the biggest man said.

Maggie sat the gun down and one of the men picked it up.

"Untie me," demanded Rex.

The biggest man struggled to untie him.

"Hurry up, you idiot. I don't have all day."

"Sorry, Boss. They tied you real good."

After several minutes, Rex was free. He walked over to Maggie and stood in front of her.

"Now we can get down to business. I have some documents for you to sign." Rex pulled out a folded stack of papers from his jacket pocket. "I took the liberty of bringing several copies of our contract in case you lost track of the one I left at the Crawfords' house."

"Why did you kidnap Uncle Max and Aunt Catherine? They've done nothing to you."

"Your selfish ways got them captured. We saw the men guarding your house last night, keeping us from you, our real target. Knowing your fondness for the Crawfords, I figured you'd come after them. Appears as if I was right. Although, I'm not quite sure how you knew to look in Mr. Madison's mansion."

"You are an evil man, Mr. Tillman. I remember my father and Uncle Max being very kind to you when you were here years ago. I thought you were friends."

"A friend would not have betrayed me when I had given so much of myself to make Mando Merchandising a success. I'm finally here to get what should have been mine ten years ago. Your father selfishly insisted on having it all. He refused to give me anything after all the hard work I had done for him. However, William did well despite my absence, likely due to how well I trained him."

"What makes you feel entitled to *my* company? You were only a subordinate, not a partner."

"Oh, I did much more for the company than a mere subordinate. I was the backbone of all major decisions. Rightfully, when your father died, Mando Merchandising should have been mine. Only a fool would leave such a large company to a woman. I must take the reins before you run the company into the ground."

"Never. My father has left me with the responsibility of overseeing what he created. No one will steal that from me."

"I'll give you a choice. Sign over your company, and I'll let you all go. Or you can watch your little acquaintances die. Your choice ... and you have about two minutes to decide."

Four shots sounded in the room as Rex and his men fell to the floor. Levi and the other Pinkerton agents ran into the room.

"Are you okay?" Levi asked, as the new arrivals tied up the men on the floor.

"We're fine, but you might need to confine Mr. Hanley, as well. I think he's working with Rex Tillman," Max said.

"I'll explain Mr. Hanley's involvement later. For now, you just need to know he's on our side."

Max looked at Levi. "What a relief to know you're safe. We worried you might have been bound or in need of rescue."

"Tillman never even knew we were here. Our search began in the attic, where we found several servants. We saw Tillman leave, then return. We stayed back until we were able to overtake all of them."

Levi pulled Rex up and grabbed him by the shirt. "You probably thought you'd never see me again, did you, Tillman? You're going to pay for all you've done."

"Levi Jackson? The coward? What is your involvement here? And who are you to threaten me? I figured you must have ended up homeless ... or dead."

Levi tightened his grip. "That is none of your business. But know this—you will lose everything you acquired illegally, which is almost all your assets. Your days of power are over."

"Doubtful. I'm not worried about a weakling like you."

"Tillman, you are a broken man in more ways than I can count."

"These men have been shot. How bad are their wounds?" Maggie asked.

"Nothing life-threatening. In fact, Rex wasn't even hit. He apparently just fell in fear." Levi stared at Rex. "Looks like *you're* the coward, Tillman. I can't wait to see you put away."

"You'll never see me defeated. I have friends in many places, including the law. Impossible to succeed against me."

"We already have succeeded. You'll soon be locked up, while your ill-gotten gains will be returned to their rightful owners, including Hanley Construction and Jackson Shipping."

Rex let out an evil laugh. "You are delusional, Jackson. No one is more powerful than me."

"Power has shifted, Tillman. Let's go."

As the men were being led out, Garrett stood in front of Rex. "Where is my father?"

"Staying away from a son he's ashamed of is my best guess." Rex cast an evil smile across his shoulder as Chester dragged him away.

Levi patted Garrett's back. "Your father would be proud of you. Don't ever doubt that."

Garrett nodded.

"Right now, all of you need to get back home to safety," Levi said. "Max, take my motorcar and I'll go with the other men."

"Mr. Jackson, before we go, I want to thank you," Maggie said. "The situation could have turned out horribly if not for your actions. My father would be pleased to know he hired the right man for Garfield."

"I'm delighted we have a positive outcome."

Max grabbed Catherine's hand. Garrett was already walking towards the doorway with Maggie.

Chapter 32

Max, Catherine, Garrett, and Maggie made quick time getting to the awaiting vehicle. Catherine moved over as close as she could to Max, then held on to him in the motorcar. Garrett and Maggie got into the seat behind them.

Garrett waited until the motorcar was heading back to Garfield before he spoke. "I owe you an explanation and apology."

"You certainly do, young man," Max said.

"Before you begin, Garrett. I know you're innocent. There is no way you would work with Rex Tillman. I believe in you," Maggie said.

"I'm glad you think highly of me, Maggie. I hope you'll keep that faith in my character after hearing everything. Know I hold you all in high esteem and want only the best for you. I absolutely would never cause you any harm. I'm sincerely sorry for my initial reasons for coming here and for allowing Rex to manipulate me."

"I'm not hearing anything to back up Mr. Jackson's endorsement. Your character remains questionable," Max said.

"I hope to clear things up shortly. First off, Rex wrote the letters you received with my name on them, Maggie."

Maggie gasped. "Rex wrote them?"

"Yes, claiming to be me. Most of what he shared was not true. In fact, Rex shared experiences from Levi Jackson's past, not mine," Garrett said.

Maggie and Max both frowned.

"Levi Jackson? What is his association with Rex?" Max asked.

"Apparently, you aren't aware of the destructive path Rex took to get here. He stole Mr. Jackson's shipping company."

"*What*?" Maggie said.

"You might have noticed Mr. Jackson is missing part of his finger. I understand he lost a toe also, thanks to one of Rex's thugs. Those men applied torture, forcing Mr. Jackson to sign away his company, Jackson Shipping. Maggie ... Mr. Jackson is the one who lost his home to a tornado and his dog to a coyote, not me."

Garrett waited for their gasps to end.

"Mr. Jackson never mentioned his difficult past," Maggie said.

"That's why he's in the business of security, to stop Rex from harming anyone else," Garrett said.

"What a horrible situation. I did not know Mr. Tillman had brought such destruction to Mr. Jackson." Maggie thought for a moment. "Perhaps that's why Papa hired him to protect our town. My father must have known Rex Tillman might try to come back here. Since Mr. Jackson had experience with Mr. Tillman, he was a sound choice."

Garrett nodded. "I'm sure you're right. Your father was a wise man."

"That gives us some insight about Levi Jackson, but your integrity is still under scrutiny," Max said.

"I'm fully aware and deserving of having my character examined, Max. As Maggie knows, my father regrettably partnered with Rex. Eventually, my father sold our construction company to Rex, then vanished, leaving Mother with nothing. We haven't seen Father in almost seven months. Rex claimed my father swindled him. Considering what I've since learned about Rex, I'm convinced my father was the one who was swindled. I now fear he's in danger somewhere."

Maggie wrapped her hand around Garrett's arm. "Your father is an honorable man."

"Thank you." Garrett felt warm inside as he patted her hand.

"That brings me to why I came to Garfield. Rex has forced me to work for him ever since my father left, making me believe I had no choice if I wanted to keep my mother in her home and protect her from his advances. He promised if I helped him get Mando Merchandising, he would finally release both of us from his web."

"You came here to steal Maggie's company?" Max asked.

"Admittedly, I did initially agree to the atrocious plan, but soon knew I wouldn't follow through. Meeting all the nice people of Garfield made me reconsider. I quickly realized leading a double life was not feasible. There is no possible way I would cause harm to Maggie. As soon as I learned of Rex's plan to kidnap Maggie, I went to Levi Jackson and informed him. That's when we decided to join forces. I apologize for not telling you sooner. I'm also sorry to have come here with horrible intentions. Although undeserved, I hope you will find it in your hearts to forgive me. I'll do anything to make up for my initial intentions."

"Forgiveness will take time, along with actions," Max said. "You were willing to partake in dastardly crimes."

"I forgive you, Garrett," Maggie said.

"Not so fast, Maggie. This man came here to harm you."

"But Garrett *didn't* hurt any of us. There's no need to make amends to me. Garrett helped stop Rex Tillman. If anything, we owe him. Garrett is a good man who was trying to protect his mother. Think what you'd be willing to do to protect Aunt Catherine."

"Maggie is right, darling. I believe Garrett's motives are admirable," Catherine said.

"Your actions of late have proven trustworthy. Don't do anything to bring doubt to your character, or Garfield will no longer welcome you," Max said.

"You have my word," Garrett said.

"We'll locate your father. I promise. Mr. Jackson will help," Maggie said.

Garrett smiled. "You're all so much better people than I am. Thank you for your forgiveness. I do want to find my father as soon as possible. He is likely in harm's way. First, I need to return home to check on my mother. I also want to see what I can do about gaining back control of Hanley Construction."

Garrett realized home didn't seem like the right word to describe Chicago anymore. Even though it was the only place he had ever lived, he didn't possess a burning desire to return there.

Chapter 33

Several weeks had passed since Rex's apprehension and Garrett's departure for Chicago. Maggie had been working harder than ever at Mando Merchandising. Sitting at her desk, she studied the ledgers with satisfaction.

Josephine interrupted Maggie's thoughts. "Mr. Levi Jackson is here to see you. Should I bring him in?"

"Yes. I'll see him." Maggie was eager for Levi's visit. She knew he had been working diligently to unravel the mess Rex created over the last several years.

Levi greeted Maggie with a surprising smile. She had never seen any evidence of happiness in him, so this must mean good news.

"I definitely have an excellent report today."

"Oh, my. Tell me details."

"Rex's lawyer, Lester Grover, is still in Chicago. He confessed to everything, hoping for leniency regarding his part in Rex Tillman's schemes. Mr. Grover has been cooperative in every way. He seems to be as relieved to rid himself of Mr. Tillman as the rest of us. We should have enough evidence now to put Mr. Tillman away forever. He's sitting in a Chicago jail cell." Levi laughed. "Hasn't had even one 'friend' come to his rescue. Mr. Grover is working with us to change ownership of Hanley Construction and Jackson Shipping back to the rightful owners."

"Wonderful news! Will you leave Garfield to go back to your shipping company."

Levi shook his head. "No. I promised your father I'd remain for a minimum of two years. I plan to honor my commitment. I'll need to split my time between here and my shipping locations, so I'll be absent more than I'd like. However, Chester, Ernie, and Rich will stay on to make sure Garfield is protected."

"Mr. Jackson, now that Mr. Tillman is gone, there isn't a need for security. Garfield is safe again."

"Are you still pursuing grooms outside of our town?"

"I anticipate resuming our search in the near future."

"Are you planning to employ new people?"

"Yes, many more are needed."

"Then, Miss Garfield, protection will remain in place."

Maggie felt her face grow hot. "Pursuant to my father's contract, I will allow your crew to stay in *my* town. Ongoing, I will evaluate our situation to decide if future indentures will be needed."

"I welcome that discussion."

"Meanwhile, Mr. Jackson, your company should be priority. My father would have insisted."

"I'm sure I can balance my responsibilities."

"What about Garrett's father. Did you locate him?"

"Yes, we found James Hanley in New York. We were fortunate to discover him when we did. Apparently, he has been held captive since Tillman took over his construction business. Mr. Hanley was being loaded onto a ship heading out of the country when we rescued him. I'm not sure we would have ever found him if he had been brought on board."

"Poor Mr. Hanley. He was a victim like you."

"As we thought, Mr. Tillman stole everything from Mr. Hanley, not the other way around. He used much trickery and deceit to obtain Hanley Construction. Mr. Grover was able to provide evidence as proof. Mr. Hanley did not leave on his own accord but was forced into captivity."

Maggie felt horrible for Mr. Hanley but ecstatic for Garrett. His father was not a dreadful man. Garrett's family would have a happy ending.

"Does Garrett know? Will they be together soon?"

Levi nodded. "Yes, Mr. James Hanley is already reunited with his family."

Maggie experienced a mixture of emotions. On the one hand, happiness for Garrett. On the selfish side, sadness, because she'd probably never see him again.

Chapter 34

As much as Sadie was attracted to Jesse, she was exasperated with him. She had thought about him and prayed all day, and now he was walking up the stairs towards her. Jesse sat next to Sadie on the porch swing, then kissed her hand.

"Hello there, Beautiful One," Jesse said. "Hungry? Meatloaf is being served tonight at the restaurant, one of my favorites."

Sadie leaned forward and looked down. She didn't want to make eye contact with Jesse, or she might lose her nerve. "Jesse, I won't be able to have supper with you tonight. I'm sorry."

Jesse frowned. "Not hungry?"

"I won't be able to see you anymore. Our courtship must end."

"Why? We enjoy each other's company. I might even see myself as a groom sooner than planned."

Sadie looked up at him. "I had hope for a union, as well. Sadly, we are not meant to be married."

"How can you say that? We have interesting conversations. We laugh and have fun. You and I are well suited. Don't be foolish."

Sadie moved to the chair next to the swing, sat down, and faced him.

"We do have fun. Maybe that's part of the problem.

Jesse, as you have told me, you rarely rise before noontime. Your days are spent riding horses, swimming in the lake, reading books, spending time in Hannibal—doing only what gratifies you. Wants drive your aspirations. This type of lifestyle doesn't have room for a wife and family."

Jesse shrugged. "I like to relax, but there's nothing wrong with that. A man needs rest before settling down. How else should I pass time while you're at Mando Merchandising all day? There's not much to do in this boring town nor anyone to spend time with while you work. If you'd leave your job, as I've asked you many times, we could spend our days together."

"Perhaps Maggie could find work for you."

"No, no, no! No one is going to chain me to a job until I've completed my sabbatical from college. I worked hard and deserve some time off."

"I desire to be married to a mature and responsible man. I see no ambition in you, Jesse, which is troubling. You're well-educated but have no desire to use what you've been privileged to learn. If we married, I would not be happy going to work while you play all day."

Jesse thought for a moment. "Sadie, you will not work outside of our home if we marry. My family has plenty of money. We can both spend our days having fun together. Maybe travel and enjoy ourselves. In fact, we could take a very long honeymoon and see any part of the world you'd like. Perhaps for a year or two. Doesn't that sound intriguing?"

"No. I don't want to travel around the world. We are very different. I want to stay here in Garfield and rear children. My aspirations are to help others while using my talents for God. I might even want to keep working at Mando before becoming a mother. I don't want to live off your parent's wealth. Jesse, perhaps you should travel and continue having all the fun you want as a single man."

"Maybe you're right, Sadie." Jesse said with a glare. "I've given Garfield a fair chance. I got myself into a courtship, which fulfills my parents' requirements. So, the time might be right to leave this town and get on with my life. I didn't want to come here in the first place. I was willing to give up my freedom for you—a mistake."

Jesse shook his head. "Think about what *you're* giving up. A wealthy educated man like me will attract many elite ladies. Sadie, you're an orphan with no known socialite lineage. Attracting gentlemen of my class with be difficult, if not impossible."

A tear rolled down Sadie's cheek. "Now I'm certain I want nothing more to do with you."

Sadie raced into the house.

Chapter 35

Garrett stepped off the train in Hannibal, happy to be close to Garfield again. He hadn't seen or corresponded with Maggie in over three months.

"Hello, Garrett Hanley."

Garrett turned around to see who was speaking to him. "Oh, hello, Jeff. Should have known you'd be working here today. Nice to see you. As usual, I need assistance. How can I get to Garfield right away?"

"You missed the stagecoach for today. There's a departure at eight o'clock every morning that makes a stop in Garfield when needed. You can purchase a fare for tomorrow."

Garrett frowned. "I'd rather get there today. Are there any other options?"

"Mando Merchandising has several cargo wagons coming and going throughout the day. Also, a motorized truck. You might be able to find a place to sit, but most of them are packed up full."

"Is there any motorized passenger transportation available?"

Jeff shook his head. "No, sir. I doubt we'll ever have that. Can't imagine choosing one of those contraptions over a reliable horse. People in Hannibal feel the same way. We do have a coach that can take you to a downtown Hannibal hotel if you'd like."

Garrett wasn't keen on waiting until tomorrow, but he didn't seem to have a choice. "Thanks, Jeff. Looks like a stay in a hotel might be best. Where can I board the coach?"

"Right here. I'll take you inside to purchase your fare."

Garrett and Jeff strolled into the depot where Max was walking towards them.

"Garrett, is that you? What a pleasant surprise."

Garrett reached out and shook hands with his friend. "Yes, finally back. I'm beyond thrilled to see you here. By chance, are you going to Garfield any time soon?"

"On my way now to retrieve Maggie from Mando. Do you want to ride with me?"

"I'd be tremendously grateful, Max. Keeps me from staying another night away from Garfield."

Garrett turned to Jeff. "You've been most accommodating as always. Doesn't look like I need to purchase a fare, after all."

"My pleasure, sir."

"How is everything?" Max asked Garrett as they left the station.

"All is well. Hanley Construction is now under my control. Best of all, my parents are reunited. Thankfully, my father is safe. I'll never doubt his character again. Surprised he still wants to claim me as his son."

"You must be quite relieved and happy to have your affairs in order again. Reconnecting with your father is a wonderful blessing."

"I couldn't have asked for a better outcome. My parents act like newlyweds. Seeing them together is sheer joy."

"I can only imagine." Max paused. "What brings you back to Garfield? I wasn't sure we'd see you again."

Garrett smiled. "In my short time there, Garfield captured my heart. If your town will have me, I sure would like to stay permanently."

"No doubt Garfield can feel like home after only a visit or two. Mrs. Crawford and I never looked back after moving there." Max paused. "Are you sure *Garfield* has captured your heart? Or could there be a certain lady pulling you back?"

"I won't deny my fondness for Maggie. Does she ... I mean ... do you think ... she misses me even a little?"

"Only Maggie can answer that question. She quite possibly does miss you but has not said. Maggie has been different since you left."

"Different? How?"

Max thought for a moment. "I'm not sure. She's quiet. Completely focused on work. Spends more hours at Mando Merchandising than I've seen in the past.

"Perhaps she's overcome with fear after Rex Tillman's ordeal. I should have been here to protect her. Women are fragile."

Max snorted. "Fragile? Not Maggie. Better not mention this conversation to her unless you want to start a battle."

Garrett frowned. "Max, you *did* say she was struggling."

"No, I said Maggie was different, quiet, focused. Didn't mention a word about fragility or struggles."

"But she *is* a lady. Even the strongest woman wouldn't be able to outdo the weakest man. She needs to realize that."

"Or you need to realize you might be wrong."

Garrett shook his head. "She's a complicated lady, Max."

"Now your mind is starting to think correctly. Ponder that thought. Try to approach Maggie with a different attitude."

"Max ... do you think Maggie could ever care about me?

"I think she already does."

Garrett turned to face Max. "She does?"

"There's an obvious attraction between you two. But also, friction. Unnecessary bickering."

"How do you think I can bring more peace to our interactions?"

"Respect ... Respect who Maggie is ... without judgment. Think before speaking. Ask yourself, 'Will my words affirm or discourage her?'"

"You give excellent advice, sir. Max ... You're like Maggie's father now. Would you give your blessing to a courtship?"

Max shook his head.

"No?" Garrett frowned.

"My answer would be yes. I like you, Garrett. However, convincing Maggie might be impossible. She's adamant the other ladies will find husbands. Maggie has told me many times she will never marry."

"Do you know why she's opposed to marriage?"

"You need to hear that answer from her."

They stopped in front of Mando Merchandising.

"We're about thirty minutes early. Perhaps you should go in to see Maggie. Seems you might have a few things to discuss. I'll wait out here."

"I appreciate that, Max. My heart is racing so fast that it might beat the rest of me into the building."

"Then it's best you hurry inside." Max grinned.

Garrett was grateful for a possibility to have a few minutes alone with Maggie. He made his way to Josephine's desk.

"Hello, Mr. Hanley. Is Miss Garfield expecting you?"

"Good afternoon, Miss Swanson. Nice to see you again. No, Miss Garfield doesn't know I'm here. Hope she isn't too busy for a short visit. Could you ask her if she'll allow me a few minutes of her time?"

"I'll check with her. Just a moment," Josephine said, walking towards Maggie's office as she pointed to a chair. "Please sit down."

Garrett was too nervous to sit. He followed Josephine without her knowledge, then he listened as he waited for an invitation.

Josephine knocked on Maggie's door.

"Mr. Hanley is here to see you. May I send him in?"

"Mr. *Garrett* Hanley?"

"Yes. Would you like to see him?"

"Uh, no ... yes ... I'm extremely busy ... I don't know ... why is he here?"

"He didn't say. Should I send him away?"

Garrett stepped into Maggie's office. "Are you truly too busy to see me? I came a long way."

"Uh ... come on in."

"Miss Garfield will see you now," Josephine said with a frown. "But you appear to already know that."

"No need to fetch me, Miss Swanson." Garrett smiled wide.

Josephine walked out, shaking her head.

Maggie walked to the front of her desk, looking even more beautiful than Garrett remembered. She wore a pink jacket over a pale grey blouse, along with pink pants. *Pants.* Garrett made a mental note not to comment. Blonde curls framed her face perfectly, with blue eyes twinkling.

Before he could stop himself, Garrett embraced Maggie.

"I've missed you, Maggie. I'm so happy to finally be back again."

Maggie pulled away and returned to her chair.

"I'm delighted to see you too, Mr. Hanley. Have a seat so we can catch up."

"Mr. Hanley? Come on, Maggie, it hasn't been that long since we've seen each other."

"Three months seems considerable," Maggie said as she looked down at papers on her desk. "How is everything?"

Garrett felt tension in the air, hurt Maggie was too distracted for him. "Things are well. If now is not a good time, I can come back."

"Now is as good as any."

"Do you think you could look at me instead of your work? Have I upset you?"

Maggie looked up. "I'm not upset. Just finishing a few things."

Garrett didn't believe her but didn't push.

"Did you get to spend time with your father?" Maggie asked.

"Thanks to you and Mr. Jackson, yes. I'm absolutely appalled with myself for having doubted my father. How could I have believed anything coming out of Rex Tillman's mouth? Thankfully, Father forgave me. Seeing him with Mother again is remarkable, as if no time has passed between them. Mother won't let him out of her sight, which seems to delight my father."

Garrett smiled at the vision of his parents being together again.

"They're going to do some traveling for a few years. Father wants to pamper Mother to make up for all she's been through."

"What about Hanley Construction? Are you now the owner?"

"Yes, my lawyer has finished all legal paperwork. I'm thrilled to be able to make decisions without worry of Rex Tillman forcing my hand. There's no question about a promising future now."

"I'm thrilled for you, Garrett. You radiate happiness." She paused. "I *am* curious. What brings you here?"

"You're back to calling me Garrett. We're friends again."

Maggie smiled. "You're impossible."

"I'm here to repay you."

Maggie shook her head. "You owe no debt. There is nothing to repay."

"Let me finish. Dr. Gibson needs a medical facility. I'd like to build her one."

"A kind gesture, but impossible. You're running a business in Chicago now. No one can be in two places at once."

"Hanley Construction will do well without my presence. I just need to get back there every few weeks, with most of my time spent in Garfield." Garrett paused. "I *need* to be here. Allow me to build the medical facility for Garfield. I can't think of a bigger honor right now."

"I'm overwhelmed with your offer. Dr. Gibson could certainly use a new building. Please know this facility is Dr. Gibson's vision, so she and I will make the decisions. That might be hard for a man who thinks women are incompetent."

Garrett thought about his conversation with Max. "Obviously, I'm not always right. Dr. Gibson and you have both proven to be completely capable. Constructing a medical facility would require your guidance."

Maggie raised her eyebrows. "Hmmm ... 'not always right' and two women are 'capable.' What have you done with the real Garrett Hanley?"

"Time away allowed me to reflect about my attitude towards ladies. I've learned to open my mind to new ways of thinking."

"So nice to hear that. Are you certain about wanting to commit to such a large project?"

"What I want is you, Maggie. Thoughts of you invaded my mind every day while I was away. Would you allow me to court you?"

Maggie's mouth opened wide. "I haven't heard a word from you in three months. If you were thinking about me, why didn't you write?"

"I wanted to but thought better. Correspondence you received from me in the past was from Rex. I worried a letter might bring back bad memories."

"Thoughtful of you to consider that. All right. You're forgiven."

Garrett wiped his forehead. "Whew! Relief. So, about courting, may I see you socially? A possible future with you would never be dull. And there's no doubt Christ would be in the center of our decisions."

"Garrett, please hear me. We can never have more than a friendship. The other ladies are looking for husbands. I'm not. If you want a wife, consider those who are available for courting."

"All right, Maggie. You win. For now, I'll be content to focus on Dr. Gibson's medical building. With such a time-consuming project, wife-hunting endeavors will need to wait. Are Sadie and Jesse betrothed yet?"

"Sadie is no longer interested in Jesse, and, there are still no prospects for Ruth and Annabelle. Guess we're back to where this started in our search for suitable grooms."

"Sadie and Jesse didn't match well? Where is Jesse?"

"Back in St. Louis. Sadie correctly decided Jesse was not mature enough for marriage. He's been gone about a month now. Apparently, advertising for husbands is not a good idea. I'll need to come up with a better way to help the ladies of Garfield find their grooms."

"Don't be so quick to declare failure just yet regarding your matchmaking efforts. I don't think Jesse will be able to stay away from Sadie for long."

"Sadie does *not* want Jesse to come back. Doesn't matter what he desires." Maggie hesitated. "Garrett, don't remain in Garfield if I'm the reason. My heart is closed to matrimony."

"You're the main reason, but not the only one. I feel at home here and missed everyone greatly. Garfield is a splendid place to live. My plans will be to remain until the medical facility is completed, then evaluate options to make things permanent. I'll honor being your friend … but … only until Ruth, Sadie, and Annabelle find their matches. Then we can reexamine that heart of yours."

"Garrett. Listen to me. I will never be married. This is not a topic for discussion."

"Why would you deny yourself that happiness?"

"For some people, there is much fulfillment in life without a spouse, so nothing is being denied. Contrary to what our world demands, not everyone should be married. In First Corinthians, Apostle Paul said to embrace the life to which God calls us, whether single or married. My father was only married until the day I was born because my mother died giving birth. If allowed the option, Father would have stayed married to Mother for a lifetime. However, after she was gone, he declared a calling to remain single."

"Maggie, did your parents have a marriage of love?"

"They adored each other."

"Was it truly a calling from God? Or was your father's heart too broken to allow in another woman?"

"Both are likely correct. Father was heartbroken, yes. But I truly believe Father was content alone, having no desire for matrimony. God wants the same for me. Please, Garrett, honor my decision."

"Promise something. Pray for God's calling to be revealed. Find out if singleness is your desire or God's."

"I seek Him daily. There is peace in this decision."

Garrett stood. "I can't argue with God. Looks like we'll remain as friends."

For now.

Chapter 36

"Miss Garfield wants a new medical building for Dr. Gibson. I hear you're the best carpenter around. Would you partner with me on this project?" Garrett said.

Hank pulled on his mustache, seeming to be in deep thought. "I was expecting you'd probably ask me. I can help."

"Excellent. I have the specifications of what Dr. Gibson is looking for. I'd like to get started as soon as possible. Do you know of any men we could hire to help us?"

"Men pass through Hannibal occasionally, wanting temporary work. We've hired some in the past. Never more than a few at a time. There are, however, capable carpenters living right here in Garfield."

"Wonderful. Where do I find these gentlemen? I didn't think there were many male residents in this town."

"Not men. Ladies. They've helped me build the houses you see all around town, furniture too," Hank said, as he nodded his head. "Right talented, they are."

Garrett felt his enthusiasm dwindle. "Ladies? You can't be serious. Females don't work on construction crews."

"They do in Garfield. Mighty efficient too. In fact, I have a crew of fifteen and others I can call upon whenever I need them. These ladies are capable of building anything with plans to view. They could be ready to work as early as you need them."

Garrett looked at Hank, feeling a bit stunned. Apparently, he wasn't joking. "I'll take a ride into Hannibal and see if there are any men who need jobs for a few months. Where would I go to locate them?"

Hank shook his head while he rubbed his mustache again.

"You could try one of the hotels or the train station. Might get lucky. Fact is, you won't find better help than the ladies here in Garfield. Up to you. Whatever you want."

"I'll give this some thought. Meanwhile, is that motorbike available to borrow so I can go into Hannibal?"

"Not today. The bike's in Max's barn. He goes over the mechanics on all the vehicles real thorough about every month. You could take a horse and wagon, but daylight would be gone before you could get back."

Not feeling he had a choice, Garrett said, "I suppose it wouldn't hurt to try out the ladies for a day. If they can't grasp the work, I can bring in some men from my crews in Chicago."

"Oh, they'll grasp the work," Hank said with a grin.

Garrett shrugged, but wanted to get the new building erected as soon as possible. "Do you have time to look at specifications and where the medical facility will be built?"

"I can squeeze you into my day. Already know where the building's going to be. Been seeing loads of lumber and supplies come in. Might be helpful to be onsite as we go over plans. Since we're already in the livery stable, let's take horses for the short ride."

The men rode to Dr. Gibson's chosen site, spending an hour going over plans she and Maggie had helped Garrett put together.

"Hank, you seem to know quite a bit about construction, something I'd not considered until just now. I won't try to take over if you're the man normally in charge of building things in Garfield. I'd be content to assist in any way you need, but I don't want to get in your way."

Hank laughed. "Oh no. Happy to see you're in charge of this one. I'll work hard on the job—helped build about all the structures here—but some days are just too perfect for fishing. That takes priority. Also have several furniture items in progress. Don't want to be obligated with additional responsibility. Besides, the hospital will be much bigger than anything I've ever built. No desire to be at the helm."

Garrett breathed a silent sigh of relief. He wanted to do this for Garfield—and Maggie. "Would your crew be ready to get started early tomorrow?"

"I'll go talk with the ladies now. I'm sure we can get several of them out here in the morning. How does eight o'clock sound?"

"Perfect. Thanks, Hank."

With a tip of his hat, Hank rode away.

Garrett envisioned what the area would look like once the building was complete, eager to get started.

A female construction crew. What have I gotten myself into?

Chapter 37

Garrett walked the mile to the job site and plopped down on a pile of lumber that would become Garfield's medical building. The structure would be a total of five thousand square feet, with thoughts of future additions. Garrett was going to build mostly with wood, since Garfield had a surplus of lumber stored and available. If there were future projects, he planned to use cast iron and stone.

The slowly rising sun formed a fiery hue across the morning sky. With each passing moment the day grew brighter, with a wave of golden arms beckoning the earth to wake up. Two hummingbirds hovered in front of Garrett, staying just long enough to flap hello.

The smell of wood urged Garrett into exercise. He climbed onto a higher stack where his breath formed clouds as he exhaled into the cool air. Perfect weather for working outside.

"You must have slept here. The sun is barely up." Hank's voice interrupted Garrett's thoughts.

"I might as well have because I didn't get much rest. My mind went over every inch of the building. Just too excited to relax. Being back in business is a satisfying feeling."

"Having a local man oversee such a large project will be a blessing to Garfield." Hank paused. "You do plan to stay, right?"

Garrett liked being referred to as a local man. He hoped to be here for a long time. Perhaps, even forever. "Staying here is my goal. I can't imagine being anywhere else."

Garrett looked back up at the sky. "Sure was a beautiful sunrise this morning. So colorful among fluffy white clouds. Gives a man a lot to be thankful for."

Voices could be heard coming closer to the men.

"Here comes your crew of fifteen," Hank said. "Maggie brought in several more orphan ladies in the last month. Likely, some of them could learn the trade and join the crew too."

"I'll keep that in mind."

The ladies walked up, all wearing colorful coveralls and hats, courtesy of Sophie Jenkins and Catherine Crawford. Garrett wanted to laugh at the sight of them but knew better. He was still having trouble wrapping his head around the idea of female builders. Several men working for him in Chicago could be here in the next few weeks if needed. Garrett wanted to wait for them but was sure Maggie would be upset if the ladies didn't get a chance to show their skills. He accepted his circumstances.

"Hello," Garrett said. "Thank you for being here. Are you ready to get to work?"

"Yes. Ready. Nice to meet you, Mr. Hanley. I'm Roxie Sinclair.

"Glad to make your acquaintance, Miss Sinclair."

"Call me Roxie. We'll be spending quite a lot of time together."

Garrett couldn't see what Roxie or any of the other ladies looked like under their enormous hats and oversized coveralls. He was glad they all wore different colors to help keep them straight. Garrett was making note of Roxie being the girl in red when she pointed to the words on her hat and clothing.

"Sophie Jenkins and Catherine Crawford stitched our names on the apparel. Might be helpful since there are several of us to remember," Roxie said.

"Yes, very beneficial as we get to know each other. I'll do my best not to rely on labels for long."

Garrett walked around to each of the ladies for some quick introductions. He went over the building plans, then handed out the assignments. The ladies quickly got to work, moving along as smoothly as ants.

Garrett was pleasantly surprised at just how well the morning went. By dinnertime, several of the frames had already been nailed together, as well as progress on the foundation. As usual, he had underestimated the abilities of these hard-working ladies.

Unexpected by Garrett, Max and Annabelle arrived at precisely twelve o'clock with a dinner she had prepared for the workers. "Time to eat. Beans and ham, fried potatoes, cornbread, and fresh catfish today," Annabelle said.

"That sounds scrumptious. Thank you. What a pleasant surprise. Max, I appreciate you bringing Annabelle to us. I'm sure we're all hungry," Garrett said.

Hank strolled over to join them.

"Thanks goes to Hank for catching the fish," Annabelle looked at Hank with admiration.

"You brought a lot of fish here. Hank, you must share your secret spot on the lake so I can catch a few," Garrett said.

"Any time. I go fishing about every day."

Annabelle and Max filled plates as the ladies lined up to get their share of delicious-smelling food. Garrett and Hank laid out some blankets under two shady oak trees.

Max sat down next to Garrett once everyone's plates were full.

"Perhaps Maggie might join us next time you come out. She might want to see some of the progress," Garrett said to Max.

"Maggie has a major order to fill. I asked her to come, but she didn't have time."

"And ... she's avoiding me," Garrett said with a frown.

"That too," Max agreed.

Before Garrett could feel too discouraged, he noticed Annabelle and Hank sit down together.

"Max, do you think Hank fancies Annabelle?"

Max laughed. "Not a chance. Why do you ask?"

"Take a look. They're deep in conversation with no one else close enough to join in. Seems a little cozy to me."

"Just two friends who enjoy each other's company. Hank is a contented bachelor. He's friends with all the ladies."

"We'll see."

Max shook his head. "I doubt we'll see much."

Max and Annabelle left after dinner. The crew got back to work on the medical building. By the end of the day, remarkable progress had been made. The foundation was fully marked, along with many frames waiting to become a part of Garfield's hospital.

Tired legs walked towards town. The women were a little ahead of Garrett and Hank.

"You were right, Hank. The ladies are excellent workers."

"Yep, best around."

"I won't doubt you again." After a brief hesitation, Garrett said, "Hank, if you don't mind my asking, would you consider courting Annabelle?"

Hank turned a little red as he snickered and rubbed his moustache. "No. I uh ... I just ... No. She's a friend like all the others."

"Annabelle's a wonderful girl. You should give the idea some thought."

"I ... I, um ... I don't think she would ... I mean ... I just don't see her being interested in a man like me. Besides, I don't have time for no lady."

"Don't sell yourself short, Hank. A talented man, kind and reliable—what lady wouldn't want that? Besides, I noticed Annabelle looking at you today."

"What do you mean, looking at me?"

"I don't know. She just seemed attentive to you. Any man would be blessed to have a girl like Annabelle at his side."

"We're friends. All the ladies around here think of me as their brother. Don't need a woman in my life to boss me around. Might cause problems with my fishing."

"Are you sure? Fishing is fun. But, why not have it all? There's no doubt you would eat well," Garrett said with a wink.

Chapter 38

Garrett had attended church services every Sunday while in Chicago and continued to do so in Garfield. Unlike the first time he walked up to the church building several months ago, he now couldn't wait to go inside. In addition to being fed with Scripture, church was the one place Garrett could always count on to see Maggie.

After each service, there was delicious food prepared for everyone. Today was no exception.

Hank and the ladies had built chairs and tables which now sat under shade trees next to the building, all within a short distance of Black Swan Lake. When the weather was warm enough, the townsfolk would eat outside and enjoy the acres of lake. Some would fish, while others would paddle around in boats Maggie had provided. For chilly days like today, dinner was in a room adjacent to the sanctuary, with many tables and chairs set up for meals.

Garrett spotted Maggie as soon as she entered. "Will you eat with me today? I have a few updates to the medical building I'd like to share."

"Since today is Sunday, I'm sure you'd like to take a day off from work as much as I would. Besides, Dr. Gibson should be a part of any conversations about the hospital."

"Fair enough. Can you come to the worksite tomorrow to see our progress? Dr. Gibson plans to be there at noontime."

"Dr. Gibson invited me as well. I'll be there."

"Perfect. Since we can't talk about the medical building today, I'd like to discuss the trip I expect to take in the middle of the week."

"You're leaving? How long will you be gone?"

Garrett detected a bit of sadness in her voice. Perhaps she cared about him more than she led him to believe. His heart leapt. "I'll give you the details between bites if you will join me."

Maggie hesitated. "All right, Garrett. I'll sit with you today. Let's find a table with Sadie, Ruth, or Annabelle. Shall we get our food?"

"Yes, please."

Garrett took Maggie's arm to help move her toward the food, then stopped, holding his hand to his ear. "Do you hear that? Miss Stoddard's fried chicken is summoning me."

Maggie smiled. "No doubt your stomach is calling out to the chicken."

"Mmmmm-hmmmm."

After filling their plates, Garrett and Maggie sat at a table next to Ruth's fully occupied one.

"So, tell me about your trip."

"First, Maggie, I've missed you. I haven't seen you since last Sunday. Please don't avoid me."

"My absence allows the other ladies a fair chance to spend time with you. They are exceptional women."

"Yes, they are, but none of them are you. Besides, there's no time for courting while building the medical facility."

Garrett changed the subject before she could respond.

"That brings me to my departure on Wednesday. Hard to believe I've already been back in Garfield for almost two months. Anyway, I must go to Chicago for a few weeks to attend several important meetings. Hank and Roxi will overcharge the crew while I'm gone."

"A few weeks? Of course, go to Chicago for as long as required. Hanley Construction's needs are priority. Don't ever let your commitments to Garfield interfere, even if the move is permanent."

"I don't plan to make Chicago my primary residence again, unless God shows me otherwise. You'll be interested to know about a stop I'll be making in St. Louis. I sent Jesse Walker a telegram to ask him to meet with me."

"Just a friendly visit?"

"Yes, along with an intended agenda. I've talked with Sadie. Although she's still angry with Jesse, she misses him a great deal."

"Sadie's heart might miss him, but common sense tells her Jesse is not a good choice. I don't see a chance for reconciliation."

"What if Jesse misses her too? Suppose he can be the responsible man Sadie needs? I believe Jesse would change for the right woman. Sadie might help him become the man God intended him to be."

Maggie frowned. "I'm not sure. Jesse is incredibly self-centered. Besides, change should come from within, not to win someone's heart."

"Just the same, being able to talk with Jesse is worth a stop in St. Louis. At least we can rest assured every effort was made to give Jessie and Sadie a chance to reconcile. Besides, I'd like to check on Jesse, see how he's been."

"Maybe the ladies of Garfield need Garrett-the-Matchmaker instead of advertisements in newspapers." Maggie smiled.

"Hmmm … Could be a new career. Do you have any potential mail-order grooms in waiting?"

"I've decided not to invite any other gentlemen to Garfield for the immediate future. Advertising for husbands has too many flaws that must be corrected before trying again."

Garrett raised an eyebrow. "I can't be expected to find spouses for everyone. You need to do your part too," Garrett flashed an ornery grin. "Don't abandon the endeavor just yet."

"We at least need a temporary pause in this undertaking while waiting for God's direction."

"I'm glad *I* made it here before you put the plan on hold. But as you know, my heart is taken." Garrett put his hand on his chest. "You could very well have two successful matches from your advertisement. Jesse and I could become your first grooms for Garfield."

Garrett didn't allow Maggie time to respond before he got up and walked away.

Chapter 39

As promised, Maggie arrived with Max and Annabelle at the worksite on Monday at noontime. Maggie helped dish out food to everyone before making a plate for herself, then sat down by Max and Garrett. Dr. Gibson soon joined them.

"Shall I pray?" Garrett asked.

"That would be lovely," Maggie said as they closed their eyes and bowed their heads.

"Lord, we come to you with grateful hearts today for your blessings and grace. Help us to please you in our daily lives. May your will be done, not ours. Thank you for what I know will be an enjoyable meal. In Jesus's name we pray. Amen."

Garrett's prayer touched Maggie. He was proving to be a man of God.

"After we eat, Dr. Gibson and I will show you around, Maggie. I'd like you to see her excellent ideas we've been able to incorporate," Garrett said.

"I am full of anticipation. No doubt my expectations will be far exceeded as indicated by what I can see already."

When Max and Garrett finished their meals, Garrett said, "Max, would you like to look around with us? You should be there to help share our surprise with Dr. Gibson and Maggie. Besides, you haven't seen the inside of the building."

"Oh, yes," Max said. "I've wanted to see what you've accomplished. And to share our surprise."

"Surprise? What kind of surprise?" Maggie asked.

"You've kept a secret from me? I'm supposed to be kept abreast of all decisions about this building," Dr. Gibson said.

"This is not a part of the building. Of course, your final approval will be needed before moving forward," Garrett said.

"I'm intrigued," Dr. Gibson said.

"So am I," Maggie said.

"As soon as you ladies finish eating, we'll show you," Garrett said.

"I'm done," Maggie said.

"Me too. Let's go," Dr. Gibson said.

"Come on, Max," Garrett said.

Once inside, Garrett and Dr. Gibson described many features in detail.

"We've added a roof over the entrance to protect patients from rain, snow, and hot sun. The doorways are extra wide to accommodate stretchers. More than one person could enter at a time," Garrett said.

"Excellent ideas," Maggie said.

"Dr. Gibson's experience and ingenuity have contributed greatly to final decisions. She's quite impressive," Garrett said.

"I appreciate your endorsement, Mr. Hanley," Dr. Gibson said. "I still remember our first meeting when my abilities were in doubt."

"I owe you and all women of the world my sincere apologies. I can admit when I'm wrong. Right, Max?"

"You've come a long way," Max said.

"Continuing on, Dr. Gibson's office will be about four hundred square feet. Hank and his helpers have built furniture to meet the doctor's specifications. The five patient rooms will each be one hundred twenty-five square feet," Garrett said.

"Soon we'll need more doctors with an excellent facility like this," Dr. Gibson said.

"Are there colleagues you can recommend?" Maggie asked.

"Oh, yes. A few come to mind. Perhaps we can discuss them soon. I'm excited to think we could meet medical needs of nearby towns as well as Garfield,"

"I agree. This would be an essential service to many. Before long, we might need to expand the building to add more patient rooms," Maggie said

"I hope so," Dr. Gibson said.

"Now, for the surprise," Garrett said. "Tell them, Max."

"Garrett and I have ordered a motorized ambulance. Horses can be too slow when patients with serious injuries need to get here quickly. With qualified personnel, an ambulance could save lives. Just imagine how important this vehicle will be to rural areas, especially as roads continue to be constructed."

Maggie was frowning. Garrett wasn't sure why.

"I want to build a barn to house our ambulance. Have we gone too far?"

"I can understand your zeal for something of this progressive nature. An ambulance sounds costly, as does another building, not to mention staffing. Mr. Hanley, you must provide me with estimates for anything that hasn't been budgeted with my approval."

"Obviously, Miss Garfield, you are not as enthusiastic about our special surprise as Max and I had hoped. I do not expect *you* to fund these items. Surprises are usually gifts, and *I* plan to pay for them."

"Garfield is my responsibility. I won't allow anyone to cover costs for anything this substantial. Please provide information about the prices so thoughtful consideration can be made."

Garrett felt his face heating as anger built inside of him. "I'm not trying to take over your town. I merely wanted to give Garfield a gift of my gratitude ... which I can easily afford."

"Just the same, provide the numbers to me. And, Dr. Gibson, perhaps you can create a list of pros and cons to having a motorized ambulance. Then we'll meet to assess the need."

"Excellent idea," said Dr. Gibson.

Garrett remained silent.

"The completed work is impressive. I'll give a motorized ambulance proper deliberation as soon as all pertinent information has been provided," Maggie said. "We better get back to Mando, Uncle Max."

Garrett walked next to Maggie. "Your unfair admonishment of a potentially life-saving gift is ludicrous. This project has been very special to me, a chance to put my mark on Garfield."

Maggie stopped abruptly. "I appreciate your enthusiasm for Garfield's medical facility. You're a gifted carpenter. Please try to remember I own this town, not Uncle Max, or anyone else. Major decisions still come through me."

"I'll not forget that fact." Garrett said no more, his focus on controlling his anger. *Maggie might be right about remaining unattached. A strong-willed woman like her would make a difficult wife.*

Chapter 40

Garrett had been in Chicago for over three weeks. He hoped his future visits would only require a few days instead of weeks. Still, much was accomplished on this trip.

Since being at the helm of Hanley Construction, Garrett worked hard to reverse the negative expectations Rex had created for employees. Rex required excessive profits each month if workers wanted to keep their jobs. That meant they were forced to put in many more hours to meet demands but without extra pay. Far too many projects were scheduled for the number of laborers at the company.

During this visit, Garrett hired forty-two men for the construction crews, for a total of eighty-eight. He was confident he now had enough manpower for all his current contracts.

Garrett's father hired hard-working gentlemen over the years. Mr. Hanley's only error in judgment had been in his assessment of Rex. Thankfully, the rest of the labor force had been dependable and honest. Leaders at various jobsites made excellent decisions while delivering quality work.

Garrett had been staying in a hotel in downtown Chicago on Harrison Street. Now that all tasks were complete, he checked out of his room, walked a few blocks to Central Station, and bought a ticket to Hannibal, with a stop in St. Louis. Within the hour, Garrett boarded the train and found an empty bench near the rear of the car.

On the way to Chicago, Garrett had met with a quite remorseful Jesse. During their conversation, Jesse was certain he could win back Sadie's heart. He would be boarding Garrett's train today in St Louis to return to Garfield.

Garrett was eager to leave the city and get back to Garfield, while apprehensive about seeing Maggie. Their last conversation was when they'd toured the medical facility. Garrett still didn't understand such a harsh reaction to accepting a gift. He wasn't sure what to expect when he saw her next. Garrett had been praying often, so he hoped God would give him wisdom to choose the right words.

The movement of the wheels along the tracks almost always made Garrett fall asleep. His eyes were getting heavy, refusing to stay open. Since Garrett hadn't slept much while in Chicago, a chance to relax was welcome. He dozed off with his head resting against the bench, waking only when he heard a shouted announcement.

"Next stop, St. Louis."

Garrett stretched, then stood and walked to the train exit. There would be about two hours before the train would continue, allowing Garrett to get off to search for Jesse.

"Hanley, over here," Jesse shouted and waved his arm.

Garrett made his way to him. They shook hands.

"Good to see you, Jesse. I'm glad you've decided to come back to Garfield."

"I've been empty without Sadie. I'm rather worried she's taken away my ability to have fun. A life without cares used to be enough, but now bores me. Sadie could be right. A man might need to have purpose and goals to drive him to get up in the morning." Jesse frowned. "Although, sleeping until noontime does still hold some appeal."

"I can't remember the last time I slept past seven o'clock except those few days after Maggie tried to kill me."

Both men chuckled.

"Let's get some dinner before boarding the train. I don't know about you, but I'm hungry."

"Famished. I'm always ready to eat."

"There's a diner not too far from here that serves the best corned beef sandwiches. A water closet is nearby to take advantage of on the way. We should have plenty of time to eat and get back on the train before departure."

The men quickly hiked to the diner and ordered their food. The service was fast, having meals in front of them in just a few minutes. Garrett prayed before they devoured their corned beef sandwiches.

"Best sandwich by far, and I've eaten quite a few in my time," Jesse said as the men got up from the stools.

"Yes, always a favorite."

The men swiftly strode to the train, sitting down next to each other on a bench.

"I can't turn back now," Jesse said. "I hope Sadie can get past being mad at me. My mother is thrilled I'm going back to Garfield. She anticipates meeting Sadie soon. I hope to see that happen too."

"From what I've seen from Sadie, she's not one to hold grudges. Odds seem to be in your favor."

"Maybe the time has come to think like a husband. Pleasure has been hard to find since leaving Garfield. Sadie must be miserable without me. I'm sure she's open to reconciling."

"Sounds like you're the miserable one. Now prove yourself to Sadie. Be certain you've made the right choice in going back to Garfield."

"Prove myself? Sadie should realize how many sacrifices I'm making to be with someone in a lower class."

Garrett glared at Jesse. "Don't ever make Sadie feel she's less than you. Regard her as a treasure. Show respect. Otherwise, don't come back to Garfield with me."

"Sadie doesn't understand how lucky she is to be offered a privileged life. I bestow more than she'll ever get from another man."

Garrett shook his head. "Jesse Walker, you're not ready to be a husband, nor do you deserve Sophie. Best for you to stay in St. Louis.

"All aboard!"

"Those are some harsh words coming from a man who has no experience with matrimony. Rest assured I care about Sadie. My intensions are admirable. This trip to Garfield should answer questions about our compatibility."

"I've not been married but have seen a proper way to treat a lady. My father has been an excellent example."

"Garrett, I have parents who love each other. You worry too much. Let's go to Garfield to see how things unfold."

The train began to roll down the tracks. The movement, along with a full belly, made Garrett sleepy again. He relaxed and fell fast asleep.

Jesse opened his bag and pulled out one of the novels he had brought with him, Bram Stoker's *Dracula*, and began to read. He hoped a good book would make time pass faster. Unfortunately, he couldn't concentrate. Winning Sadie back was all he could think about.

After what seemed like an eternity, Jesse finally heard, "Next stop, Hannibal."

A rush of anticipation swept through Jesse with thoughts of soon seeing Sadie.

Garrett sat up straight and rubbed his eyes.

"Sleep well, Hanley?"

"Yes, I did," Garrett said as he stretched out his arms and legs. "I can't believe we're here already."

"Already? I read almost half a novel while you slept. Even with a book to distract me, I've been quite restless."

"I found the ride to be completely restful. Perhaps you should have relaxed and closed your eyes."

"I'm far too anxious to sleep, while optimistic about a favorable outcome of this visit. Sadie will be overcome with delight at a chance to reconcile."

"I'm not sure that should be your mindset. My encounters with the ladies of Garfield have proven they're strong in their decisions. Best to focus on showing Sadie how much you missed her rather than the other way around."

"She's lucky to get a second chance with a gentleman of wealth and education. Sadie Stoddard could do no better. For that matter, no woman could."

"Jesse, my optimism is fading. That attitude will not win Sadie back. Make her feel cherished, or you might head back to St. Louis before nightfall."

"Don't worry. I can be quite charming when needed."

Garrett shook his head. "I'm not confident of seeing a happy ending."

When the train had come to a complete stop, Garrett and Jesse gathered their bags and stepped onto the platform.

"Garrett. Over here."

Garrett looked in the direction of the familiar voice and saw Max.

"Glad you're back. Pleased to see you again too, Jesse. Garrett informed me of your arrival. Will you stay long?"

"I'm not sure. Depends on Sadie's attitude. Our last encounter was not good. I hope she's had time to gain some wisdom in my absence."

Max raised his eyebrows. "I hope you gained wisdom as well."

Jesse shrugged.

The men were soon on their way to Garfield.

"Max, are we set for supper tonight at Slumber and Vittles? Will everyone invited be there?" Garrett asked.

"Yes, although no one is aware Jesse's in town. How do you want me to handle your arrival, Jesse?"

"Let them know I'm here and would like to have a meal with them. They can find out more when we're all together. In the meantime, I plan to wait on Sadie's porch swing until she returns home from Mando. Sharing my intentions with her before anyone else is important. Besides, if she's not receptive, there's no need for a supper meeting."

Garrett asked to be dropped off at the medical building jobsite.

"Amazing," Jesse said. "That is a big building."

"So much has been accomplished in my absence. Thank you, Max, for the ride. See you both for supper. Best of luck, Jesse."

Hank hurried toward them when he heard the motorcar. "Nice to have you back, Garrett. Things are moving along."

"Glad to be back. Impressive work has been accomplished."

"Dr. Gibson is inside waiting to catch you up on everything."

"Excellent. Let's go talk with her."

Chapter 41

Max, Catherine, Maggie, Ruth, Annabelle, and Hank were already at the table when Garrett entered Slumber and Vittles restaurant. He was wearing a new suit purchased in Chicago, along with a sandalwood cologne his mother had given him. Garrett wanted to look and smell his best for Maggie and hoped she would notice.

"Hello everyone. It's great to be home," Garrett said.

Those in attendance shared welcomes.

With greetings over, Garrett moved to a chair next to Maggie. "Wonderful to see you, Maggie. I've missed you. You look exquisite. May I sit here?"

"Yes. Thanks for the kind compliment. Nice to have you back."

Maggie didn't look at Garrett, so he was sure she must still be be harboring some anger toward him from their last meeting. He'd deal with the situation soon. For now, he wanted focus on why they were all together tonight.

Garrett turned to the others. "Looks like I'm not the last to arrive, after all. Where are Jesse and Sadie?"

"They aren't late yet. Should be here soon," Max said.

"I hope Jesse was able to convince Sadie," Garrett said.

"Convince her of what?" Catherine asked.

Ruth and Hank looked at each other and shrugged.

"Why is Jesse with Sadie?" Annabelle asked. "Maybe I need to check on my sister."

"Here they come now," Garrett said.

Jesse and Sadie walked in, with her hand wrapped tightly around his arm. Garrett wondered how Jesse had gained such closeness from Sadie so quickly. After the way Jesse talked earlier today, Garrett did not expect a reconciliation.

"Hello, everyone. I apologize for our tardiness," Jesse said. "I needed to discuss some important matters with Sadie, which took a little longer than expected."

When Jesse and Sadie joined the rest of them at the supper table, Annabelle asked, "What important matters?"

Jesse looked at Annabelle and said, "Learning opportunities. Sadie thinks you'll be pleased."

Annabelle kept her worried gaze on Sadie.

"Tell us what's on your mind so we can get on with supper," Garrett said.

"I would like to bring education to Garfield. Maybe begin with a college for current residents. Eventually, when we have children," Jesse turned and grinned at Sadie, "we could open a school for them. Maybe some of the women would like to be teachers, and the college could train them."

"First a hospital and now a school. Garfield is becoming a place no one will want to leave," Ruth said.

"This town does need more to keep people entertained. Being a city man, I can bring ideas to liven things up," Jesse said.

"Do you plan to stay in Garfield, Mr. Walker? What are your intentions toward my sister?" Annabelle asked.

"Yes, living here is my desired path for now, with hopes of some modernizing. As for Sadie, I've asked her to be my bride."

Annabelle's mouth opened wide. "Sadie, I hope you did not accept a proposal from a man who merely weeks ago you deemed not ready for matrimony."

"I've missed Jesse very much. Establishing a college is a step in the right direction to show he accepts responsibility to take care of a wife."

"Absolutely not! As your sister, I won't allow you to make such a huge life decision without talking to me first."

"My sweet Annabelle, know I've spent many nights on my knees praying about Jesse. Don't worry, a courtship will happen before the wedding."

"We need to talk, just the two of us," Annabelle said. "Very soon. Tonight."

"I agree," Sadie said. "Jesse might become your bother-in-law, so your approval is imperative."

"Excuse me, Mr. Walker," Maggie said. "I won't deny educational opportunities excite me very much. From the looks on faces here, this idea seems to have seized their interests as well. However, before proceeding with anything of this magnitude, we need a formal evaluation of your proposal. Put together details, and we can schedule a meeting."

Jesse scowled. "A formal evaluation? Are you serious? I'm giving up my freedom to educate Garfield. You're preposterous to question my offer."

Sophie frowned at Jesse, but he didn't seem to notice.

"Absolutely not preposterous. You seem to have forgotten I own Garfield, which means I approve all changes. I will always consider the opinions and ideas of those living here because I want what's best for them. However, final decisions fall on my shoulders."

Jesse rolled his eyes.

Garrett felt like he was reliving their encounter at the medical facility. Maggie's declaration of power was unnerving.

"Miss Garfield, everyone here knows you own Garfield. Perhaps being open to new ideas could bring about positive changes," Garrett said.

Maggie glared at Garrett. "Changes are constant in Garfield. I embrace them, but always with proper consideration. As a business owner yourself, I would think you would understand this is necessary."

Garrett didn't want to have this discussion now in front of everyone. "Your point is valid, albeit, a bit rigid."

Maggie shook her head and looked at Jesse. "Mr. Walker, undoubtedly educational pursuits would be a tremendous amount of responsibility and hard work. Are you prepared for such an undertaking?"

Sadie's pleading eyes stayed on Jesse.

"If overseeing a college will make Sadie happy, I accept responsibility."

"You seem sincere about Sadie, but building an educational system will not succeed based merely on the love of a woman. Is this vocation a genuine desire?"

"Sadie, along with my parents, seem to think I have not lived up to my full potential. They believe life needs purpose to be fulfilling. This might be a way to appease them."

"I'm not convinced you're fully committed to such a responsibility but put together a proposal. Then we'll meet. Much should be contemplated before proceeding. No need to worry about children for a while. Our search for grooms has not gone as designed up to now."

Jesse put his arm around Sadie. "This lady is the inspiration for creating a school. I am passionate about education. Ask any of my professors. My scores have always been at the top of every class."

"Jesse, what if courting Sadie does not lead to marriage? Would you stay in Garfield to continue leading educational endeavors?" Maggie asked.

"No," Jesse answered. "Without Sadie, there's no reason to live here. But this courtship will end in marriage, no doubt."

"For now, focus your proposal on offering a few classes in an available room at Mando. We'll not plan for a formal college until things are more permanent with you," Maggie said.

"Likely our courtship will be short, so a few classes will be fine for now," Jesse said.

"My sister will be courted for as long as she requires, which could be a considerable amount of time," Annabelle said. "Or, shortly terminated, if need be."

"Sadie and I will decide the duration, with all due respect," Jesse said.

Annabelle looked heated.

"Oh, my goodness, Maggie, our advertisement for husbands does work. Looks like we have a connection on our first attempt. Will there be anyone else invited here?" Ruth said.

"A few gentlemen have corresponded with me. I think it's best to see how things work out with Garrett and Jesse for now. Obviously, Jesse's situation appears promising," Maggie said.

"I, too, have every reason to believe my outcome will be positive," Garrett said. *Unless Maggie continues to be controlling and bossy. I might need to help her see how unbecoming these traits are for a lady.*

"Jesse, what about your degree as a lawyer? Have you abandoned the desire to open a practice?" asked Ruth.

"I can still be available for any legal advice to the townsfolk. There doesn't seem to be much need for lawyers in Garfield." After a glance around the table, he continued. "Meanwhile, many of you might decide to be students at my new school."

"At *Garfield's* new school, *if* I decide to proceed with this endeavor," Maggie said.

"If we proceed, sign me up," Ruth said. "I've always wanted to learn more about the business world and how to be an excellent leader. Will you offer any courses to help me?"

"With your leadership skills, courses like those could be taught by you," Maggie said.

Ruth beamed with pride.

"Do you want to include culinary subjects? Maybe I could teach a class," Annabelle said.

"I'll be the only instructor for now. After you've passed a few classes, we can see if any of you qualify to be a teacher," Jesse said.

Annabelle and Ruth looked at each other with dejection showing on their faces.

"Talented ladies like both of you will make wonderful instructors," Maggie said.

"Possibly," Jesse said.

"Will your wedding take place in Garfield?" Catherine asked.

"Yes," Sadie said. "Jesse wants to contact his best friend, Benjamin Meier, who is a pastor, to inquire of his availability to officiate the ceremony."

"Wait a minute," Garrett said with a raised eyebrow. "You mean to tell me, Jesse Walker, that you, the one who burned down a barn, is best friends with a pastor?"

Jesse nodded in agreement. "Yes. For some unknown reason, we formed a close friendship. There's more to me than some people might think. To have Ben officiate my wedding would be special."

Annabelle shook her head. "Now is not the time to be planning for a wedding. You two have much to work out before you're ready for that."

Sadie held Annabelle's hand. "Rest assured there will be no wedding before we're absolutely certain the time is right."

Sadie looked at Maggie and Max. "Jesse would like to invite Pastor Meier here for a short stay."

"Having a pastor in town would be splendid," Max said. "Perhaps he could preach a sermon on a Sunday or two. What do you think, Maggie?"

"Lovely idea. Uncle Max, please make Mr. Jackson aware of Pastor Meier's invitation. Jesse, what can you tell us about your friend? What are his credentials?"

"We met while students at Transylvania University. As you already know, I studied law. Ben focused on ministry classes. We hit if off immediately, even though he would never join me in any questionable activities. I spent a lot of time with friends who, like me, enjoyed having a bit of fun. Ben kept me grounded as much as possible. I didn't appreciate his conservative nature at the time. Looking back, my best memories of that time were with Ben. He's smart, both in knowledge and common sense. He has a big heart too. Ben preaches often, filling in for other pastors, but doesn't have a congregation yet. This allows for a flexible schedule right now. Ben will absolutely adore Sadie. I can't imagine getting married without him. He'd like a small town like Garfield. Never cared much for big city life."

"Pastor Meier sounds like a wonderful man whom I hope we get to meet," Maggie said.

Jesse smiled wide with pride. "I'll write Ben tomorrow and see what can be arranged. He'll likely agree to preach. Ben will be surprised to know I'm getting married, especially to a lady like Sadie. He gives excellent advice. He counseled me about Sadie. Must have worked because she's giving me another chance."

"Has anyone noticed that Jesse has not mentioned being hungry for the entire thirty minutes we've been in Slumber and Vittles? Love does strange things to a man," Max said.

Laughter broke up the serious conversation.

"Oh, I'm always ready to eat. Let's order supper," Jesse said, waving to a server.

After making food selections, conversations filled the room.

"Maggie, can we talk about our last encounter? No one can hear us with everyone talking," Garrett said.

"There's nothing to discuss as my position must have been clear to you."

"Quite clear, but also misunderstood. I merely wanted to give a gift to Garfield that would have great meaning. The motorized ambulance was not meant to cause you any loss of control."

"For as long as we've known each other, you've never minced words about your view on women's abilities, which can be frustrating. Admittedly, I might have misunderstood your kind gesture as disregard for my authority. Until you can respect ladies' capabilities, there will likely be more disagreement between us."

"Let's agree on something. I'll work on changing my thoughts on competences of females, as well as choose words more wisely. Meanwhile, will you try not to jump to negative conclusions about my intentions? We should think better of each other."

Maggie nodded. "Yes, agreed. By the way, you smell nice and look handsome in that suit."

Garrett felt his heart melt. "I hoped you'd notice."

"I noticed. Ruth and Annabelle might have as well ... I hope."

Garrett ignored Maggie's comment. "One more thing. Please accept a motorized ambulance as a donation by the Hanley family. Allow this gift to honor my parents as well as Garfield."

Maggie closed her eyes seeming to be in deep thought or prayer. Garrett sat silent, waiting for her response.

Maggie opened her eyes. "In homage to your parents, thank you for this very generous gift."

"I'm pleased we're on good terms again. You're very important to me."

"Your friendship is important to me, as well, Garrett."

Friendship? For now ...

Chapter 42

Garrett knocked on the door to Maxwell Crawford's house. He was glad Levi's men had stopped following him, especially today, when privacy was needed. His hands were sweaty, heart racing, as Max opened the door.

"Hello, Garrett, what brings you all the way out here today?"

"Good morning, Max. My apologies for arriving without an invitation. I hope you aren't too busy to talk for a few minutes. There's something important on my mind."

Max crinkled his brow and stared at Garrett. "Important? Come in. We can go back to my library."

Garrett followed Max, as he led the way down the hall. The room was somewhat extravagant for a gentleman's room. Uniquely styled hats hung on the brightly painted red walls.

Max noticed Garrett's puzzled expression as he looked around the room.

"I was not in charge of decorations," Max said with a grin. "My wife is rather found of hats and the color red. I find her taste appalling, yet fascinating. Truthfully, the walls me think of Mrs. Crawford often throughout the day, which pleases me. Besides, the decor doesn't interfere with my research. Or writing. I've been fortunate to correspond and consult with car manufacturers such as Charles Duryea and Alexander Winton. We learn much from each other."

"Impressive. This explains more about your love of motorized vehicles."

Garrett smiled. He felt a yearning inside when thinking of sharing a home with a wife. He probably wouldn't mind a few hats on red walls for a love like the Crawfords seemed to share.

Max looked serious. "What's on your mind today, young man?"

Garrett sat up and cleared his throat. He looked down and prayed for courage, then gazed directly at Max.

"Sir, as you know, I have grown quite fond of Maggie."

Max grinned. "I might have noticed."

"Maggie obviously doesn't need anyone to care for her financially, but ... maybe a devoted partner could be nice."

"Who would be this devoted partner?"

"Uhm ... maybe *me*?"

Max raised his eyebrows. "I see."

"I don't need her money, because my company is doing well. I *do* need her heart and presence in my life. Max, a future without her is unimaginable."

Garrett raked his hands through his hair. "You're a father figure in Maggie's life, which is why I'm here. So ... um ...what I want to ask is for your blessing to ... ask her to marry me. I would only proceed with your approval."

Garrett took a breath and waited.

Max was silent for several minutes. "You say you need Maggie's heart and her presence. What about her needs? What can she expect to receive from you?"

Garrett was taken aback by the question as he realized how selfish he had been in his presentation to Max. "I ... uhm ... I hope to give her ... whatever she desires."

Max's stern face told Garrett he expected more. Garrett cleared his throat.

"Uhm ... she already has my heart. So ... if I'm ... honored enough to become her husband, I will do my very best to ... uhm ... always put her needs above my own."

Max's stern face was not getting any friendlier, so Garrett continued.

"And ... uhm ... sir ... I will try to make her smile and feel loved unconditionally. And ... uhm ... Together, we will put God first ... uhm ... above all else. Oh... and I will continue to build whatever she needs or wants in Garfield. And ... if we are so blessed ... I will ... uhm ... be a ... tender father who ... leads our children by example. I won't be a perfect husband but ... uhm ... will try my best to always make fair decisions. And, will be ... uhm ... honest and dependable, unlike the man I was when I first came to Garfield."

The room was silent when Garrett's voice faded. Max finally spoke.

"Do you love Maggie?"

"I do."

"I like you, Garrett. You're an honorable man who appears to have become a man of God. You and Maggie might match well. I feel certain she cares for you. However, Maggie would never leave Garfield. Do you view Garfield as a permanent home, long-term?"

Garrett was happy to hear Max thought so highly of him. And especially that Maggie might care for him.

"I have no intention to lure Maggie away from here. Garfield is home. My parents will be traveling for a couple of years, which leaves me with no family in Chicago. There are reliable men to oversee my company and day-to-day activities. I will need to take trips back there throughout the year but could be here most of the time."

Max stood and walked around the room. He turned back towards Garrett. "My dear son, Garrett, it is obvious to me that you want what's best for Maggie."

Garrett's hope rose when Max called him son.

"You absolutely have my blessing if—and this is a big if—she's agreeable, and you promise not to try taking her away. I hope you two can get together." Max paused. "I think her father would have wanted a man like you to be her husband."

Max's comments overwhelmed Garrett. "Thank you, Max. Your endorsement is extremely important to me, especially to hear Mr. Garfield would have approved."

"My approval might be important, but now for the hardest task—Maggie. She will not be as quick to agree as I have been. Maggie's quite adamant about never marrying."

"Yes, I know, Max. I plan to be persistent. I won't give up easily. Maggie's too important to me." Garrett paused. "Sir, can you provide any details as to why she has such a strong stance against matrimony?"

"Find out from Maggie. Her news to share, not mine."

"Thank you again, Max. I'll see myself out." Garrett exited the room.

Max smiled as Garrett made his way through the house and out the door.

Catherine stepped into the study. "Well?"

"Maggie might get her a husband, after all," Max said.

"Does Maggie know about this?"

"I think her heart knows, even if her mind fights the idea. Let's hope she comes around."

"Garrett Hanley might be the man who can win her over. He certainly seems to be a worthy opponent."

"He obviously has no idea how tough Maggie can be once she's made up her mind. Garrett might not have the stamina to remain in the fight for Maggie's heart."

Chapter 43

Garrett rode the motorbike down to Black Swan Lake after leaving Max's house. He followed a trail that eventually led away from the water into open field. Garrett's curiosity wanted to see where this path would lead. Maybe Hank's horse, Charley, or any number of the other horses could have created the route. Perhaps even Maggie's horse, Blaze.

The trail ended at what appeared to be a gravesite. Garrett got off the motorbike and walked closer. He read the names on the headstone, William and Amanda Garfield.

Maggie's parents' resting place.

Garrett turned to walk away, feeling intrusive. Then he stopped, realizing he had something important to do before leaving. Strolling in front of William's name, Garrett got down on his knees.

"Sir, you've never met me, but I want you to know Maggie will not be alone anymore if she'll have me as her husband. I want to take care of her, as you did while alive. Maxwell Crawford has given his blessing. Yours would have meant the world to me. Maggie's a special lady, as you already know. I wish I could have known you while you were here on earth, sir. I'm certain spending time in your presence would have been an honor. Thank you for the opportunity to introduce myself."

Garrett returned to the motorbike and was about to start the engine, when he heard gallops in the near distance. Blaze carried Maggie towards Garrett, who got off the bike to greet her.

Blaze stopped a few feet in front of Garrett. Then Maggie quickly jumped to the ground, running to where he stood.

"Hello, Maggie." Garrett smiled.

"Why are you here, Mr. Hanley?" Maggie asked, with hands on hips. "How did you find this place?"

Garrett shrugged. "I just followed a path. I haven't been here long. I was leaving but saw you and waited."

"You have no right to be here. How dare you treat my parents' graves like any old public place at your disposal. You must leave."

Garrett's eyebrows scrunched. "Hold on, Maggie. I'm an innocent man already being convicted. Your reprimand is unmerited. I did not come here to invade your privacy. Anyone could freely arrive here, no matter how unintentional."

Before she could speak, Garrett continued. "I wonder when you will start to think more highly of me rather than jump to negative conclusions about my character. I remember you said you would try but I've seen no evidence of that. Now, excuse me, and I will be on my way."

Garrett sat back down on the motorbike to take his leave.

"Wait, Garrett. Forgive me. I was startled to see you but should not have spoken in such a harsh way. Other than myself, only Uncle Max and Aunt Catherine have ever been here … at least, to my knowledge. Sharing this special place with anyone else is difficult."

Garrett got off the bike again. "I understand. These are your parents, and I should not have come. This was truly an innocent mistake."

Maggie bit her lip. "I'm certain you meant no harm. I come here at least once a week to talk with them, even if they can't speak back." She hesitated. "It might be nice if you want to stay for a few minutes."

Garrett was eager for the invitation. Perhaps a little progress with her, after all. "I would be honored."

Garrett wanted to take her in his arms and hug her tight, but knew such an action would not be appropriate. They shouldn't be out here alone. He wanted to make sure she felt safe with him.

"Maggie, my heart breaks to think about how much you must miss your parents. I don't want you to feel alone. There are many people who care about you."

Maggie nodded. "Yes, I'm humbled by the wonderful people God has brought into my life. Blessed beyond measure."

Garrett reached out and took Maggie's hand. He felt her wobble and helped her to the bench near the gravesite. "Are you all right?"

"I'm fine." She pulled her hand away as he sat next to her.

"Did you ever see Dr. Gibson? You do seem to lose your footing quite often."

Maggie shook her head. "I do not need a doctor. I was just startled to see someone out here. Besides, the long ride on Blaze probably took a little bit out of my step."

Garrett studied her for a moment. "Your color is better. I suppose you're fine now."

"Thanks for the analysis, Dr. Hanley. I'm glad you can see I have made a full recovery."

Garrett grinned. "Yes, I probably would have made a fine doctor."

Maggie shook her head. "You're hopeless. We've established I'm fine. What about you? What brings you out today?"

"I, like you, enjoy a long ride through the country. Only, I prefer two wheels while you fancy the four-legged type."

Maggie laughed. "Be glad about that fact. You don't like it when I'm in charge of a motorcar."

Garrett nodded. "Quite true. I'm delighted to hear you choose transportation that keeps cows, horses, and trees safe from any potential danger."

"I do what I can." They both laughed.

Garrett spoke again after a few minutes of silence. "Maggie, what do you talk to your parents about when you come here?"

Maggie thought for a moment. "I catch them up on what I've been up to. Ask for advice. Remind them how much they're loved and missed. Even though there's no response, I always come away with wisdom."

"Why aren't you open to the idea of marriage?"

"We've already discussed this, Garrett."

"I still don't understand."

A tear rolled out of her eye. "Sorry. I tend to cry out here."

Garrett wiped her cheek with his thumb. "You don't always have to be so strong. I'm extremely fortunate to have never lost a parent. I wish you had not endured that pain."

More tears flowed. "Do you remember how my mother died?"

Garrett shook his head. "Yes. You shared with me she died giving birth."

"Mama and Papa wanted children very much. Mama lost three babies before the little ones were ready to be born. I'm not sure God's plan was for her to be a mother, but Mama never gave up. Sadly, neither did I, which left my father to rear me alone." Maggie closed her eyes and a few more tears fell out.

Garrett took her hand into his. "Your father honored her well by raising a beautiful daughter, inside and out."

"My father had to lose Mother to give me life—not a fair trade."

Maggie got up and walked over to the headstone. "I'm sorry, Papa."

Garrett made his way to stand beside her.

"Father adored my mother more than anything. They had a wonderful love story and marriage. Do you know why the company is named Mando Merchandising?" Maggie said.

"No, I don't. An interesting name, though."

"My mother's name was Amanda. My father affectionately referred to her as Mando. She was his everything." Maggie wiped her eyes again. "And I took her away from him."

"No, Maggie. You didn't. That wasn't your fault."

"Why did God allow me to be born? I've heard she was an amazing person. And those who knew my parents said they were perfect together."

"Maggie, you can't blame yourself. If your mother and father were here, I know they would tell you the same."

"No, Garrett, I caused her death. I heard Papa was devastated after he lost Mama. He did everything he could to keep her spirit alive. She's the reason Papa built Garfield for orphaned women. Since he couldn't take care of Mama, he would at least help other ladies who were in need."

"Your father sounds like a wonderful man, and you are an amazing lady, but don't try to carry this guilt. I never met your parents but am certain they would agree. You make such a difference in so many lives. Your parents would be incredibly proud."

Maggie looked down at the ground. "I try to make them proud. But, proud or not, they're one of the reasons I will never marry. Those precious years of matrimony were stolen from them. I have no right to the wedded bliss they deserved.

"Maggie, you must know you're not meant to bear such a burden. Did you ever express these feelings with your father?"

"Only after he died. Father would have felt obligated to forgive me. I didn't deserve his exoneration."

Garrett took her hand and led her back to the bench. "You must let go. God forgives us for everything while loving us unconditionally. Forgive yourself, Maggie. You cannot serve him well if you let unmerited burdens guide your life."

"I've tried to find ways to use my circumstances for his good. At the very least, I'll do my best to complete Papa's work, even with flaws and mistakes."

"I promise to pray for God to release you of guilt."

"Thanks, Garrett. But I'm willing to carry this to my grave."

"I plan to do everything in my power to convince you otherwise." Garrett paused. "May I share something important with you, Maggie?"

Maggie bit her lip. "Yes, of course."

"I went to see your Uncle Max today. I think God led me out here to see your father too. I was able to speak to both important men in your life."

"What did you talk to them about? Why do you feel God led you here?"

"I asked Max if I could marry you."

Maggie gasped.

"I shared my desires with your father too."

"As we have discussed many times, marriage is impossible for me. In addition to the burden for my parents, I feel God has called me to be single. *I don't want to be married*. My mission is to find suitable husbands for the ladies who want to start families. My priority is them, not me. My mind will not change."

"Perhaps your reasons are true for now. I'll wait for you and God's timing, no matter how long that might be. Max gave his blessing. He told me he thinks your father would have approved, also."

"I cannot marry anyone regardless of any blessings."

"I love you, Maggie. I think you might feel the same about me."

Maggie opened her mouth, but no words came.

"Don't worry. You've made it clear the other ladies come first. I'll ask you to be my wife only when the time is right. You're worth waiting for. Just promise me you'll open your heart. Ask for God's peace. He'll clearly show you if we're meant to be together. I believe he's still in the process of preparing us for each other."

"Or preparing you for someone else."

"God's will be done." Garrett stood. "I'll leave you alone to have time with your parents."

Chapter 44

"I do *not* enjoy fishing, nor going anywhere at this unreasonable hour of the morning," Jesse said with a jaw-breaking yawn. "A sensible idea would be to meet your sister for an afternoon tea or a meal. Undoubtedly Annabelle would prefer a more civilized jaunt. As for Hank, he can fish all morning alone. I'm not entirely sure why Hank is involved in this 'family outing.'"

Sadie's glare left no uncertainty about who would win this battle.

"Hank is like a big brother. I want the two of you to be friends. Annabelle and Hank both have extremely busy schedules but managed to arrange this morning's excursion to spend time with us. Sacrificing a little sleep is not asking much considering Annabelle will be your sister-in-law. She is my only family. I would think you'd like to get to know her much better."

"*I'll* be your family soon. Annabelle needs to understand things will be different after you become Mrs. Jesse Walker. She should want to form her own family."

Sadie frowned. "You're being unreasonable. I would hope marrying you does not require giving up my sister. Annabelle will always be a big part of our family."

"I'm too tired to argue. Let's just get today over with. There's Hank and Annabelle now."

"Good to see you Jesse ... Annabelle." Hank said. "I don't usually get many folks to join me before six o'clock when fish are biting good. I've never had any ladies want to come along. Makes me proud to see a couple of my girls give fishing a try."

"Seems like fish might be more awake after noontime. No one should be up this early," Jesse said.

Hank laughed. "Now is best if you want to catch a lot of fish in a short amount of time. Do you fish much, Jesse?"

"Not if I can avoid it."

"Might change your mind after today. Come on everyone."

The four of them strolled to the edge of the lake along with a quacking duck wobbling to get to her ducklings.

"Ladies first," Hank said. He baited the line on a pole for Sadie, then cast it into the water. "All you have to do is holler for me if you feel a tug. Hold on tight until I can get here."

"Will I be strong enough? How big of a tug?"

Hank smiled. "You'll be able to handle it. Besides, I'll be right here as soon as I hear your call."

"This should be interesting," Sadie said.

"You're next, Annabelle." Hank baited her line.

"I want to throw it myself. I paid real close attention when you were helping Sadie."

Hank raised an eyebrow. "Are you sure? Casting a line can be tricky."

"I'm a quick learner. Just give that ... what did you call it?"

"This is a rod."

"Please give me that rod." Annabelle held out her hands.

Hank reluctantly handed the rod to Annabelle, then stood still to observe.

"Go get after those fish waiting to be caught. It's nerve-wracking having you watch."

Hank didn't move. Annabelle flapped her hands to shoo him away. "Go. I can do this."

"I'll be close by if you need anything."

"Yes, I heard you tell Sadie that very fact. Now go."

Hank reluctantly walked over to Jesse. "Need help to get started?"

"No. I'll just relax a while."

"Up to you."

Jesse laid his head on a rolled-up blanket and fell asleep.

Annabelle flung the bamboo rod behind her, then whipped it forward, sending the silk line high into the air, landing just shy of the water.

Sadie laughed. "Might be harder than it looks, huh, sister?"

"Just takes some practice. I want to see if I can throw this line out as far as Hank did. Watch this, Sadie."

"Might be best to let Hank get that thing into the water. We can sit and wait as Hank suggested."

Annabelle reeled in the line. Then repeated her casting routine. This time the baited line landed into the lake, albeit after wrapping around a tree branch.

"Right in the water! I knew I could do this. Fishing isn't so hard. You should try this, Sadie."

"What are you planning to do about all that string wrapped around that big old tree?" Sadie asked.

Annabelle twisted her mouth, appearing to be in deep thought. Then she climbed onto the unsteady branch that was holding her tangled line. Just as Annabelle was making progress with freeing the tangled mess, the line was being pulled by what must be the only whale in Black Swan Lake. She probably regretted her dedication as she found herself splashing into the lake below, still holding on to the unreliable twig, as well as the fishing line. Annabelle's head resurfaced when she stood in water up to her shoulder.

"Help! Jesse. Hank. Annabelle fell in the lake," Sophie yelled.

Jesse remained sleeping, but Hank hurried over.

"Annabelle, here, grab my hand," Hank said as he ran into the water to save her.

"No, Hank, you're scaring my fish. Go away. I don't want anything to make me lose this big boy."

Hank immediately stopped his pursuit as he waited in the water, watching to make sure Annabelle wasn't about to drown.

Annabelle held her arms up, feverishly pulling and wrapping line around the branch, happy to see this twig had become valuable, after all.

"Annabelle, let me help you," Hank said as he waded towards her.

"Don't you dare come any closer, Hank Rothstadt. This is my first caught fish. I'm determined to bring it out of this lake."

Annabelle continued wrapping the line until she screamed.

Hank raced through the water, making his way to Annabelle's side in no time. He wrapped his long arm around her waist, then started pulling her towards the shore.

"Hank! Stop this very minute. Look! Look! Look what I have!"

He stopped and looked, letting her go. Annabelle was smiling with pride as she held up a crappie that could not have been more than six inches long.

"You need to throw that fish back in the lake. Way too small to keep."

"I will not throw my fish back into the lake. This big guy is coming home with me. I think he'll make a mighty fine supper."

"You better add some of your scrumptious cornbread, as well as potatoes and beans, if you want to have enough for your supper."

Hank stepped up onto the shore, holding out his hand to Annabelle, then helping her out of the lake.

"I'm certain this fish will be enough for me, but the day is just starting. I plan to catch several more."

"Considering we're both soaking wet and likely scared all the fish away, we should probably head back home."

Sophie was laughing so hard she snorted. Soon Hank and Annabelle were laughing too. All three of them laid on the ground until they finally composed themselves.

"I brought a blanket to sit on. Here you go, Annabelle. Use it to dry off."

Sophie pulled the blanket out from under Jesse's head and handed it to Annabelle. Jesse barely moved, never waking even though his head was now laying on a rock.

Sophie wrapped the blanket around Annabelle and sat next to her.

"Thank you. I must be a sight with my wet hair and clothes."

A dripping Hank leaned down to face Annabelle. "Are you hurt?"

"No, just wet. Don't let my fish go. I mean it, Hank. As soon as I warm up, there will be more just like him in my bag."

Hank shivered.

"I'm more than willing to share this blanket, Hank. Come on over here," Annabelle said.

Hank sat down on the other side of Annabelle and pulled some of the blanket around him.

"Fishing is so much fun. Why haven't you taken me before today?" Annabelle asked.

Hank raised his eyebrow. "Can't say a lady has ever shown interest. Besides, look what happened. You're soaking wet. You could have drowned out there. I'd never forgive myself if that happened."

"The water was not deep enough for me to drown, Hank. Besides, I'm a good swimmer. No need to worry."

Jesse sat up, rubbing his head. "Has anyone heard fishing is best when it's quiet?"

Sophie glared at Jesse. "Our time out here was supposed to be a chance for you to get to know Hank and Annabelle better, not for sleep."

"Why are you two so wet? Kind of chilly to be swimming," Jesse said.

"Annabelle fell in the lake. Hank gallantly jumped in to save her while you snored, missing all the fun."

"I didn't need saving. My fish did. So sorry for getting you wet, Hank. Quite gallant of you to look after me," Annabelle said with a twinkle in her eye.

"You certainly gave me a fright. Better not climb trees and hang on any branches again." Hank looked down. "We should get you home before you catch a cold."

"Yes, going home is a sound idea." Jesse stood. "Come on, Sophie."

"But I want to catch some more fish," Annabelle said between chattering teeth.

"I promise to bring you again," Hank said. "Right now, dry clothes are a priority. You're freezing."

Hank helped Annabelle up.

"Tomorrow?"

Hank nodded. "Tomorrow ... but only if you stay out of trees."

"Promise."

Chapter 45

Pastor Meier had preached every Sunday for three weeks, with only a few days left until Jesse and Sadie's wedding. Townsfolk were chattering about being blessed to have a consistent voice in the pulpit, especially such a godly one.

When today's service ended, Max stood. "I hope you won't mind, Pastor. Would everyone stay for just a few minutes?"

The crowd remained seated as Max walked up front, then stood behind the pulpit next to Pastor Meier. Max put his arm around Pastor's shoulders, while scanning the crowd's smiles.

"Thank you, everyone, for your attention. I smell delectable food in the next room, so this will be brief."

Max turned to face Pastor Meier. "Pastor, I've spoken with several members of our community. You've brought new life to Sunday services with inspirational sermons, as well as kind deeds. Garfield is a small town right now, but growing. We want you to be where God directs, selfishly, hoping His path leads here. Our congregation took a vote. By a unanimous decision, we would like to ask you to become our permanent Pastor."

Everyone shared their agreement at once.

"When the room quieted, Max continued. "We know you will want to pray about this before giving an answer.

Take what time is needed to prayerfully decide. We'll continue praying as well."

Pastor Meier shook his head in disbelief. "I'm quite humbled by this offer. And must confess to have already spent time in prayer about God's will for an opportunity to be your pastor. I've felt at home here since arriving. God has been gracious to lead me to Garfield. I would be honored to be Garfield's pastor."

The townsfolk stood while clapping.

"As you can see and hear," Max said, "we are beyond thrilled.

Max shook Pastor Meier's hand.

"Let's not forget about our special wedding next Saturday at two o'clock," Pastor Meier said. "A wonderful celebration with Jesse Walker and Sadie Stoddard. Now let me pray over the awaiting food so we can eat.

"Dear Heavenly Father, thank you for this wonderful opportunity you've bestowed. I pray I will never get in the way of your good works here in Garfield. Use me, as well as our congregation, in mighty ways to complete your will for each of us. Thank you for this food you have provided and the special hands that prepared it. In Jesus's name, I pray. Amen. With that order of business taken care of, let's be dismissed to eat."

Everyone took turns congratulating and thanking Pastor Meier before going into the adjoining room to eat dinner.

Maggie was overwhelmed with happiness as she sat down by Ruth, Annabelle, and Hank. She thought about how wonderful God had been to bring Jesse and Pastor Meier to Garfield.

Garrett walked up next to Maggie. "Mind if I join all of you?"

Maggie instantly felt warmer as he brushed against her arm.

Hank looked up. "You don't need a formal invitation."

Garrett grinned as he sat down. "Wonderful. Can't think of better company. How is everyone?"

"We've been blessed with an amazing week," Annabelle said.

"Made even better by gaining a new pastor," Ruth said.

"Annabelle caught eight fish yesterday," Hank announced.

"They were all big enough to keep too." Annabelle beamed with pride.

"Did you know Pastor Meier is unattached, with no special lady in his life?" Garrett asked.

Ruth looked up. "How do you know?"

"Because I asked him. Thought the ladies would be glad to know there's an eligible bachelor in our midst. There might be someone who would find Pastor to be an admirable choice for a husband."

"Pastor Meier just moved here. No need to infringe on his private life when we barely know him," Maggie said. "Let's not get ahead of ourselves, Garrett."

"Well, regardless, I was sure the information needed to be released in case of any interested ladies. Have you found other potential grooms for Garfield, Maggie?"

"There are a few unopened letters I've received. Maybe the time has come to invite more gentlemen here. Some additional ladies have shown interest since Jesse and Sadie got betrothed."

Pastor Meier walked up to their table. "May I sit with you?"

"Please do, Pastor Meier," Garrett said.

"We'd love the pleasure of your company," Ruth said, uncharacteristically showing a bit of nervousness.

Pastor Meier sat down. Maggie noticed Ruth stared at him with a look of enchantment. Ruth rarely smiled, but her grin couldn't get any larger right now. Maggie could see Garrett had created a potentially uncomfortable situation. She hoped Pastor Meier hadn't noticed.

"I'm thankful for these Sunday dinners. In addition to tasting so delightful, they're a nice way to get to know everyone. Since we're family now, please call me Benjamin. Pastor Meier just seems too formal. Some people call me Pastor Ben when they feel less comfortable with Benjamin. I like both."

"Pastor Ben, did you know Miss Ruth Calvin is the main supervisor at Mando Merchandising?" Garrett asked. "She's excellent with organization. Perhaps she could help you settle in. If you can find the time, Miss Calvin."

"I'd be honored to offer any assistance. Just let me know what you need."

"Thank you, Miss Calvin. I'll keep that in mind and greatly appreciate the offer."

Pastor Ben looked around the room, "The people of Garfield are the best I've met, many with servants' hearts. I can see you're no exception, Miss Calvin."

Ruth's face turned a soft shade of pink as she looked down with a smile.

"I want to stop by each table today. Better move on before folks start leaving. Thanks for the visit," Pastor Ben said as he stood and walked away.

Ruth kept her eyes on him until he was out of sight. Maggie hoped there would not be any hearts broken because Garrett was apparently playing matchmaker again.

"Only six days until our first wedding in Garfield," Ruth said. "I'm thankful Jesse turned out to be the perfect match for Sadie. Such excitement awaits us."

"Sadie will be a beautiful bride, I'm sure." Annabelle said, "Perfect is a strong word that only Jesus deserves. Jesse is far from perfect. Sadie seems to adore him, so I'll learn to see the best in Jesse too."

"None of us are perfect, but apparently capable of finding a perfect match," Maggie said.

"This is the first of many successful pairings, I'm sure. I wonder who will be next," Garrett said.

"I'll go through any letters from potential grooms in the next day or two," Maggie said. "Perhaps we'll find other suitable gentlemen for our ladies."

"Maggie, what about Garrett? He's an honorable man who deserves a bride. What do you plan to do about him?" Annabelle said.

"Yes, Maggie, what are your plans for me?"

Maggie was at a loss for words. She felt all eyes on her from all four of them: Ruth, Annabelle, Hank, *and* Garrett. She stared down at the table and tried to come up with a response. What *would* she do with Garrett?

Maggie looked up. "As we all know, Garrett is a grown man who can court one of our ladies or remain a bachelor. That's up to him."

"Hmmm ... Up to me?" Garrett asked.

Maggie was just about to respond when Annabelle spoke up. "I don't mean to get into your private affairs, but it's obvious you and Garrett might be well suited. We all see it."

"Yes, I agree," Ruth said.

"As do I," Garrett said.

Maggie could feel the heat rising on her face.

"Garrett and I are friends, nothing more. As I've said many times, I'm not looking for a husband. My priority is to help you ladies find suitable matches."

Garrett batted his eyes as he stared at Maggie. "We are *very* good friends, right?"

Maggie stood. "I must leave now as there is an issue that needs my attention."

Her words faded as she walked away.

Chapter 46

Garrett turned the knob on the doorbell to Maggie's house. After a few moments, Emma opened the door.

"Good evening, Mr. Hanley. What a pleasure to see you. What brings you here? I don't believe Maggie is expecting you. We were just about to sit down to supper."

"I apologize for arriving unannounced. Would you mind asking Maggie to see me for a short visit? I promise not to stay long. Or I could return for a scheduled visit at another time if that would be best."

"Come on in. You can wait in the library while I check with Miss Garfield. Our parlor is being renovated."

Garrett followed Emma to a davenport, then sat down, watching her leave the room.

Hundreds of books lined a wall. Garrett wondered how many of them Maggie had read. He imagined quite a few.

The grandfather clock brought a methodical sound to an otherwise silent room. "Tick tock. Tick tock. Tick tock," said the clock repeatedly while Garrett waited.

Garrett rose to study a large portrait hanging on the wall of what appeared to be a family of three. The man looked strong, yet kind, with his hand resting on a lovely lady's shoulder. She cuddled a baby. The lady's face was striking, looking just like Maggie. Garrett wondered who this man was with her? Did Maggie have a baby? Then Garrett understood.

No. Not Maggie. Mrs. Walker. The baby is Maggie. What a captivating family.

Emma strolled into the room. "Have you eaten, Mr. Hanley?"

"No, but I plan to stop by Slumber and Vittles before retiring to my room at the boardinghouse."

"You must dine with us. Maggie insists."

"Thank you for your gracious offer. I don't mean to impose."

"Nonsense. Please follow me to the dining room."

Maggie was already sitting at the long table when Garrett walked in. Three places were set.

"Hello, Garrett. Please join us for supper. We're having cream of potato soup, along with cheese and fruit."

"If you'd like something heartier, we have some ham," Emma said.

"Potato soup sounds excellent. My mom used to make that. Haven't had any in quite some time."

Garrett and Emma sat down on opposite sides of Maggie, who was seated at the head of the table.

"Would it be all right if I pray?" Garrett asked.

"Yes. That would be lovely," Maggie said.

"Dearest Lord, we're grateful for your provisions, as well as your peace that passes understanding. Thank you for the meal we're about to eat. We pray we bring you glory in all we do. Amen."

"Emma makes excellent soup. Nothing like it on a cool fall evening."

Garrett ate a spoonful of soup. "This is as good as my mother's, but please don't tell her I said that, Emma."

"I've always said the highest compliment is when a gentleman says I cook like his mother. Don't worry. I won't tell Mrs. Hanley, especially since she's out of the country."

"Garrett, what brings you here? Something on your mind?" Maggie asked.

"Yes. Perhaps it can wait until after we're done eating. The soup has captured my attention."

"I can understand. Think of how spoiled I've been over the years with Emma taking such good care of me."

Emma smiled. "I can't think of anyone else I'd like to spoil more."

After supper, the three of them went back to the library. Emma sat at a desk in the far corner working on her nightly letters, while Garrett and Maggie settled into two chairs across from one another.

"Is that a picture of your parents and you?" Garrett asked, pointing to the portrait he had seen earlier.

Maggie looked at the picture. "Yes, sort of. As you know, Mother died giving birth to me. Father wanted a family picture, so he paid an artist to add me to this existing painting. This is my most treasured possession."

"You look exactly like your mother. She was certainly pretty."

"Those who knew her have said we have a resemblance. That makes me very happy because I feel more a part of her. Mother was much more sophisticated in her beauty."

"I'm honored to be allowed to see such a charming family."

"What did you want to discuss?"

"Have you been praying about us?"

"Yes. Have you?"

Garrett nodded. "Have you gained any clarification?"

"I have."

"Will you share this with me?"

"Garrett, I already have, many times. You're an incredible man. I've enjoyed our friendship more than you'll probably ever know. My hope is for both of us to be happy. For me, right now, God has called me into singleness. I'm content with my life. The peace he has given me is undeniable. What has God shown you through your prayers?"

"My answer might come as a surprise. I'm in agreement. As much as I adore you, I can finally clearly see we're not meant to be together. I was pushing you, but you never budged. I was being unfair to both of us by trying to make you see things my way. I can't say I feel called to be single. However, I'm not ready to be married yet, especially to any of the strong ladies of Garfield. My ideas about women's roles are very different from the realities of this town. God still needs to work on me."

"When did you discover this?"

"Maybe I've always known, but my eyes were on me instead of God. I must apologize for not listening to you or to him. Tonight is when I finally knew without a doubt." Garrett paused. "Maggie, did you notice how easy our time together has been this evening?"

"Yes. There wasn't our usual tension."

"Exactly. When I finally gave us to God, the conflict in my heart went away. I, too, feel complete peace about us."

"Will you stay in Garfield?"

"That's something I wanted to discuss. After the wedding, I'll go back to Chicago, at least for a while. One of the crew leaders at Hanley Construction, Mr. Brady Quenzer, will come to Garfield to oversee completion of the medical facility. I'll make a few trips back as well to make sure Garfield has a hospital to be proud of. In the future, God might lead me back to Garfield. I just need a little distance for now."

"I understand," Maggie assured him. "Please know, you'll be missed by everyone. We must always go where God leads us."

"Yes. Even though I came here in a deceptive way, I'm certain God led me to Garfield. I'd stopped praying when my father left. Maggie, you inspired me to get back in touch with God. I have more peace now than I've ever had. Thank you for pushing me to be a better man."

"I didn't do anything. God did."

"Your walk with God inspires me. I plan to spend the rest of my life living for him."

"I'm so proud of you, Garrett. God must be too. Please stay in touch. If I get correspondence from you, I promise to believe you're the author."

Chapter 47

Saturday, the twelfth of November—Garfield's first wedding was about to begin, with most of the townsfolk in attendance. Maggie sat on the front pew as Sadie's honorary mother for today's ceremony. Maggie wasn't much older than Sadie, but she was delighted to be asked.

Jesse's parents had been in town for over a week. Mrs. Walker's fingers gave a stunning voice to the lonely piano that sat for years waiting for someone to help it sing. Music made the sanctuary seem to dance with excitement.

Pastor Ben stood in front looking down at his Bible. Maggie's heart skipped a beat when Garrett and Hank joined Pastor Ben, both looking handsome in their suits. Maggie wondered if Jesse might have slept in. Late as usual.

Pastor Ben motioned for Mrs. Walker to stop playing.

"Welcome to this joyous occasion of uniting in matrimony a special couple loved by everyone in attendance. Please stand for our bride to enter."

Mrs. Walker again magically filled the room with enchantment, playing, "Here Comes the Bride."

Everyone stood, then turned to watch Sadie Stoddard walk down the aisle. But wait ... this wasn't Sadie.

Gasps could be heard above the music, with stunned looks on all faces.

Annabelle Stoddard, fully dressed in bridal attire, held onto Max's arm, not seeming to notice anyone else was in the room, as she stared straight ahead at ...

Maggie turned to see who the recipient of this beautiful bride could be. *Garrett? No, he was leaving ... Pastor Ben? No, barely knows her... Not Hank? Oh my goodness! Hank?*

When Annabelle finally made it to her groom, Maggie saw a tear roll down Hank's cheek.

Along with almost everyone else, Maggie continued to be confused. *Annabelle is marrying Hank? Wait, where is Sadie? Oh my, where is Jesse?*

The music stopped, and Pastor Ben began to speak. "Although Annabelle is not the Miss Stoddard everyone anticipated to marry today, let's continue with the wedding at hand between Miss *Annabelle* Stoddard and Mr. Hank Rothstadt. Please be seated. Hank would like to share a few words.

Hank turned to face the crowd. "Surprise!"

Those in attendance spoke at once. Pastor Ben motioned for silence.

Hank rubbed his mustache. "Friends, thanks for coming today. Sorry we aren't who you expected. But ... Uh ... I lo ... love Annabelle very much." Hank rubbed his mustache again. "Gosh ... likely for a long time, even though I only recently realized this fact. Probably what's even harder to believe ... is ... Annabelle loves me too."

Annabelle looked up at Hank with a smile, nodding. The audience cheered.

Annabelle turned to the crowd, waving for silence. "Hank is a marvelous man. Of course, all of you know that. He has been adored by each of us for a long time. I've had the honor of spending a lot of time with Hank lately, even fishing."

Laughter filled the room.

"When parting ways became difficult, with my thoughts remaining on him, I knew Hank was the man for me. Friendship was replaced by a strong love. I began to hope we would marry one day. Apparently, God granted that desire sooner than any of us realized was possible."

Sadie walked down the aisle, and stood next to Annabelle. The crowd looked nervous, as did Sadie.

"Today belongs to my sister and Hank, so please don't allow me to take away from that. Annabelle asked me to speak briefly since all of you care so much about us. Jesse and I decided we were not well-suited. We care about each other a great deal, but both of us feel marriage is not God's intended path. However, God *has* decided marriage is right for Annabelle and Hank."

Sadie turned to Mrs. Walker. "Thank you to Jesse's wonderful mother for playing such beautiful music for Hank and Annabelle. Such a selfless gift. Now, please, everyone, enjoy the wedding of my dear sister, Annabelle, and our wonderful Hank, my soon to be real brother."

Sadie sat down next to Maggie, who grabbed her hand.

"You are so brave and look absolutely stunning," Maggie whispered.

"Thank you," Sadie whispered back.

Pastor Ben stepped forward. "Let's continue with our ceremony as I'm sure Hank and Annabelle are anxious to wed."

Maggie was still trying to comprehend what was happening as the vows were given. Hank and Annabelle looked at each other with tender admiration, both with wide smiles.

How did I miss this? How did all of Garfield miss this? Maggie thought of Garrett. *He didn't miss this. Maybe Garrett is the true matchmaker, much more intuitive than the rest of us. I'm going to miss him—aggravating though he was too often.*

Pastor Ben said a prayer over the couple, then proclaimed, "I now pronounce you husband and wife. Friends, allow me to introduce Mr. and Mrs. Hank Rothstadt."

Everyone clapped and cheered.

"Mr. and Mrs. Rothstadt would like each of you to join them next door for refreshments."

Pastor Ben led the way with the new couple following close behind.

Maggie turned to hug Sadie. "Your dress is a perfect shade of blush. Makes your green eyes look like emeralds. How are you?"

"I'm doing very well. I'm sorry to disappoint you by not marrying Jesse. He's in Hannibal waiting for his parents to go back to St. Louis."

"Sweet Sadie, I'm not disappointed in you. Not all courtships end in marriage. Thankfully, the ladies of Garfield have choices. You certainly gave Jesse a fair chance. More importantly, you're strong enough to walk away when things aren't right. I'm proud of you.

"I feel bad to have not succeeded in your plan to find grooms for Garfield."

"I would say we've done quite well. Bringing in Garrett and Jesse might have helped Hank to gain enough courage to pursue Annabelle. God's plan is always better than mine. If more gentlemen are brought to Garfield, there will likely be more broken courtships along with successful pairings. Spending time with each other is how couples determine if they should be together."

"Maggie, I'm thankful for you."

"And I, you." Maggie gave Sadie a hug.

"Can I get in on this?" Mrs. Walker asked, before embracing Sadie.

"Oh, Mrs. Walker, words cannot express the gratitude I feel for you for playing the piano after what Jesse and I put you through."

"Sadie, I have lived with my Jesse for twenty-three years. I was optimistic, but he's not ready to be married, especially to an amazing girl like you. One day he'll grow up, I hope. As much as I wanted a daughter-in-law, you made the right choice by not marrying Jesse. I will continue to pray for both of you. I love you, dear."

"And I adore you. Thank you, Mrs. Walker. I hope to see you again."

Mrs. Walker wrapped her hand around Mr. Walker's arm, then they exited the church.

"Let's go celebrate with Annabelle. She's probably wondering where you are," Maggie said.

Annabelle hurried to Sadie and Maggie as soon as they stepped into the room. "Sadie, how are you doing? Are you sure Hank and I marrying on your day is what you wanted?"

"This is your day now and I couldn't be happier. My heart is full. There's no better man than Hank."

"I can't help feeling bad about your broken engagement. Hank said you can stay with us if you'd like."

Sadie laughed. "Outlandish! Newlyweds need time alone to get to know each other, take time to create a home. Honestly, Annabelle, I'm fine. Better than fine. I love you, Sister. Now, go be with your new husband."

After hugging Sadie, Annabelle embraced Maggie.

"When did you decide to get married?" Maggie asked.

"About an hour before the wedding," Annabelle said with a big smile.

"God works in mysterious ways. Congratulations. You are so beautiful. How did you manage to borrow such an exquisite gown that fits you so perfectly?" Maggie said.

"Do you remember when Ruth and I had fittings with Sophie?"

"Yes."

"I was embarrassed to say at the time, but I was purchasing this wedding gown ... just in case."

"Sounds like a wise decision. You have wonderful taste because I've never seen you look lovelier. All the lace is very feminine, making you look so elegant."

Maggie looked closer. "Is that lace actually an apron over your dress?"

"Yes. Sophie wanted my love of cooking to be represented in my gown, so she made the most delightful lacey apron for me to wear." Annabelle turned. "Not to mention this magnificent bow tied around my back to keep the apron attached."

"Sophie thinks like no other when it comes to our attire. I love that about her."

"Yes, and by making the lace a removable apron, I have a versatile dress to wear beyond today, plus an apron to dress up any other plain old dress in my closet."

"You certainly do. Apron or no apron, you look gorgeous today."

Hank joined them. "Couldn't agree more. Mrs. Rothstadt is always beautiful, just extra special today. I'm a lucky man."

"Yes, you are," Sadie said. "Welcome to the family. Now my official brother ... in-law ... the first groom for Garfield. And we didn't have to send for you through the mail."

Garrett spoke from behind them. "I wonder who the second groom with be? And who will be the lovely bride next time?"

About the Author

RONDA SIMPSON grew up on a farm in Kansas and spent her childhood summers writing stories full of her own imagination, dreaming of being published one day. Ronda's childhood "claim-to-fame" was a Christmas play she wrote in fifth grade which was presented to the students.

Many years later, Ronda is debuting her inspirational historical fiction romance novel, *To Steal Maggie's Heart*, the first in a series, Mail-Order Grooms for Garfield. Ronda is drawn to books and history about the gilded age, and especially those which bring glory to God.

Ronda was a corporate trainer for thirty years and cherished the experience. She is excited to make writing her next career and hopes to produce many inspirational novels for readers to enjoy.

Ronda now lives in a house near a lake, which offers a breathtaking setting to be creative. The sunsets are beautiful, and the lake is tranquil, providing inspiration from the beauty God has provided.

Readers can find Ronda on Facebook and at https:// rondasimpson-author.com/.

www.ingramcontent.com/pod-product-compliance
Lightning Source LLC
Chambersburg PA
CBHW070443030726
47503CB00004B/868